## He didn't know how to say it more clearly: she was *his*...

Arousal was flowing through his body, and her fear dragged sharp claws over his skin.

Calm down," he managed, in a voice that had precious little humanity left in it.

She quieted, her breath hitching as she tried to swallow the tears. And she stopped struggling, which was good. Except that he still wanted to press against her, despite the irritating layers of cloth in the way. She was sweating, he could taste it, and the urge to press his face against her throat and lick his tongue delicately against her bare skin to taste it even further made a fine tremor run through the center of his bones.

Fur receded. The claws prickling out through his fingertips receded, as well. He won the battle with himself by bare inches, and the animal retreated snarling back down to the floor of his mind, curling up and promising trouble later...

Dear Reader,

I always wanted to write a story where the were-creatures weren't wolves or big cats. Which presented an interesting dilemma, until one morning when the hero of *Taken* sauntered onstage and started telling me his story. Characters. They always act like they own the place.

Anyway, I had a great deal of fun writing this. I hope it's good for you, too…

*Lilith Saintcrow*

# TAKEN

## LILITH SAINTCROW

MILLS & BOON

First published in Great Britain 2011
by Mills & Boon, an imprint of Harlequin (UK) Limited,
Eton House, 18-24 Paradise Road, Richmond, Surrey TW9 1SR

© Lilith Saintcrow 2011

ISBN: 978 0 263 88014 4

89-0711

Harlequin (UK) policy is to use papers that are natural, renewable and
recyclable products and made from wood grown in sustainable forests. The
logging and manufacturing processes conform to the legal environmental
regulations of the country of origin.

Printed and bound in Spain
by Blackprint CPI, Barcelona

**Lilith Saintcrow** was born in New Mexico, bounced around the world as an Air Force brat, and fell in love with writing at the tender age of nine. She is the author of the Dante Valentine and Jill Kismet series, as well as the bestselling author of the Strange Angels YA series, which she wrote under the name Lili St. Crow. She lives in Vancouver, Washington, with two children, three cats and assorted other strays. Please check out her website at www.lilithsaintcrow.com/journal.

For Mel Sterling,
best friend and beta reader.

# *Chapter 1*

"Half my ass is hanging out." Sophie tugged on the skirt's hem. There was nothing like wearing your friend's clothes to remind you of your shortcomings. "I'm, what, only an inch taller than you?"

"Oh, you look fine." Lucy swept her short, sleek dark hair back, blotting her lipstick. Luce even lit a cigarette before opening her door, the brief flare of the lighter painting her face with gold. "You look *hot*. Why don't you ever loosen up and wear a miniskirt?"

"I wear appropriate attire for my job." Sophie pushed her glasses up, wishing her curls weren't falling in her eyes. Lucy insisted she leave her hair down. The car was nice and warm, so the touch of cold wind on her bare legs was shocking when she stepped out. She pulled the back of the skirt down one more time and wished she'd just worn jeans. Jeans covered up a lot. "There's a dress code, you know." *And I don't have anything else in my closet. Food first, clothes later, that's the rule.*

Luce was already tapping her foot, eager to be off down the cracked sidewalk. "Oh, please. Margo the Battle-Ax wears scrubs all day. You could, too, you know." She'd squeezed into a short evening-blue silk sheath that showed off her ample curves, and her legs looked long and beautiful in a pair of fishnets, ending in a lovely pair of glittering silver heels.

Heels, for a night of dancing? Well, Lucy had more endurance than Sophie did in a lot of areas. Sophie could stay, have a drink, watch everyone making fools of themselves, then catch a cab home.

Though cabs were expensive.

Lucy slid her arm through Sophie's. "Besides, you need to put your toesies in the dating pool again, sweetheart. It's been six months since the decree came through. You're a free woman."

*A free woman. I wish someone would tell Mark that.* "I guess so."

"You *guess* so? Come on, Soph."

"Okay, okay. I'm a free woman." *As long as he can't find where I live. Stop worrying so much, dammit!* But that was like telling herself to stop breathing. And good God, but she had no intention of ever dipping a toe—or any other appendage—in the dating pool ever again.

Once was enough.

The street pulsed with neon. Here on Broadway, Jericho City's nightclubs were all clustered for warmth, a long row of them on either side of a square bounded by leafless trees and trellises with strings of decorative all-weather lights woven into them. A chill wind came up Fifth Avenue and teased at Sophie's bare legs. Her back was already aching from the low black heels Lucy had talked her into, a familiar pain she put up with during the week but could have happily done without on a weekend. "Why am I doing this again?"

"Because I need to practice my *lambada*, and it won't hurt you to get out from under all those books," Lucy said sharply.

*Thank God for you, Luce.* Sophie straightened her shirt. Well, maybe *shirt* was an ambitious word for a silk spaghetti-strapped tank top that showed a slice of midriff. This was Lucy's, too. Sophie didn't have anything that satisfied Lucy's exacting standards for a night out.

She had precious few clothes at *all,* and was sneakingly glad her best friend had rolled right over the top of her objections and squeezed her into something she didn't have to buy or wash. Luce wasn't always the soul of tact, but she almost never referred to Sophie's situation—except to note that Mark had been a bastard, and to lament that Sophie hadn't taken him to the cleaners.

"I'm having *one* drink, and I'll stay to drive you home. Okay? That means that we have to leave at a reasonable hour." Which would solve the whole problem of getting a cab, too.

*I want to get some sleep this weekend. And I have rent due. Jeez, I can't even afford to go on a drinking binge.*

"Reasonable?" Lucy's laugh belled out again. "What the hell? Who's reasonable on a Friday night, out on the town with a hot babe? Live a little, honey."

Luce thought "safety" and "reliability" were highly overrated. It was one of the things Sophie loved about her—and the same thing that drove her to tooth-grinding distraction.

Still, Lucy was a good friend. And she never asked questions, even when Sophie had showed up at her door, bruised and bleeding, terrified and—

*That's an Unpleasant Thing. Don't think about it.* "Seriously, Lucy. I have stuff to do this weekend." *Like sleep. And figure out next month's budget. If they don't give me some overtime I don't know how I'll make it.*

"For Chrissake. Don't think about that. Think about how good you look right now." They reached the entrance to the Paintbox. Pounding music spilled out, neon lights flickering, cigarette smoke and sweat exhaling into the cold.

The night was chill, but Sophie's heart was already galloping along uncomfortably hard. It was strange to be out in public at night. And unsettling. The sky was too big, and there were too many people to keep track of.

Sophie kept breathing. The therapy books all said deep breathing was key. You couldn't control a lot of things, but you could control your breathing.

On Friday nights, if you paid ten dollars, you got to go into every club and bar on Broadway

Square without a door fee—*and* get a free drink in most of them. It wasn't worth a whole roll of laundry quarters, to Sophie's mind. And the thought of so many people clustering around her made her a little sick. *Just keep breathing,* she told herself.

"God, Soph, you're *divorced,* not dead. Come on."

*I'm wondering if one is analogous to the other, really.* She dropped Lucy's keys in the teensy plastic-jeweled purse at her hip. Lucy pulled Sophie through the door into blessed muggy warmth full of pounding bass played *way* too loud to be healthy. The bouncer wolf-whistled; Luce swished her hips in response and laughed.

*This is going to be trouble.* Sophie sighed, but the sound was lost under the music. What the hell, right? Lucy was just being a good friend. The only friend she had left, really, since the others had fallen away one way or another during the first year of her marriage to an egotistical bastard. *Stop thinking,* she told herself as Lucy actually hopped with excitement, aiming straight for the crush of people around the bar. The Paintbox's major attraction was its dance floor, blocks of light in the floor turning different colors in time to the beat. The place was packed and only going to get more so. Sophie kept her arm carefully over the tiny jeweled purse, borrowed from Lucy—just big enough for ID, keys, cash, and a tube of pale-pink lip gloss—and let her friend tug her along. *That's an Unpleasant Thing, and it's in the Past. Leave it there, for God's sake. Look at how hard Lucy's trying.*

She plastered a smile on her face and followed her friend, wincing every time the music hit the decibel level right before "jet takeoff."

*This is going to be a long night.*

# Chapter 2

"Now, all of you *behave*." Kyle's eyes glittered with a random reflection of silver, catching the glow of a streetlamp. "This is for food and supplies. We can't afford another incident."

"Aw." Julia rubbed at her forehead, her long dark hair falling forward over her shoulders. The pale streak at her temple, just beginning to grow in, glowed dully. "Can't we have a little fun?"

*Fun is one thing. Almost eviscerating a man because he's patted your ass is another.* "Kyle says to behave." Zach looked back from the front passenger's seat of the blue minivan.

"That means *behave*." His tone was soft, but the windows in the van rattled.

"Sure." Julia ducked her head to the side. So did Brun, mimicking her submissive posture. "You got it, big brother. Behave." She made a low, soft sound, the *please-don't-rip-my-throat-out-I'll-be-good* sound. Zach's nostrils flared. She was overacting just enough to be sarcastic, and her pheromone wash was spiked with thinly veiled aggression.

"We can have fun just fine without blood," Kyle said. His hair stood up in soft spikes. "We're Carcajou. Eric?"

"No blood," Eric said from the backseat, his bitten leather jacket creaking. "Brun?"

"No blood," Brun said, his light tenor almost piping. "We're not savages."

"Good." Kyle took the keys out of the ignition. "Everyone's dressed?"

"Quit fussing." Julia tossed her head impatiently. "Let's just *go*. I'm hungry." She was whining a little, already. Brun rubbed at her nape, and she shoved her twin's hand irritably away.

*It's not her fault*, Zach told himself. She was young, barely past her first Change, and a spoiled brat to boot. Kyle pretty much allowed

her to run wild, because she was the only female in the Family. It was his call…but she was
getting harder and harder to control.

*You're not the alpha, either. It's not your
job.* Zach settled himself, one boot on the dash-
board, and waited. He wouldn't move until his
little brother did. Ky stared out the windshield,
the glass beginning to fog up with five healthy
young animals breathing inside. Little brother
was wearing his scruffy face today, a shadow of
stubble across his cheeks, the circles under his
coal-dark eyes attractive instead of worn down.
Women liked him with a little bit of rough on;
otherwise, Ky was too pretty.

*Better to be tough than pretty,* Zach reminded
himself for the thousandth time. He studied his
boot toes, ran over the situation again inside his
head. They needed cash, and the kids needed to
bleed off some energy. It was dangerous, especially with the young ones in such a state.

He'd almost talked Kyle into letting him and
Eric do it alone. They had the quickest fingers
and the best control of their tempers. But Kyle
didn't want to be left home to babysit, and he
*especially* didn't want them separated if Julia
had another one of her fits. It took a lot to control her sometimes, and Zach was the best at it.

Though sometimes he wished Kyle wouldn't always take the easiest way out.

But thoughts like that were dangerous. They were the thoughts of someone who was about to challenge the alpha, and Zach had made up his mind. No challenging Kyle, that was the rule.

It had been the rule ever since the night of the fire, when Zach held his little brother back from plunging into the flames.

"All right," Kyle said. It was the signal, and they got moving.

It was an autumn night full of rattling naked branches and the faint smell of dry-cinnamon leaves. The sound of thumping bass was clearly audible, running under the concrete like a pulse in the throat of sweating prey, and Zach breathed deep, rolling the cold air over his tongue. There was danger on the wind tonight, and it wasn't just the danger of starvation haunting their little Family.

The beast in the floor of his mind stirred restlessly. Instinct blossomed into certainty. *Something's gonna happen.*

"I don't like this," he murmured. Kyle paused as the others preceded them—slim dark Julia, Brun trailing in her wake as usual, Eric hunch-

ing his shoulders and glancing from side to side
warily. "It smells odd."

Kyle agreed silently, his chin dipping in the
facsimile of a nod. "Wish we had a shaman."

*You and me both. We could settle down if we
had one.* And Zach wouldn't be half so tempted
to do something drastic.

But resisting temptation was getting to be his
middle name. "I'll keep an eye on Julia." *I'm
such a diplomat.*

The half-blind, animal part of him raised its
head, interested in a thread of scent. Brunette
and young, tantalizing in its evanescence. *Hmm.
Wonder who that is. Smells interesting.*

"Good. We can blow town if we get enough
tonight." Kyle glanced up at him, as if Zach was
the alpha. "South, I'm thinking."

*Nice and warm. Easy pickings, too, if we
just stay under the radar.* "Sounds like a good
idea." *Except we're traveling blind, without a
shaman. Nobody to throw the bones, and Julia's
unstable. She's too headstrong. She should
marry into another Tribe, if we can find a male
strong enough.*

But good luck finding a mate for her without
a shaman. Good luck finding *anything.* None
of the other Tribes would so much as give them

the time of day if they didn't have a shaman of their own. Not even the Tanuki would talk to them, and Tanuki were some of the most gregarious around.

He sighed, a cloud of breath hanging in the cold air, and Kyle gave him another one of those odd sidelong glances. *Quit looking at me that way. You're the alpha, I'm the second—that's the way it's going to stay. God, I wish Dad was here.*

"You've got the quickest fingers," Kyle finally said. "You take point tonight."

Zach nodded. "By this time tomorrow we'll be driving toward orange groves and white-sand beaches." *And still running one step ahead of disaster.*

# Chapter 3

She meant to have fun. Really, she did. But the gin and tonic was watered down, the dance floor was so crowded she'd gotten elbowed and damn near molested in the five minutes she'd spent on the floor, and the pumping, throbbing music was going straight through her head with glass spikes.

*Great. All I need is a migraine. Why can't I enjoy myself like everyone else?*

Lucy was having a fine time, shaking her thang on the dance floor with a guy who looked like the epitome of Latin Lover, right down to the poufy white shirt. She looked good, and the guy was leaning in, talking in her ear or nibbling. They were rubbing hips, and Lucy had her hands up in the air, abandoned to the dance in a way Sophie couldn't even dream of being.

*I was like that once, though, wasn't I?* She couldn't remember. Instead, the image of copper-bottomed pans hanging over a kitchen island rose up, their bright shapes moving slightly, and a cold rill of fear slid up her back. A half-guilty glance around showed nothing out of the ordinary.

Still jumping at shadows. She couldn't even remember what it felt like to dance without being afraid. And her nerves tingled, whether it was from weak gin or the infrequent pins-and-needles feeling that meant something bad was about to happen.

Those pins and needles had saved her from a car crash once. Or, at least, she firmly believed so. The feeling had made her sit at a four-way stop until a car zoomed through the intersection, not even pausing. Whether the driver was drunk or just careless didn't matter.

The trouble was, that feeling would never warn her when she was, say, about to marry a man who thought "wife" meant "slave." Or "punching bag."

Sophie sighed. She could have left her

glasses in the car, making the world into a soft fuzz much easier to deal with, but then she'd be half-blind. She probably *should* have left them, this was just the sort of crowd who would accidentally knock them off her face and step on them, and there went two hundred bucks' worth of frames she couldn't afford to lose. They were cute, yeah, and they didn't require the care and expense contacts did.

*I'm all new now. Except the inside, where I'm the same old Sophie. Scared of my own shadow.* She took another gulp of gin and tonic, and someone bumped into her from behind. The drink slopped, splashing, and cold liquid landed on her cleavage. The pins and needles swept over her skin and retreated.

Sophie sucked in a breath, nearly choked, and looked up as the person bumping her settled against the bar less than a foot away.

*Oh, wow.*

He was tall, and dark, and rough-looking, stubble crawling on his cheeks under high arched cheekbones. His mouth was a little too thin, as was his nose, but his eyes—so dark pupil blended into iris in the uncertain light—were nice. And the shelf of dark hair falling stubbornly across them looked like it was just waiting for fingers to smooth it back. A streak of pale blondness winging back from his temple should have looked ridiculous, but didn't.

*Hello, stranger.* Sophie quickly looked back down at her drink. Lucy would have grinned at him and said something witty. *Jeez. I'm such an idiot.*

"Sorry about that," he almost-yelled in her ear, easily heard over the music. His breath touched her hair, and a bolt of heat went through her. It was the closest she'd been to a man since…oh, two months before she filed for divorce?

The tingling feeling had gone away. It was probably just the weak gin.

"No problem." She pitched her voice loud enough to be heard, as well, but yelled into her drink. Being this close to *anyone* made her nervous. And he was *big*. The physical size meant danger, and she nervously checked where his hands were with quick little peripheral glances.

*You can't tar everyone with the same brush,* she told herself for at least the five thousandth time. *Not all men are like that.*

The sense of someone breathing on her didn't go away, and she slid to the side, bumping a tanned woman in a white dress. *Too many people in here. I'm going to suffocate.* Her gaze swung up, and she found the man looking at her again. A drink had appeared in front of him, and he handed the harried bartender a ten without looking. Black T-shirt, jeans, a belt with an oddly shaped silver buckle.

He was standing too close, too. It was packed three-deep here at the bar, but he was still way inside her personal space.

Like, leaning in so far they were almost rubbing noses. A breath of male scent, some musky cologne, enfolded her.

Her heart gave a nasty, nervous thumping leap. *Jesus!* Sophie flinched back, dropped her gin and tonic on the bar, and retreated. The glass turned over, sending a tide of watered alcohol across the polished plastic, and a flash of terrified guilt burst reflexively under her rib cage.

*Stupid. You're stupid.* Mark's voice hissed inside her head, and she made it to the dance floor, going up on her toes to look for Lucy. She pushed her glasses up, and hoped they wouldn't get smudged. That would just cap everything.

*Dammit, Lucy. Where have you gone now?* But her friend was nowhere in sight. Sophie canvassed the whole dance floor, glanced at the emergency exit, and decided that was silly. Lucy wasn't at the bar, either—and it wasn't like her to vanish completely.

Her heart was pounding like it intended to explode, and her breath came short and fast as she checked the ladies' room and found no Lucy.

*Don't have a panic attack now. Luce wouldn't bail on you.*

But, oh, her body wouldn't listen. It was bracing itself for something terrible.

Outside, the night was clear and cold, and the wind brushed the back of her sweating legs. It was too hot inside the club, and hypothermic outside. What a choice. Her glasses fogged briefly and cleared. Her breathing eased a little, and the tight knot of squirming panic inside her dialed back a little bit.

There was a group of smokers in a knot around a parking meter, all laughing easily. One of them was a college-age boy, doing some sort of jig to the beat coming through the walls for the enjoyment of his buddies.

But no sleek dark head or jingle of gold bracelets. Sophie stood, irresolute, on the pavement, and someone bumped into her from behind.

She thought it was Lucy, and turned around, opening her mouth to scold her. Instead, her jaw dropped even farther as she looked up—and up...he was at least six feet tall—at the man who had jostled her at the bar.

*Oh, for Christ's sake.* "Watch where you're going," Sophie snapped, and took two nervous, skipping steps back. *Leave me alone. Go away.*

"Sorry." He smiled, showing incredibly white teeth, but the expression was like a grimace. "You okay?"

She didn't have to reply. A scream punched the night, a high feminine note cut sharply off the moment it reached full-throated terror, and Sophie almost leaped out of her skin.

*I know that voice!* She was already moving, her heart hammering and her heels clattering. The bouncer at the Paintbox's door had his head up, staring down the street as if trying to figure out where the sound had come from.

"Lucy!" she yelled, and paused for the barest moment before plunging into the alley. *"Lucy!"*

The alley ended on a blank brick wall, and

there was a crumpled pale shape moving weakly in the gloom. A hand closed around her naked upper arm, hot fingers like steel bands driving in. Whoever had Sophie's arm yanked her back as another shape—slim, male, with a blotch of blackness down its white shirt—looked up from its crouch, eyes running with crimson hellfire and darkness smeared across its lips.

Sophie screamed as the hand on her arm pulled her farther back. Another slice of golden light opened up, and slim graceful bodies piled through, crouching and leaping. They swarmed the thing with the red-gleaming eyes, and Sophie's legs turned to noodles. She sagged, the hand on her arm the only thing keeping her upright, and when the iron fingers loosened she actually fell, the shock of her knees meeting filthy concrete jarring up through her hips and shoulders.

The pale, weakly moving shape on the ground wore Lucy's face, and it was gasping, rattling breaths drawn in. Its throat bubbled and gaped, and as Sophie stared, it stopped moving—and the thing in the white shirt, snarling, turned away from the back of the alley and lunged for her.

## Chapter 4

It shouldn't have happened.

They'd hunted *upir* before, of course, while the old alpha was alive. But the farm had burned, their sleeping shaman and alpha dead in the flames, and now they were on their own, scrabbling to survive. They had cut both Tribe and *upir* a wide berth since.

And Zach shouldn't have followed her, but she smelled too good to be true. Brunette, yes. Human, which was all right but not exactly appetizing. But young, female, warm—and with an edge of moonlight and snow, something cold and crystalline. Zach hadn't smelled that in *forever,* and certainly not with the tantalizing musk of something that belonged to him over-laying it.

He'd leaned close and gotten a good lung-ful, and she *was* probably what he thought she was, which made it incredibly lucky, and incredibly—

But she'd flinched away as if she knew what he was, and searched the inside of the nightclub as if she'd lost her purse. She hadn't; he'd kept his fingers well away from it, despite fleecing at least four people at the bar while he watched her. Pale skin and pale eyes. Nice hips, a glory of curling sandalwood hair, a pair of cute little steel-rimmed librarian glasses, and that ridiculous purse she kept clutching. She'd walked right out the front door while he was still cutting across the dance floor, harvesting another few wallets and emptying them by touch. It was almost too easy when you had the training and quicker-than-human reflexes. The rest of them had been working the crowd, Julia concentrating on businessmen and Brun sliding through knots of college boys with fat rolls to spend on killing their livers. Those fat rolls would keep the Family fed and moving.

But here, in the alley behind the nightclub, the smell of blood drenched the air, plucking at the beast in his bones. Zach yanked her back as the *upir* snarled, and the emergency door flew open, smacking against the brickwork so hard dust puffed out. Kyle was first through, his head up and nostrils flared, the Change rippling under his skin, and he leaped for the *upir* without pausing.

*Oh, holy shit, no!* Kyle shouldn't be doing that, even if he was the alpha; he could get not just hurt but unzipped.

Kyle just hesitated too much.

The woman fell as he let go of her. He promptly shelved her as a problem to solve later and leaped, a fraction of a second slower than Kyle—who met the *upir* with a bone-shattering crunch, driving it sideways and down as it twisted and snarled. It had a white, loose shirt on, and was probably rabid if the just-spilled blood painting its front was any indication.

Not that the bloodsuckers needed much inducement to get really savage. But if an *upir* was hunting here, going after all the healthy young ones under bright lights and in the middle of crowds, it was either a baby, which was all right—or too burnsick for them to handle.

Snapping, growling, making a hell of a lot of noise, Kyle feinted and Zach's bones made crackling sounds as the Change touched him, too, running through his body like fire. The animal in him snarled, lifted its head, and clawed at the blind-root thing in front of it, the enemy who twisted like a snake and spat, slashing with hands turned to shovel-shaped claws. If he could just hold it long enough, it would make a mistake and he would get it safely put down before it hurt any of the others. And before it made any more noise to attract witnesses.

But Julia was suddenly there, too, crowding her brothers aside as she let out a chilling glass-throated howl. The fight tipped and shifted, the *upir* kicked and slashed again. Kyle backhanded his sister, throwing her out of the way—and catching the claws meant for her, full across his unprotected belly.

Blood burst again. The smell of it, loaded with the terrible reek of a gutshot, smacked Zach across the face. He descended into the red welter of combat, the animal in him roaring, and didn't care that there would be witnesses.

The *upir* died, shredded and shrieking, the rot of its last exhale throttling the alleyway. Zach landed, foul liquid staining his fingers, and his bones crackled again as he looked for more to kill.

They pressed against him, those of his kind, and a thread of scent tried to cut through the reek of death and decay. It was a reminder, something he had to attend to, some problem his human side had to solve.

The animal didn't care. It smelled food, and blood, and suffering, and it wanted revenge and hot meat, bones cracking between its teeth.

"Zach—" someone said, a word that had no meaning.

He thumped back into himself as the Change receded. Julia was sobbing, as openly and messily as a child, and sirens pierced the night with diamond stitchery. There was other noise, too—people, crowding around.

The instinct of hiding among prey all his life prodded him. The *upir* was dead, and he had to get his Family out of here before they were seen, or, God forbid, *caught*. A Carcajou couldn't be held for long, but if other Tribes caught wind of their presence after this, it could get ugly.

*You mean uglier than this?* The Change trembled inside his bones, spikes of pain.

"Zach," Brun whispered again. It was the sound of a child in a nightmare.

The *upir*'s body was already just a stinking sludge inside a sodden white shirt and the ragged remains of a pair of leather pants, a pair of boots full of nasty black liquid falling over, skooshing out in a tide of corruption over Kyle's half-Changed body. Fur receded into his little brother's skin, his entrails a mass of grayish-blue tangled in a spill, the jet of blood from the abdominal aorta's cutting black as the *upir*'s leaking.

His corpse would be fully human—what parts of it the *upir*'s caustic sludge didn't eat away.

*Another alpha, dead.* Zach's stomach cramped. He hadn't eaten yet tonight, and the smell was enough to make him glad. *My fault again, I should have—*

"Come on." Eric pulled at his arm. "We have to *go*."

*Where is she?* He glanced around, but the woman he'd followed here was gone. A crowd of people had magically appeared—*prey,* his animal side whispered, casting around for that thread of light brunette scent that he somehow knew.

She was nowhere in sight. He had to find her.

*What the hell is going—*

"Come *on!*" Eric yelled, and dragged at his

arm. Julia let out a keening sound, and it was like a jolt of fresh bloodscent, jarring him into alertness. He showed his teeth, still searching for the woman, and he and his Family leaped, Julia catching a high-hung fire-escape ladder and bolting, Brun right behind her, Eric using the full measure of his strength and speed to hop onto a Dumpster's top and land behind the knot of people who had somehow clustered in the bottleneck of the alley. Their surprise echoed off the brick walls.

"Did you see—"

"Holy *shit!*"

"Jesus!"

Zach's throat ached, denied another growl and the hunting cry. *We are Carcajou, and you are our prey. But not right now. Not when there's likely another predator around.*

He moved among them like a cold wind, quick fingers plucking, and grabbed a few more wallets as he did. They would see only a blur, and the instinct to grab what he could was very close to the surface. Along with other instincts—like the urge to rip through flesh instead of clothing, to spill blood instead of cash.

A few feet clear of the alley he paused, because he smelled *her* again, very close.

The animal in him snarled. Two drives, possession and revenge, were forcing it to run in circles—and thankfully, giving him enough room to reassert control. *Kyle. Goddammit, why? You should have waited, we could have baited and trapped it, and we could have killed it together. And kept Julia out of it.* The howling hit, Julia's voice lifted in a paroxysm of grief, and he had to go. She was likely to hurt herself or someone else, and he was the only one who could control her when she got like this.

But he had to find that woman. She smelled like ice and moonlight, like salvation.

She smelled like a shaman potential.

The scent drifted across his sensitive nose again. He glanced down the alley again—more people were crowding, spilling out of the emergency exits and pressing into the confined space, most with cell phones out.

Stupid herd animals. He could probably scare them, scatter them like the bleating sheep they were.

But the scent of her, close and sweating, filled his nose. He drew in a deep lungful and took off at a lope.

*Christ, Kyle, why didn't you wait?* But he knew why. His little brother had taken on the responsibility of an alpha—first into battle to defend his own.

And it was Zach's fault.

## Chapter 5

Her heels hit the cracked pavement with a clattering tattoo, and she didn't know she was screaming until she had to whoop in enough breath to keep running. Lucy's little jeweled purse bumped against her side, something in her back tore and ran with pain, and the cold whipped through her throat as she dragged in another breath, suddenly very sure she was going to scream *again*.

Her legs flew out in front of her as the rest of her was wrenched violently back, a hard hand clapped over her mouth, and she was too stunned and breathless to do more than start kicking and let out a choked cry—a muffled sound, not worth much with the wind rattling the empty branches of a tree overhead.

A motor started. "Get us out of here," the man said, and tossed her into the van as if she weighed nothing. She landed on something soft, her elbow sinking in, and there was a yelping as if she'd kicked a puppy.

"What the hell is *this?*" A girl's voice, young, and there was a sudden sound like a sheet popped smooth before being laid over a bed, resolving into a low rumbling growl much different than an engine.

"Keep your mouth *shut*, Julia, until I tell you to open it." He sounded furious. The voice was familiar. Sophie struggled to sit up as the van—it was definitely a van—pulled away from the curb.

*What the hell?* Someone grabbed her shoulders, shoved her so she half flew across the narrow space and landed *hard* on something softer than metal but more solid than upholstery.

"*Ooof.*" A hard huff of expelled breath. "Careful, there," the man continued. "Be easy with her, dammit!"

"Who is it?" Another male voice.

*I've been kidnapped. Oh, God. Lucy—* "Lucy!" she gasped, and erupted into wild motion. Her elbow whapped something soft, and he *oof*ed again. It might have been funny— if it hadn't been happening to her. Her wrists were grabbed, and the hand clamped down over her mouth again. He held her still as if she was a little kid.

He was terribly, hurtfully strong, and fresh panic turned everything behind her eyelids red.

"This is our new shaman." Silence greeted this statement. The sound of growling swallowed the hum of the engine, shook through her before settling down into something like a purr. "You can smell the potential on her. She was back there, near the *upir*. I think it ate her friend."

*Lucy!* She got a good mouthful and *bit,* as hard as she'd ever bit anything in her life. So hard her jaws ached, and there was a hiss of indrawn breath. Her eyes rolled in her head, and she worried her teeth back and forth. Something warm and coppery filled her mouth. It was too thick and slippery to be spit.

"And she's blooded me," he continued, without any discernable change in his tone. "Which takes care of that. So all of you behave yourselves, or I'll have your hides."

A sharp intake of breath passed through them all, like wind through wheat. The charged silence reverberated. The van's tires hummed.

"A shaman?" A very young male's voice, and it sounded shocked enough for everyone involved. "A real one? A real live one?"

"A potential." The man's voice rumbled against her back. "She'll trigger to us soon enough."

It was dark inside the rocking van; it took a corner at high speed and she was tipped back against whoever was holding her. *Lucy, oh, God.* The image of Lucy's body on the pavement just wouldn't go away. Sophie made a low, despairing sound in the back of her throat and struggled, getting exactly nowhere. Her skirt was riding up, adding a whole new problem to the situation.

The stuff in her mouth coated the back of her throat. He didn't move his hand, and she felt his skin quiver against her lips. A weird, slight movement, as if it there were small legs under the skin.

There were glitters of eyes. A reflection of streetlamp light boiled through the interior, outlining a young girl with long dark hair, her hand clapped to her cheek as if it hurt, and a slim young man who looked enough like her to be a twin, with the same narrow nose and winged eyebrows. The young man was actually crouched on a bench seat, easily swaying back and forth with the motion of the vehicle, the pale streak over his left temple reflecting streetlight.

"Slow down, Eric," the voice behind her rumbled. The growl was coming from his chest, and his hand jammed her glasses uncomfortably against the bridge of her nose.

It was *him*. The guy who had bumped her at the bar.

The van slowed. "What the hell just happened?" the driver asked.

*Think, Sophie!* Three men and a woman. They'd just *kidnapped* her, for God's sake. And Lucy…Lucy was…

"Kyle took on a rabid *upir*. Least, I think it was rabid—it acted like it was." He paused, his hand peeling away from her mouth. "And Julia had to go and get involved."

"I didn't—" The girl cowered back as the man holding Sophie made another deep, weird sound.

It was definitely a growl. She froze, her brain struggling, attempting to deal with this new absurdity. It was more distant and dreamlike the more she thought about it.

Lucy's white face, the horrible gaping below her chin, the blood-drenched thing with the twisting, plum-colored face—it was the Latin Lover who'd been grinding with Lucy on the dance floor, there was no mistaking that white shirt. What had he *done* to her?

The taste in her mouth, Sophie realized, was blood. She'd bitten him hard enough to break the skin.

*Oh, God. What is he going to do to me?*

"Kyle's dead? Really dead?" The very young male voice again. "What will we do?"

The man sagged a little bit. His arms were still iron around her. "I'm working on it. For right now we're driving, and we're going to get the hell out of Dodge with our new shaman." The arms around her loosened fractionally. "Now. What's *your* name, honey?"

The blood smeared over her mouth crackled as cooler air hit it. Sophie took a deep breath, filling her lungs, and screamed.

He silenced her almost instantly, his bleeding hand over her mouth again. "All right, we'll do it the hard way. Head south, Eric. Don't stop for a while. What's the take?"

Immediately, the two on the seat began digging in their pockets. The boy wore a denim jacket and the girl reached down into her bra, coming up with an impressive roll of bills. "Good pickings," the boy said, his eyes glowing in the dimness. Tears glittered on his cheeks.

The girl bit her lip. She was visibly shaking, her hands jittering as the money fanned out. She threw the rest of it down as if it burned her fingers.

"Kyle..." The driver sighed. Banged his fist sharply on the wheel, once. "What about his body?"

*Body?* Sophie tried pitching away from the man. It was no use at all.

"He died in battle. The *majir* will take him home." He didn't even have the grace to pretend he noticed she was trying to squirm free of him. Her nose was full and the blood and spit smeared across her mouth sealed her up pretty effectively. Her lungs burned, her throat crawling with iron-tasting slickness.

She'd tasted blood before. Plenty of times. It always made her sick and light-headed, bracing herself for the next punch and hoping Mark would run out of steam. The past threatened to close over her head, a weight of black water against every muscle. Her ribs heaved as she tried to breathe, the panic attack looming over her.

*Breathe, Sophie. Breathe. Don't think of the past.*

But she literally *couldn't* get any air in with his hand over her mouth and her nose full, and the blackness was so close.

Then, thank God, he eased up on her a little. "Be nice and quiet, shaman. Take a deep breath."

*Shaman? What the hell?* She sucked in a lungful of blessed air. The panic retreated, with a vicious little thump under her breastbone that promised it would be back.

Sophie's eyes were beginning to get used to the inside of the van. It smelled of musk and fast food, and with each mile slipping away under the tires she was farther and farther away from Lucy's car—and Lucy's body. The police would be there soon, but nobody would know she'd been out with her friend.

If she could just escape, get to a phone, something, anything—What did these people *want* with her? She was a nobody. At least, *now* she was.

*Mark?* Maybe. He had money. But why

would he want her kidnapped? He'd want something far more personal, wouldn't he?

Oh, yes, he would. Unless they were taking her to him. Oh, God. If they were taking her to Mark, it was all over.

"I've got a little over a thousand," the driver said. "Could be more or less, I wasn't keeping close track."

"We'll drive for a while, then we'll stop for food." The one holding her loosened up a bit as the van took a sharp turn and accelerated. "We're on the freeway now, sweetheart. Just be nice and easy—you're safe." He let up on her mouth again, but kept his hot fingers on her cheek, ready to gag her. The wet warmth slicking her cheeks and fogging her glasses was tears, she discovered, and blood smeared around her mouth. Had she drooled, too?

Did getting kidnapped and half suffocated make you drool?

*I've gone insane. It's the only explanation.*

"Please don't hurt me." Much to her surprise, she sounded steady. Her tank top— *Lucy's* tank top—was all rucked up, her bare skin against his T-shirt. He was warm, and the van was heating up. Her naked legs prickled with gooseflesh.

"We're not going to hurt you." The young boy crouched on the seat swayed as the van kept going. He swiped at the tears on his cheeks, scrubbing them away angrily. "Zach, are you *sure?* She's a bleeder."

"She's got the mark, I can smell it on her. If I can, you can, too." His hands fell away, and Sophie was suddenly aware she was half lying on him; he was wedged up against the closed side door. Her eyes flicked toward the passenger's side in the front—there was an open seat there, and maybe she could signal or get away somehow, if she could just *get* that far.

*Think, Sophie. Think!*

"A shaman." The driver sighed. "God*damn*it." There was a sound—palm striking steering wheel, sharply. "Kyle."

"We'll sing him to the moon as soon as I'm sure we're safe. We'll hold Silence for him until then." The guy she was lying on—Zach— sighed, too. "It's just us now. But we've got a shaman. Julia, find her a coat. Brun, gather up the money. You'll hold it for me."

The crying boy hopped off the seat, grabbing the roll from the girl's hands. He paused and ducked his head when his gaze drifted across Sophie's. That streak in his hair looked oddly familiar. He seemed not to notice he was weeping, even while the tears dripped on his denim jacket.

"Please," she whispered. "You can just let me go. I won't tell anyone, I promise."

"She's whining." The girl's lip lifted. White teeth glimmered. "What a *bleeder*."

There was a confused sense of motion, and Sophie landed hard on her side, her head hitting something. A burst of starry pain rocked through her skull, and the weird rattling growl crested again, drowning out the engine.

Her ears roared, too, like a high wind in acres of trees. A familiar sound, one she'd heard many times before, usually while Mark was yelling. It was always so *loud* when he started in on her, the screaming robbing her of breath and light, closing down her vision into a tunnel.

"Shut *up,* Julia!" Zach snarled, but Sophie slid down into a darkness starred with weird spangled lights, and was gone.

## Chapter 6

An hour later, they stopped at a drive-through at the city limits.

They held the Silence for Kyle, none of them speaking unless absolutely necessary. It was to keep his spirit from lingering, but it meant Zach had too much time to think.

It also meant he couldn't explain much to the new shaman. Not that she seemed disposed to listen. She shrank frantically away any time one of them came near her, and her eyes roved the inside of the van when she thought he wasn't watching her.

Looking for escape.

He cursed to himself every time he saw her

flinch. She had an oil-stained rag clasped to the side of her head. She really was a pretty little thing, curved in all the right places, her hair a tangle of sandalwood curls and those little librarian glasses—thankfully not damaged; Brun had picked them up from the carpet—perched on her adorable little nose, over two wide, pretty eyes. It was too dim to tell what color the pale irises really were. Something too light to be green, and the wrong shade for blue.

He wanted to find out.

Unfortunately, the bruise spreading down the side of her face from hitting the seat didn't do much to help her looks. But he'd had to shut Julia *up* before he was tempted to hurt her. So many times now he had glanced over to gauge Kyle's reaction to the new shaman, to Eric's driving, to Julia's soft sobbing in the backseat, curled up in a ball—and found an empty place where his little brother should be.

*This is your fault, not Julia's. He wasn't hard enough to lead, and especially not to rule a traveling Family without a shaman. You know that. You still let him take the alpha, because... why?*

He knew why. Because of the smell of smoke and the sound of Kyle's agonized howl as Zach held him back, as the fire ate their home and their parents. It was right after a fight with a small wandering band of *upir,* both the alpha and the shaman wounded, the shaman too deep in a healing-trance to wake up in time. Smoke inhalation could kill any Tribe, and the old alpha had thrown Zach clear with the last of his strength. Dad had succumbed with his last mate, their deaths an agonizing rawness in the center of Zach's memory.

The fire had left them homeless, without shaman or kin. And it had left Zach with the deep shame of failure. He was strong enough— he should have saved Dad or gone up in flames with the shaman. He'd made the instinctive choice, not the *right* one.

And an alpha couldn't ever afford to be instinctive instead of right when it came to choices like that.

Eric handed the bags of food to Brun, who had settled in the passenger's seat, not daring to comfort his crying twin. The shaman potential, who wouldn't give her name, perched on the other side of the bench seat, dry-eyed and dazed. She smelled too good to be true, and he had to stop himself from taking deep lungfuls every time the air in the van shifted.

*I have screwed this right up, haven't I?* But he hadn't been *thinking,* just reacting to the beast's roar of possessiveness. It had happened so quickly, and she smelled so *good,* brunette and cold silver light. That smell meant comfort to a Carcajou. It was the shamans who could hold the beast in check, the ice and moonlight in them taking the edge off sharp claws and blood-hunger. Already it was easier to think clearly, even with the numbness in his chest, the part of him that didn't believe his little brother was gone.

And as soon as she was triggered, she'd belong to them. It wouldn't take long, not with as strong as she smelled of the potential now. A stray gust of air brought him another load of the silver-smell, and he inhaled gratefully.

*Kyle. I wish you were here to see this.*

But he wasn't. And they broke the Silence temporarily to break their fast. Maybe he could talk to the girl, coax her somehow.

"Dead cow ahoy," Brun said, thrusting three huge wrapped loads of overcooked, oversalted meat and processed bread into his hands. The van started again, Eric wolfing double hamburgers almost whole. The tank was full, courtesy of the stop-and-rob across the street, and they were ready to strike out south. As soon as they finished eating they could keep the Silence again.

"You want some?" Brun had crouched, his head well below the woman's, submission and conciliation evident in every line of his body. His pheromone wash was submissive, too, tinted with softness. He was the one she was least likely to be terrified of. And the closer he could get to her, the more they could all get their pheromones on her, the sooner she'd trigger and be theirs in truth.

She just blinked at him, holding the rag to her head. "I won't tell anyone," she whispered again. "Please just let me go."

"Don't worry." Brun was trying to sound hopeful and soothing; Zach watched carefully, hoping she'd respond. Her scent was alternately far too pale and choking-strong. It could have been shock; it could be that she wasn't triggered yet. "We're not going to hurt you. We need you."

She blinked again, as if she was having trouble focusing. It would just cap everything if she had a concussion. "Did…did Mark pay you? Whatever he promised you, please, don't believe him. He lies."

*What?* Zach didn't like the sound of that. But he had to take it one thing at a time right now. "Just give her some food. You'd better eat, sweets. You look like you need it." He almost glanced at the passenger's seat to gauge Kyle's reaction, stopped himself only by easing forward and snagging a milk shake. Eric slurped at a root beer, flipping the turn signal and setting the drink in a holder with a practiced motion. He was the best driver, but he would have to be spelled about dawn.

Zach didn't want to stop at a hotel and give everyone time to think for a little while. He wanted to wait until he had some sort of plan in his head. Besides, he felt better when they were moving. When they were on the road and he didn't have to think about anything other than the next food stop, the next rest stop, the steady revolution of tires. Driving felt more natural than anything else, and if they stopped he might have to face the mess he'd made of everything.

They had a shaman now. But Kyle was gone. *The spirits take with one hand and give with the other,* the Tribes always said. But still. Why did they have to take so *much?*

Brun pressed a cheeseburger and a huge clutch of fries into the woman's lap, ignoring her flinch, and moved over to Julia, bending over and whispering in his twin's ear. Julia's sobs were beginning to grate. She had reason to cry, they all did. But the racking sobs were beginning to take on a whipsawing note that meant Julia was working herself up into a fit or literally crying herself sick, and neither of those things would help the situation.

The floor of the van was littered with clothes, the leatherworking supplies stacked in cases behind the passenger's seat. Here was his chance. Zach made it to the girl's feet and offered her the milk shake. "Here. You really need to eat something." He tried to sound conciliatory. Soothing.

Those pale eyes met his, and he found out they were gray, like a winter sky. He got a good lungful of her, spice and beauty overlaid with the hot grease from the bag in her lap. The thread of ice and moonlight was stronger now, twining through the warp and weft of her aroma like a jasmine vine coming into bloom, but the rest of it…she smelled damn near edible. And familiar, in some way he couldn't quite place.

She smelled like *his*. It was that simple. It was a mate smell, and *that* was going to make things even stickier.

*Why couldn't you have come along earlier, huh?*

But that was unfair. She probably had no goddamn idea what she'd just landed in. Which meant it was his job to keep this whole train on the tracks for a while, at least until he could make a stab at helping her understand.

And keeping her here until she was theirs.

She shifted on the seat, pulling her knees back, and the fries were headed for the floor until he caught them, his hand blurring. Quick fingers and quicker reflexes, the Tribe birthright.

It was sometimes the most useful part of the animal inside each of them.

Her eyes were very big, and glazed. Fringed with dark lashes, and behind her smudged glasses he saw fear.

"What's your name?" He kept his tone nice and even. He had until they finished eating to calm her down a little. Eric slurped at his root beer, and Julia made a little hitching sound. Trying to steal the limelight, again.

The woman stared at him like he was speaking German or something. Finally, she stirred. "Sophie," she whispered.

"Sophie. That's pretty. What's the rest of it?" *Nice and easy. Good job, Zach.*

"Harr—I mean, Wilson. My maiden name's Wilson."

*Married? Huh.* He didn't see a ring, but he supposed anything was possible. And maiden name usually meant divorce. "Nice to meet you, Sophie. Listen, you really should eat. You just saw an *upir* kill two people." He couldn't put a nicer shine on it than that. And the more he kept a tone of normalcy, the better she might respond.

Or so he hoped.

She shook her head, and tears stood out in those big dark eyes. "Lucy." Her lips shaped the word, and he had to stop staring. It was goddamn indecent, how soft her mouth looked.

"Was that her name?" *Christ. It* was *her friend.* Hard on the heels of that thought came another: Sophie *was* a really pretty name. He liked it.

*Pay attention to what you're doing, Zach.*

She nodded. Her fingers curled around the milk shake, brushing his, and a jolt of heat slid up his arm from the contact. Married or not, hopefully divorced or not, the animal in him thought she belonged to him.

It was a tricky situation if she was married, but it did happen. Especially with "found" shamans. There were ways to fix it.

Lots of ways. Especially if you made up your mind not to be too overly concerned with playing nice.

She took a long pull off the straw and a tear tracked down her cheek. "She wanted me to have a little fun, that's all. Since Mark…" Another flinch, and his sensitive nose caught the discordant note, an acridity in her scent.

Fear. More fear than she was already in. It smelled like old fear, like prey. Like blood in the water and an easy meal.

He pushed down the anger threatening to bubble up inside him. Slow and easy was the way to handle this. Her eyes stuttered to his face and she flinched, as if she'd read the emotional weather there and didn't like it.

A swallow, her vulnerable throat moving. "Whatever he's paying you, please don't do this. Please don't hurt me." She looked away, toward the milk shake, as if she couldn't quite figure out how it had gotten in her hand.

*What the hell?* His jaw was threatening to clench down hard enough to break a tooth. The fear in her was all wrong. If she was terrified, it would completely negate the soothing aspect of a shaman's scent, and *that* would open up a whole can of worms—not just for him, but for the younger ones, too.

"Get this straight." He took a deep breath, leashed the animal in him, and continued. "We're not going to hurt you. We need you, and I'm sorry it happened this way, but from now on, you're one of us. You're *ours*. The sooner you accept it, the better off you'll be."

It would take a lot of repeating before that sank in. Might as well get it out of the way first.

"I have to go back to work on Monday." She blinked again, swallowed hard, and more tears slid down those pretty, curved cheeks. "I've got night school, too. I'm studying to be a social worker."

*Well, Christ, honey, we've got tons of field-work for you right here.* "We'll settle that later. For right now, you have to eat." *And stop smelling like a downed deer.*

She just stared at the milk shake. Zach retreated, settling on the floor behind the driver's seat, the rhythm of the road soaking into his bones as he tore open a fresh bag and found a burger. The Silence folded around all of them again, and he didn't think he'd done too badly.

There was no easy way to handle this. But goddammit, she was a shaman. He could *smell* it on her, the potential some humans and fewer Tribe carried. Once she was triggered, she could be the nucleus of a new Family, a way to rebuild everything. With a shaman they could settle down even in a territory held by others. They were no longer rootless, wandering non-persons, dangerous because they lacked the thing that kept their kind from running amok.

They could be somebodies again, instead of fugitives. She would *make* them somebodies.

That was worth a little kidnapping, he decided. Whatever life she had back in the city they were now leaving, she would just have to learn to let go of. His little Family needed her too much.

## *Chapter 7*

The van jolted, and Sophie clawed up into full wakefulness, biting back a scream. Someone had draped a coat over her, and it was warm. Thin winter sunlight showed leafless trees, a few ragged pines, not blurring by but merely ambling. The vehicle made a deep turn, braked to a halt, and the engine cut off.

Finally. They were stopping. The eerie quiet in the car was breaking up, too, like ice in a river. Her ears had felt stuffed with cotton wool, but maybe it was the crying.

"Wake up." The girl shook her shoulder, fingers biting in. Her voice was rusty, as if she'd spent weeks instead of hours not talking. "Time to wash, bleeder."

Sophie sat up, blinking, and found the tank top had ridden up and twisted around, and the skirt—never very decent in the first place—was hitched up to show her panties, for God's sake. Her entire face was crusty and aching, and she had to use the bathroom like nobody's business. Her stomach rumbled.

The side door opened and the van cleared out. It was amazing, how people could fit in here. Clothes tangled across the floor, one bench seat had been taken out, and the back was stuffed with plastic bags. It didn't smell bad, though, just musky and close.

Sophie clutched the coat to her chest. The girl made a spitting sound of annoyance. "Come on, will you? I've got to pee before my kidneys float away."

*You're not the only one.* Mechanically, she pulled the skirt down, tried to straighten the tank top. Lucy's black heels were on the floor, and the way her back ached she didn't think she could stand to put them back on.

But she did, because cold air was pouring in through the open side door. Frost rimed the slice of a parking lot she could see, and as soon as she hopped awkwardly out of the van, pulling her skirt down and shivering, she found out they were at a rest stop off the freeway. A brick building housed restrooms, a creek wandered on the side away from the freeway down a short hill, and another building had vending machines behind iron grating, a wall full of maps in plastic cases, and—*oh, my God*—a Kiwanis booth selling coffee.

An old man sat in the booth, reading a newspaper, occasionally glancing out over the empty parking lot. The van, she now saw, was an older maroon Chevy, and her eyes came back to the man in the coffee booth.

The girl—Julia—jostled her from behind. She had dark eyes, long straight dark hair starred with that single streak that turned out to be white, and a sweet face, with the type of clear pale skin only found on the very young. Amazing skin. She was pretty, but there was an unfinished look around her mouth, like she was trying to be hard and not quite succeeding.

And she looked, for some reason, spoiled. Sophie couldn't put her finger on quite *how*, but she had the same overprivileged look as the mean-girl cheerleaders from Sophie's high school years.

"Come on." The girl slung her arm over Sophie's shoulders and started hurrying her to the bathrooms. She was a good head taller, and skinny, but strong. Sophie struggled to keep up, stumbled, and almost turned her ankle. And the girl began to whisper, very fast and low, as if she'd been bursting to talk. "Jeez. You *are* useless. Don't worry, I've got some stuff that might fit you. Zach'll take care of anything else later today, probably. We had a good haul last night." Julia took a deep breath, squeezed Sophie's shoulders roughly. "He was my brother. Kyle."

*What?* Last night was distant and dreamlike, receding like the van. Her heels clicked. Her stomach cramped, and her back was made out of aching concrete. There seemed nothing to say.

"The one who got killed last night. He was my brother." Julia cast a glance back over her shoulder, her voice dropping even further.

"Oh." Sophie couldn't think of anything else to say. *My best friend got killed, too, I guess we're even* didn't sound, well, very useful. It was what Lucy would call Not Helpful.

"It's not your fault," Julia continued softly, and she sounded magnanimous, condescending, and outright miserable all at once. "I'm stupid.

I've always been stupid. I just don't *think*. Not like Zach. And our alpha's dead and all we've got is a stupid bleeder to show for it." She paused, and cast another quick little glance over her shoulder. "Even if you do smell like Mom. I never… I was just… I thought I could kill it. The *upir*. I'm good at that."

*What, you mean you're good at killing? God, what a thing to say to someone you've kidnapped.* Sophie shivered. The thing in the white shirt. She'd stuck around long enough to see something awful, something so unreal, her mind even now shivered away from it. She flinched all over, inside and out, and stumbled again.

*It was dark and I was just confused. That's all.*

It was, Sophie reflected, a bad time to start lying to herself. She needed to think clearly if she was going to get out of this mess, and part of thinking clearly was figuring out last night.

What actually *had* happened? The only thing she was sure of was that Lucy was dead, and she had started running, screaming, a confusion of panic roaring through her. Lucy's white face, the terrible gaping hole where her throat should be, the thing in the white shirt snarling as its face twisted up, white teeth too big for its livid-lipped mouth—

"Watch where you're going," the girl said as Sophie tripped, and hauled her up over the curb. "Jeez. Heels. Why didn't you wear something practical?"

*You little...*Sophie found her voice. "I didn't know I was going to be kidnapped." The sarcasm surprised her. "Or watch my best friend get killed. I kind of forgot to put it in my day planner."

"Huh." Julia let go of her. She studied Sophie intently for a long moment, and stopped whispering. "I guess." She held up her free hand, which was full of cloth. "I've got something you can change into. If you want."

*Oh, God. I've been kidnapped and she wants me to dress appropriately.* "Fine." The side of her face hurt, but it didn't seem to be too bruised. She didn't dare glance at the old man in the Kiwanis booth. *If I can get over there— he's got to have a phone, right? Or something.*

The bathroom was cold and industrial, but well-lit and actually clean. The clothes turned out to be a pair of jeans that fit if she rolled up the legs like a little kid, and a long-sleeved thermal shirt that clung embarrassingly. There was a flannel button-down, too, with the same smell of musk and laundry detergent, but no socks and absolutely no undergarments.

The girl steered her toward the handicapped stall; Sophie shivered through changing and spent a blissful few minutes getting rid of the pressure on her bladder. When she came out, clutching Lucy's clothes to her chest, she looked longingly at the sink. It would feel so nice to wash her face, even if the water was freezing.

But Julia was still in a stall, humming something off-key. Sophie clutched the sad, small scraps of clothing and the heels, hugging them, and caught a glimpse of herself in the scratched piece of metal passing for a mirror. Wide eyes, her smudged glasses, and a wild mop of hair. She probably looked like a bag lady, though the side of her face wasn't that badly discolored. There was just a tender spot under her hair and puffy redness down her cheek, and she'd had worse.

*Much* worse.

She stared at the mirror for a few seconds, trying to clear her head. A rattling sound echoed in the depths of her memory, and she shivered. But it made her start moving, impelled by the sure intuition that had saved her more than once. It didn't happen often, that tingle along her nerves. Since leaving Hammerheath, it had always been accompanied by the rattling buzz of copper-bottomed—

*Did I feel it last night, and just not pay attention?* She pushed the question aside and took the first few tentative steps.

Her purse was still in the van. *Stupid, stupid, stupid!* she chanted inwardly as she edged, heart hammering, for the entrance. Cold tile gritted under her bare feet, and she eased out of the hallway and into the chill of a winter morning. Without the heels, her footsteps were silent.

She set off for the Kiwanis booth, not daring to look over her shoulder. *Don't act guilty. But walk quickly. Walk determined. Catch his eye.*

Her stomach rumbled. If she could catch the man's attention and ask him to call the police, she could get free, she could…what? Give a statement?

What statement could she *give?* She hadn't seen anything she could swear to, just things out of a nightmare. Things with fangs, and a confused impression of something leaping, something covered in hair like a…

Like *what,* exactly? She couldn't put it into words. And the rattling in her head got louder.

Forty feet away, the man coughed behind his newspaper. Her feet were numb; she stepped on a pebble and winced. Going barefoot at home was nothing like this. The jeans were raspingly unfamiliar, and she really wanted nothing more than her own kitchen, her ratty chenille robe, and a hot cup of coffee. And a Danish. A warm one, dripping with icing and with chunks of brown-sugar-drenched apple.

She could almost taste it, and hurried up. Thirty feet. Twenty-five.

The air was still except for the hum of traffic from the freeway. What was she going to say? *This isn't a joke. I've been kidnapped. Please help me.*

She practiced it inside her head, clutching the clothes to her chest. Cold morning wind touched her hair, and the sky was still orangeish in the east from dawn. If she was at home she'd probably still be in bed, and if Lucy stayed over—

Pain jabbed through her chest. *Oh, Lucy. Luce. God.*

The rattling in her head got worse. Fifteen feet. Ten.

She opened her mouth—and let out her

breath in a sigh when the man looked up, his hazel eyes caught in a net of crinkles, his smile immediate and genuine.

The buzzing rattle stopped.

A heavy arm fell over her shoulders. "Cup of coffee, sweetheart?" Zach said, as if it was the most normal thing in the world.

Everything in her cringed away. She stared at the old man, willing him to realize she'd been about to ask him for help. The sore spot under her hair throbbed, and her cheek was on fire.

The old man grinned even wider, if that was possible. She saw the glasses dangling on a chain at his chest, and her heart sank. "What a pretty young miss. I call all the young girls 'miss.' Hope you don't mind."

"Not at all." Zach's arm tightened. "Make that three coffees, please. And probably a doughnut for her, too. We've been driving all night."

"Family trip?" The man eased off his stool and shuffled around the small booth. "Reason I ask is, I heard your van door."

Zach grinned easily. "Yeah, heading south. Warmer down there." His arm tightened again, and he—of all things—bent down and kissed the top of Sophie's head, inhaling deeply. As if *smelling* her. She writhed inwardly with embarrassment; what was she supposed to do? Start screaming?

What would he do if she did?

A sudden crystalline image from last night, right before she'd run off like a panicked idiot, burned through her brain. It was the thing that had killed Lucy, snarling and champing its too-big teeth, while Zach's shape changed like clay under running water.

Growing *fur.*

Sudden certainty nailed her in place, the chill concrete biting into her feet. *I didn't imagine that. I saw it. That's what made me run. I saw it all.*

"Oh, I hear ya, I hear ya." The old man shrugged inside his jacket, setting out three foam cups, putting a pink bakery box on the small counter. "Honey, why don't you just peek in there and see if there's a doughnut you like? I got apple fritters, and Bismarcks, and all sorts of good things. Fresh this morning, too."

Sophie swallowed hard, her throat making a little clicking noise. Zach bumped her, gently, and she was suddenly very sure that if she didn't try to act normally, something would Happen.

*Like something "happened" to Lucy? He said they weren't going to hurt me.*

He could have been lying. She'd heard "I'm not going to hurt you" before. If she had a quarter for every time she'd heard it, she wouldn't have to worry about scraping together rent for a year.

Zach used his free hand to open up the top of the bakery box. "See anything good?" He sounded concerned. Morning light was kind to him, running over the shadow of stubble on his face, the thin nose, dark eyes a lot of women probably liked. His hair was a soft mess except for the wiriness of the white streak. One stubborn wave of it fell over his forehead, and he actually grinned down at her like he was having a great time.

Sourness rose in her throat. He'd kidnapped her, and had the effrontery to smile and put his arm over her shoulder like he owned her?

"I'm not hungry," she managed through the stone in her throat. "But thanks." She stared at the old man, her eyes burning. *Look at me. Please see me. Please help me.*

"Dieting? Never did anyone any good, honey. First three letters of *diet* are a warning, that's what they are." He wasn't looking at her; he was pouring the coffee, frowning a little. She tried leaning away from Zach's arm, but it was useless. Her feet went numb, aching from the cold. "My wife used to say that. Cream and sugar?"

"Only in one." Zach peered into the bakery box, pulling her with him. "And I think we'll take two of these apple fritters. They look nice."

"You go ahead now. That'll be three dollars for the coffee, young man. You just take those fritters as a gift from me."

"Why, thank you." He sounded so normal, so nice, as if he hadn't kidnapped a woman and killed—

*Oh, my God. He killed that thing, didn't he? "Upir,"* he'd said. Her head hurt just *thinking* about it, spikes of glassy pain through her temples.

Nobody would miss her for another twenty-four hours, and by then, who knew how far away they would have taken her? Her ferns would die, she wouldn't be at work Monday morning, and Battle-Ax Margo, the office manager, would have a conniption. Nobody knew she'd gone out with Lucy, and Luce was between boyfriends. What was happening right now? Were the police trying to find her? Trying to find Lucy's car keys?

*If I hadn't divorced Mark someone would be missing me right now—but if I hadn't run away in the first place I wouldn't have been out last night. God.*

Zach moved again, and she almost flinched, but he was handing her two monstrous apple fritters wrapped in a napkin, tucking them on top of the clothes she clutched to her chest. "Here. Hold these, sweetie. Why don't you head on back to the car, and I'll bring your coffee?"

The old man chuckled. She realized he was not just shortsighted; he just really wasn't interested in anything she might say. "My wife was like that. Bit of a bear in the morning without her coffee, God bless her."

"Go on, now." Zach gave her a meaningful look, and when Sophie snapped a glance over her shoulder she saw the two other men at the open van, watching intently. They all had those weird pale stripes in their hair, like a dye job gone wrong. Maybe it was a gang sign?

*Yeah, like the badass Lady Clairols. Come on, Sophie. Think of something!*

There was nobody else around, and what could the old man do?

Nothing. She was just as helpless now as she'd been last night.

"Fine." She backed up as Zach's arm fell away. Her feet felt frozen, and if she stepped on anything sharp now she'd probably be too numb to care. Each step was another jab of freezing pain up her legs, and her toes felt clumsy.

The younger boy, sitting crouched just inside the van door, eyed her. He was a male copy of Julia, but instead of looking spoiled and unfinished he had a perpetually worried grin and a way of hunching his shoulders as if he was painfully uncertain. "You okay?" he asked, softly, tilting his head to the side. His eyes were red-rimmed and his nose a little chapped from crying.

The other one, bigger and broad-shouldered but not as tall as Zach, had odd, piercing blue eyes. He regarded her warily, hunching inside his tattered leather jacket. He had one hand raised, and as she glanced at him his strong white teeth worried a little at the leather cuff of his sleeve.

*No, I'm not okay. How could I be anything like okay?* But some instinct made her hold out the fritters with one hand freed from the clothes, despite the way her stomach growled. "Here. These are for you."

"Hey, thanks!" The younger one grabbed one, took a huge wolfish bite, and grinned. The blue-eyed one took the other more slowly, but at least he stopped snacking on his sleeve. "I'm Brun. This is Eric. He's our cousin. Gee, aren't your feet cold? Come on up." He moved aside, and Sophie mechanically climbed into the van. It still held a ghost of warmth.

They both peered at her, the one in the leather jacket nibbling at his fritter now.

"These are really good," Brun continued. "Are you really a shaman?"

"She's a found shaman, not even triggered. She wouldn't know, not yet." The blue-eyed one—Eric—eyed her speculatively. "This means we can settle down somewhere."

"You think? It'd be nice. We haven't settled anywhere since the farm..." Maddeningly, he stopped, and gave her a shy smile. Dark puppy eyes glimmered at her. "It's nice to meet you. You're going to take care of us?"

It was too absurd to even guess at an answer. "You kidnapped me." She sounded flat and unhelpful even to herself. "I'm supposed to take care of you?"

"We're Carcajou." Eric shrugged. "Makes no sense to you now, but it will. And Zach's—"

"Zach's what?" Zach was at the door suddenly, his shadow filling it, and the other two fell silent. "Coffee, Eric. Courtesy of our new shaman. Isn't she sweet?"

"Breakfast?" Julia arrived, looking fresh as a daisy, her glossy hair combed and her face pink from scrubbing. Sophie's skin crawled, and her mouth tasted like ashes. "Where's mine?"

"You don't get any," Zach said pleasantly. "I told you to watch her."

"She's right here." Julia's lower lip stuck out, and she looked supremely confident that she would get her way.

"Get in the van. If we lose our shaman like we lost our alpha, I'm holding *you* responsible. Even if it's not on your watch." Zach's pleasant tone and even smile didn't change, but something in his face shifted, and the morning grew a little chillier. Sophie eased back, suddenly very sure something awful was about to happen. She'd felt the same way before, whenever Mark was a certain type of quiet or smelled too strongly of liquor when he came home.

But Julia just bowed her head and hopped into the van. They all moved so gracefully it was unreal. The rest of them piled in, and Sophie was suddenly in the middle of a press of bodies. Zach thrust a foam cup into her hands. "Cream and sugar, sweetheart. And then we'll figure out getting you a toothbrush and everything. You're probably not ready for life on the road."

*That is such an understatement.* Sophie stared at him. The van door heaved shut, closing the empty parking lot outside. It might as well be the surface of the moon. It was just as far away—and just as useless to her.

The weird crackling quiet folded over all of them. She was about to say something—plead, maybe, or point out that they were kidnapping her, or something equally useless. But the odd silence filled every corner of the van and stopped the words in her throat.

The van started up again, and she found herself huddling against the wall on the far side, the coffee in her numb hands and her face aching. It was no use.

She was trapped. At least, for now.

## Chapter 8

A day's worth of driving had them a safe five hundred miles away, even with bathroom and food breaks. It was far enough that he couldn't avoid having them stop, and a comfortable distance from a rabid *upir* attack.

They kept the Silence unless they were eating, and there seemed no reassurance that would get the new shaman to open up. After a few tries he gave up. She didn't even respond to Brun's gentle mealtime questions.

She even refused to eat, just huddled in the back under his coat and stared reproachfully at them all. When the Silence came back she trembled and closed her eyes, pretending to be asleep. It was a good pretense, and he let her keep it.

Julia loftily ignored the girl except for a bathroom break, and Zach saw his sister pinch her as she was hurried toward another rest-stop bathroom.

He let that go. Another night in their company, smelling them, would trigger her—if the biochemical process hadn't been started already by their proximity. Found shamans took longer than born shamans to adjust to life in a Family, to the responsibility and the shock of finding out the world held more than just regular old humans.

Then again, most found shamans were taken into a regular Family and trained by another shaman, finding and shifting to a Family of their own later. They weren't taken off the street right after an *upir* attack by a half-wild shaman-less Family who had just lost their alpha. It was the worst possible scenario.

And there was another thing. The instinct that had compelled him to grab her was circling the bottom of his mind even now, whispering other things.

Things like, *Look at that hair, even all tangled up it's pretty and it smells like sunshine.*

Or, *Those hips have a nice curve to them, don't they?*

Or how about, *Her lips look pretty kissable when she purses them like that.*

And something less pleasant. *We're being followed.*

Night fell in cold streaks of scarlet and orange, the Silence breaking naturally on its own. Clouds massed on the horizon along with the glow of a good-size city. A hotel on the fringes wasn't hard to find. They were flush with cash, so he sent Eric in to get a room, then shepherded his weary Family up the stairs to a nice little room with two queen beds and a kitchenette, not to mention a television Julia immediately turned on and a bathroom the new shaman looked longingly at.

The flannel shirt was too big for her, and it was his. The sight of her wrapped in something he owned was guaranteed to distract him—just like the smell of her mixing with *his* smell and rolling off the fabric. Right into the middle of his head, and right below the belt.

Brun hopped out the door to get food, and Julia and Eric were sent to get toiletries, things the new shaman would need. That left him alone in the room with her, and as soon as the silence closed around them she edged for the bathroom, shutting the door with a bang audible even through the television's yapping.

He turned the idiot box down and pulled the curtains, spending a few minutes watching the parking lot. The animal in him crouched watchfully. There was no reason to think they were being followed...but there it was. The itching between his shoulder blades and the nagging feeling in his gut just wouldn't go away.

*Trust that feeling, son,* his father's voice growled inside his head. *It's your best friend, and it'll keep you and your Family safe.*

His father.

That wasn't a good thought, so he shut it away. The smell of smoke and the crushing weight of responsibility wouldn't quite go until he took a few deep breaths and reminded himself that he had problems in the here and now, and thinking about the past wouldn't solve them.

Kyle's spirit was safely over the border now, into the shifting realm of the *majir*. Which meant he *had* to talk to her, and try not to screw it up too badly.

He gave her ten minutes, then turned the television off and tapped at the bathroom door.

"You can come out, sweetheart. We need to talk."

*We definitely need to talk. The sooner you understand a few things, the better off everyone will be.*

Nothing. No sound of running water, no sniffles, just a deathly silence. He was sure there was no window in there; he'd checked. But still, his hand hovered above the doorknob. It would be a simple matter to snap a cheap hotel-door lock and walk in.

He didn't even know who this girl was. Sophie, okay. Married once, possibly married still. Curly hair and steel-rimmed glasses, vulnerable wintry eyes and curves to make a racetrack die of envy. She smelled good, but among Carcajou there was such a thing as courting a female. Even when she smelled like she was his already, her pheromones striking sparks against his sensitive nose.

He knocked again, suddenly acutely aware that he was unshaven, smelling of unwilling attraction and acrid worry, still wearing the same clothes he'd been in last night. She was bound to be confused, upset. He'd have to handle her carefully.

*Yeah. Like you have a clue how to handle a*

*woman carefully. You've been doing a bang-up job so far.*

He'd been too young to even think about mating while his parents were alive, and the gatherings where young people of each Tribe eyed one another and courted were closed to them once they were on their own. And human women smelled like food, not mates. His entire knowledge of what to say to a human woman came from television. Julia was no help at all, either.

There was a slight scraping noise. *What's that?* He listened so intently he could hear her pulse, quickening now, and the soft soughing of her breathing. *Up to something in there. Huh.* He knocked again, softly. "Look, I'm not going to hurt you, no matter what you think. I'll explain everything. Just come on out, Sophie. Is it short for Sophia?"

Another soft sound. Was it a laugh? The animal in him perked its ears, expectant. It was like hunting, waiting for the prey to appear.

Only she wasn't prey. She was something else. Something he wanted to run down and fill his mouth with. Something good.

He touched the doorknob, running his fingers over it. "Come on. At least say something."

"Go away," came the muffled answer. But her breathing was high and harsh now, and her pulse thudded, as if she was in some sort of pain. There were other scratching, wrenching noises under the thunder of her stress-laden breathing.

*What the hell?* He twisted the knob and pulled the door open, opening his mouth to ask her if she was hurt.

The blow came out of nowhere. Faster reflexes saved him; he ducked and caught it in one hand, her surprising strength sending a shock all the way down his arm. She was screaming like a banshee suddenly, trying to wrench it away—a cheap hotel towel rack, pried loose from the wall. He smelled blood, too, and instinct woke in a red blur. He ripped the thing out of her hands and caught her wrist as she flew at him, still screaming.

She beat at him with her free fist until he caught it, trapping it in his much-larger hand and yanking her around as if she weighed less than a feather. There was a clear space next to the bathroom door, between the jamb and a closet space holding an ironing board and hangers attached to a rod.

He shoved her back; her shoulders met the

wall with a tooth-rattling thump, and trapped her there. She kept struggling until he got her arms up over her head and pressed against her, bloodscent teasing and taunting at the animal, and the acrid reek of a shaman's fear tearing at his control.

*Goddammit.* She pitched from side to side, mad with fear, and tried to bite him. Her mouth landed against his shoulder, she drove her teeth in again, and he froze, fingers clamping down until she made a small hurt sound, an interruption in her screaming.

She was biting him. Teeth in flesh, a promise and spur all at once. A red tide washed through him, and he almost lost it right there.

*Control.* Memory rose—he was twelve years old, and the alpha's fingers were crushing the back of his neck, holding him still. *Control the beast. We are human, we are Carcajou. We are not savages.*

Still, with a shaman in an ecstasy of fear, accidents could happen. *Bad* accidents. And she had no idea that her teeth in his skin were an enticement.

She tried kneeing him, but he was pressed so hard against her, a slim soft thing between him and the unforgiving wall, she couldn't get any leverage. The ice-and-moonlight smell broke over him in a cresting wave, and confusion between the obedience bred into every Carcajou's bones to that smell and the response to the feel of her against him, the sunshine aroma of her hair filling his nose and its softness rubbing against his stubble as he buried his face in the tangled curls, gave him bare seconds to take a breath before drowning.

He came back to himself piecemeal, a sobbing woman between him and the wall, his fingers bruising-tight around her wrists and violence just a hairsbreadth away.

*Oh, God. Get out of this one. Control yourself, goddammit; nobody can do it for you! You're not a savage. You're Carcajou.*

The animal in him didn't believe it. Arousal was a lead bar in the lowest part of his belly, her fear dragging sharp claws over his skin. "Calm down," he managed, in a voice that had precious little of humanity left in it. It was a snarl, pure and simple. "Calm the *fuck* down, girl, or we are going to have *problems*." *Problems that make this look like making out in the back of a Chevy. Jesus, don't think about that. Control.*

She quieted, her breath hitching as she tried to swallow the tears. And she stopped struggling, which was good. Except that he still wanted to press against her, irritating layers of cloth in the way. She was sweating, he could *taste* it, and the urge to press his face against her throat and flick his tongue delicately against her skin to taste it even further made a fine tremor run through the center of his bones.

Fur receded. The claws prickling out through his fingertips receded, as well. He won the battle with himself by bare inches, and the animal retreated, snarling back down to the floor of his mind, curling up and promising trouble later.

"I am not going to hurt you," he whispered into her hair. "You hear me? We need you. You have no idea how much. Nobody's going to hurt you. I promise."

"Why are you doing this?" Tears crowded her voice, but she didn't move. Maybe she was smart enough to know that if she moved right now, he might very well snap and do something he'd regret. "Just let me go and leave me alone. I'm *nobody,* why are you doing this to me?"

*What the hell?* "You're not nobody." There was a rock in his throat; he managed to clear it and she almost flinched. So he pressed forward again, holding her still. "If you'll be quiet, and sit down, I'll explain a few things. We're

Carcajou. We were born different, and sometimes we come across people like you. We call
you found shamans. You're different, too, just a
little bit. You can keep us calm, make us better."
He inhaled, drawing the smell of her all the way
down into the bottom of his lungs. *And I don't
know how to tell you this, but you're mine. Fight
it all you want, but we'll come to some sort of
understanding. Sooner or later.* "I'm the alpha
now. The boy you saw get unzipped fighting
that thing—the *upir*—that was my brother. I let
him take the alpha because…" Shame rose hot
and tight in his throat. "Because I was afraid,
and because of…other things." Inch by inch,
his bones creaking in protest, he eased away
from her, his flesh still holding the sensation of
hers. "Now you know something none of them
knows. You know I let him take it, even though
he wasn't strong enough. I suppose that makes
me a coward, but I'm done with that." *I have to
be done with that. There's nobody else left.*

Another deep breath. She was still afraid,
and the taint of blood still maddened the
thing crouching in the floor of his mind. His
eyes traveled up her arms, her thin wrists
caught in his fingers, pale against the darker
tone of his skin.

That was where the maddening tang of blood had come from. Her fingertips were raw, probably from working the towel rack out of its holder. She must've been damn motivated to get it free, disregarding the damage to her skin.

"Goddamn, girl. Look what you did to yourself." He brought her hands down, flipped them palms up, studied the ragged, bloody edges. "Jesus. What were you going to do after you brained me with that thing, huh?"

She swallowed, her throat moving. Her glasses were smudged, knocked astray, and she was biting her lower lip so hard he thought she might start bleeding from there, too.

If she did there was going to be even *more* of a problem. But her teeth eased free, thank God.

"I was going to dial 9-1-1 and get the hell out of here. Let the police come and keep you busy while I ran." She sounded steadier, calmer, but hoarse. This was a fragile peace, the eye of the hurricane. If he handled her carefully enough now he might be able to make her understand a few things.

"Good plan. It would have delayed us for about half an hour. Then we would have tracked you and brought you back. You're *ours* now. Get used to it." *The sooner we get that through your head, the sooner we can all breathe easier.*

He realized just a little too late that sheer stubborn repetition might not be the best way to handle a terrified woman who flinched at all the wrong times. If he'd had a hand free he might've been tempted to smack himself in the forehead.

But it was too late. Her chin lifted a little, stubbornly. Then, the dam burst. "What was that thing? It killed Lucy, goddammit! And you—you're not *normal!* None of you are normal! You don't even *smell* human!"

Perceptive of her. "The thing that killed your Lucy was *upir.* That's what we call it. They... you can call 'em vampires, if you want. We kill them where we find them and they return the favor, only most of them stay out of our way unless they're stupid or rabid. That one was probably rabid. They go nuts if they get a batch of bad blood, and they act just like dogs foaming at the mouth." He dragged in another deep breath, still holding her wrists. *Come on, Zach. Give her something reasonable to hold on to.* "We aren't human, not like you are. Score one for you. We're different but we're still people.

And we need you. I'm sorry I haven't been nice about it, but—"

"*Nice?* You fucking *kidnapped* me!" Her eyes were all but spitting sparks. She drew herself up to her full height—still a little too short to be anything but adorable—and gave him a glare that would have done even Dad, the old alpha, proud. "You're holding me *hostage!*"

"No, we're not. We're not asking anyone to pay for you." It was out of his mouth before he could stop himself, taking refuge in the reflex of sarcasm. "Is there anyone who would?"

"The only person who might have is dead in a fucking alley—let *go* of me!" She wrenched her hands away and he let her. Her chest heaved, tears slicking her cheeks, and the sudden urge to press her against the wall again was stunning. It warred with the urge to put his arms around her and tell her everything was going to be all right. "I have a job. I have a life. It's not much of a life but it's *mine,* and I worked too hard for it to let you or anyone else take it away! I started out with *nothing!* And I'm not going to do it again, you hear me? You'd better let me go. You'd just…" She almost ran out of steam, put her shoulders back and her chin up. "You'd just *better.*"

*That's good.* It gave him more to work with, and if she was angry she wasn't crying or afraid of him. Anger he could deal with.

Anger he could understand. "All right, so you had a life. You want to go back to it? Work with us. We'd like a life, too. You think we *want* to live this way?"

"It looks like you like it, especially if you're kidnapping innocent women." She clutched her bleeding hands together. Her eyes were still glowing.

*What? That makes absolutely no sense.* "Well, we don't. We lost our brother, our alpha, killing the thing that killed your friend. You could cut us a little slack here." He suddenly began to get the idea he wasn't controlling this situation nearly as well as he thought he was. "We don't like this. We want to settle down. Once I know I can trust you, we can go back to your city and do it there. How about it?"

"Are you *insane?*" Her voice hit a pitch right under "scream," and the ice-and-moonlight smell intensified. A flush spread up her throat, blooming in her cheeks, and he could *smell* the balance of her internal chemistry shifting. It was like smelling Julia's sudden drift of estrogen once a month. Only much, much nicer.

Bingo. She was triggered. High emotion and proximity to Carcajou pheromones setting off latent potential. By midnight she'd be a Carcajou shaman, and it would take weeks to shift her to another Tribe. By next morning she'd be *their* shaman, and it would take months to shift her. The first critical step had happened.

Everything else would follow. It had to. She was their only chance, and he couldn't fail this one last test like he'd failed all the others. There was nobody else around to take the fall for this one.

And God, how he hated what that said about him. He *had* to get this one right.

Her hands had curled into fists. "You've *kidnapped* me." A very low, dangerous tone, stroking his skin until he felt the urge to shiver. "What you're doing is illegal and wrong. You let me leave right now and I won't go to the police. I'll go home and forget about this, and go to work Monday morning. If you don't, I swear to God I'll—"

*You'll do what? Leave us to die one by one?* His temper almost snapped. "What? Try to kill me? We can hold you for years until you calm down, shaman. Play nice with us. You said yourself nobody would pay for you. What the hell is back in that city you want so much? Your husband, maybe?"

Her immediate flinch, and the sharp note of fear cutting through her scent, warned him just before the animal lunged for freedom again. Her eyes turned big and wounded; her hands pulled back toward her chest and raised a little as if to ward off a blow—

The Change ran through him like a sword of hot glass, bones crackling and fur rippling. He fought it, desperately trying to retain control, but the animal knew better than he did, had seen something he hadn't.

*Your husband, maybe?* A flinching woman. A flinching, frightened woman. His claws stretched, sliding free, and his left-hand ones sank into the flooring as he crouched. She'd lost all her air, backing up until she hit the wall again, not even screaming, the wash of terror from her glands enough to send him careening over into pure madness.

Control *yourself!* Clapping a lid on the beast wasn't easy to do, especially when it smelled fear on something that belonged to him.

*She doesn't know that, she doesn't know anything—just fucking control yourself!* Words almost vanished in a sheet of red, but the ice and moonlight sent a silver thread through the crimson, stitching it together. It was a fine thread, a thin thread, and his human side clung to it with every ounce of strength it could scrape together.

Fur receded, claws slid back home, and she was staring at him, glassy-eyed with terror. Her mouth was slightly open, as if she'd forgotten everything she wanted to say. His jaw crackled, taking on a shape fit for human speech again, bone moving under the skin, muscles stretching and shrinking. Hunger tore across his midsection—it took a lot of energy to fuel the Change, even more to hover just on the edge of it.

He backed away, despite the howling of the thing inside him that wanted to leap on her. Her legs went; she slid down the wall and sat with a bump, her teeth clicking together hard.

"I'm not crazy," she whispered, between deep whistling breaths. "I'm not. I'm *not.*"

"You're not," he agreed hoarsely. *At least, you seem pretty normal to me. But what would I know?* That was a good thought, a rational human thought, and he clung to it. The sharp bursts of terror from her were like painful static across his sensitive nose, cutting through the blandness of hotel room and the comforting blanket of fading musk from his brothers and sister. "I promise you're not."

"You're a werewolf." She said it flatly, like she'd watched all the movies and had everything figured out.

Great. Sometimes he wondered if the movies were worth it. They made Tribe into fairy tales, so nobody went hunting them anymore. But on the other hand, they made things like this…difficult.

"Carcajou," he corrected. "It's different. You don't know how different. And we need you, Sophie."

"I'm not crazy," she repeated. "You're a *werewolf*."

"The Wolf Tribe's different. We're *Carcajou*." It probably didn't mean squat to her, but still, the comparison rankled. *We're not dogs, for God's sake. We're allied with the Ursa Tribe, and we are finer than the Felinii. But we're not dogs.*

"Are you going to…eat…me?" she whispered. It was impossible for her gray eyes to get any bigger. Fever spots stood out high on her cheeks, and her smudged glasses were askew. She didn't even seem to notice.

*Jesus.* A bolt of revulsion shot through him.

It killed the animal rage, which was a good thing, but that she could *think* that was horrifying. "Of course not. We don't eat people. We're not savages."

"You don't…" She blinked, going pale almost as rapidly as she'd flushed. "That's a relief." Amazingly, she looked—and sounded—calmer. "But why would you want to kid—" Another thought crossed her mobile little face, and he congratulated himself on making some progress. "Oh, my God," she breathed. "That thing that killed Lucy. That was a—"

*Not too shabby. Quick on the uptake, even.* "Like I said, you'd call it a vampire. But it's not like the movies, honey. Running water and crosses won't stop them, and a stake will only make them mad. Unless it's wielded by a Djombrani." He shrugged, cautiously. Maybe the movies were good for something, if they gave her a handle on what was happening. "But we don't mess with that Gypsy shit. We're Carcajou."

"Vampire." Her pupils were so dilated her eyes looked black, rimmed with silver. "Right." She paused, licked her lips. "Werewolves." Another long pause. "Right?"

"Right," he echoed. *Are we finally making some progress?*

*"Right."* And she scrambled to her feet and bolted for the door.

He caught her halfway there, taking her legs out from under her and shoving so she landed on the bed. Which was *all sorts* of tempting, so he followed, pinning her, careful of his greater density. The mattress groaned once, sharply, its springs taking a sudden load it probably wasn't designed for. "Keep trying," he said, his nose inches from hers. "We'll catch you every time, shaman. We *need* you."

"Nobody needs me." Her pupils shrank, her gaze losing its shock and fuzziness. "The only person who needed me is dead in that alley and you've kidnapped me. I am *not* going to be trapped again. I won't do it. You'd better let me go. You'd just *better.*" Her voice broke on the last word, and he cursed himself.

Here he was scaring the hell out of her, when he should be explaining, gently and patiently, that she could do more good with them than with anything she'd left behind. That she was their passport to rejoining their entire fucking species. That they couldn't afford to let her go, that they would do anything she asked except let her go. That she was a *shaman,* for God's sake, and all she had to do was snap her fingers and they would jump.

That she would keep them—and especially him—human.

Human enough that he wouldn't terrify a woman who probably needed gentleness more than anything else. Human enough that he wouldn't feel the slip-sliding tug of rage and grief plucking at his control. Human enough that he could get through five or six breaths without wanting to beat his head into the walls and keen for his brother, for his Family, for the whole goddamn messy situation.

It would take so little from her to do so much for them—but why should she? He was doing everything exactly wrong, and he couldn't figure out how to do it right for the life of him.

And here he was on top of her, on a bed, and she had gone very still.

Too still.

She'd closed her eyes, tears welling out from under her lids, her glasses tilted, and visibly braced herself for the worst. So he let go of her, an inch at a time, and as soon as he could stand to lose the feel of her under him he leaped free of the bed and put his back to the door.

She curled into a small ball and sobbed, each small hitching breath tearing at his heart.

Maybe one of the others could make her understand. Because he had a sinking feeling he'd just fucked up his one chance. She didn't have a shaman to train her, and if they ran across other Tribe who found her in this state of abject misery and terror Zach would have a lot of explaining to do—and there weren't many Tribe who would listen. He might end up being put on trial, and who would look after his Family then?

In other words, he was right back where he started. And she was worse off than ever.

## Chapter 9

She was awake when the window broke.

Well, maybe not *awake* but certainly not asleep. Instead, she was in a fuzzy half state, cried-out and wishing for her own bed and her own kitchen instead of yet another clutch of un-eatable fast food. For people who ate junk all the time they were awfully slim and energetic, each one of them long and lean and graceful.

Apparently, being werewolves was good for *something*. Jesus.

She'd refused to eat or speak to them, with-drawing inside her head the way she used to when Mark was on one of his rampages. They left her alone after a while and she just curled tighter and tighter around herself, becoming all elbows and knees. Julia had kept turning the television up, and Zach kept turning it down, and the smell of food made Sophie's head ache and her stomach rumble.

*Werewolves. Oh, my God.* Little shivers would race through her at the thought. But she'd *seen* it, his flesh melting and reshaping, hair sliding free, and that sound—a thunderous growl that couldn't come from a human chest, with weird clicking stops at the end. And oddly enough, he told *her* she wasn't crazy.

But *werewolves,* for God's sake. And poor Lucy, and Lucy's body, and the terrible gaping hole in Lucy's throat…and Sophie would flinch again, pull herself together more tightly, and try to find some way to fit all this inside her aching head.

It wasn't working.

They had arranged themselves either on the other bed or on the floor to sleep, Julia whining that Sophie had a bed all to herself and Eric saying, "She's the *shaman,*" just like someone would say, *It's raining.* Zach stood near the door for a long time, his head down and his arms crossed. The others whispered and glanced at him until he shook his shaggy hair as if he was dislodging a bad thought. They quieted as if he'd shushed them, then Zach settled down cross-legged like he was going to sleep sitting up.

Sophie turned over, drew her knees up, and tried in vain to sleep. Her head wouldn't let all the horror fit inside it—she would try to put everything together, and one piece would fall out, sending a zing of pain through her aching skull. Lucy's agonized gasping would echo inside her, or the thing snarling with its white shirt blackened and wet down the front. And she would flinch, her stomach churning.

It didn't help that her skin felt like it had been scrubbed raw. Everything was so *loud,* the rustle of clothing and sheets rasping like jagged metal edges. The sough of breathing, like bellows. Her skin hurt, each sound sandpaper over ragged nerves. Her entire body flushed and tingled oddly. She wondered if you could get an allergic reaction from just the smell of MSG-laden food, and tried to find a comfortable way to lie.

Sleep was an utter impossibility.

So when the window shattered and the noise started, she sat bolt upright. A terrible reek of old dirt and rotting spice-rubbed fabric blew into the room like a tidal wave. The door shattered, kicked inward, and someone ran into her, grabbing and rolling.

The confusion ended with her on the floor between the beds, Zach untangling himself from her and barking, *"Stay down!"* before he vanished. The lamp on the table between the beds shattered as something hit it, and the growling, snapping, screams shading into yowls like a huge enraged cat reached a pitch just short of madness. Habit sent her fishing around for her glasses—thankfully, they were right on the night table where she'd left them, though the shards of the lamp were sharp against her frantic fingers for an endless, nightmarish second.

She might have stayed there, crouched with her hands over her ears, if she hadn't heard a gurgling noise, like water swirling down a recalcitrant drain.

It reminded her of Lucy's throat and the terrible bubbling, gaping wound there. And her knee was on something small and pebbled—Lucy's tiny jeweled purse, the keys inside spearing her kneecap.

Sophie grabbed it and threw herself toward the end of the bed. Something flew over her head, snapping and snarling, and hot drops of foul-smelling liquid spattered her. She screamed, miserably, a small sound lost in the cacophony boiling around her, and crawled for the door. Someone tripped over her, a booted foot sinking solidly into her side, and all her breath left as her stomach backed up, trying to flee out her throat.

Cold air drenched the carpet as a coppery stink roiled around her, and she scrambled through the shattered door on all fours, crying out again as a sliver the size of a tree trunk pierced the meat of her left hand. That sound was lost in the huge noise, too, and the sliver was pulled free as she raised her hand.

She made it outside, to the pebbled concrete walkway, and scrambled to her bare feet. Ran, the little jeweled purse clutched in her bleeding fist and her feet slapping the concrete so hard she felt the reverberations in her teeth. The stairs unreeled under her, and a sudden vivid image of tripping, cartwheeling over and over and smashing her skull on the pavement below, managed to slow her for only half a second. The parking lot blurred by, a Coke machine screaming red, and she made it to the entrance to the parking lot, framed with high holly bushes. Her breath plumed white in the frosty air.

And there, looming out of the night like a fresh yellow beacon of hope, was a taxi. *Riverside Car Service* was painted on the side in orange, with a cheery decal that looked something like a mushroom and was probably intended to look like a car.

*"Stop!"* she screamed, waving her hands like a maniac or a drowning woman and, wonder of wonders, the cab braked smoothly. She reached for the back door just as the passenger's window rolled down.

"Lady, you on drugs?" The cabbie, a short, thick, bristled man, peered through Coke-bottom glasses at her. Her own lenses were smeared and smudged, and her head hurt, a spike driven through her temples. The tingling, flushing weirdness on her skin was better outside in the cold air.

"Of course I'm not." Her throat was raw, and she winced, groping for something to say. The noise wasn't nearly as overwhelming out here in the parking lot, but in another few minutes that might change. "There's a party going on here and I want to go home. Can you take me to the train station? Please?" *Please?*

She tried to look drug-free and vulnerable at the same time, digging in the purse and pulling out a random handful of cash—all she could afford to take dancing with her last night. She'd been grousing to herself over the waste—it was half her grocery bill for the month, dammit. "Look, I can pay and I'm not any trouble, honest. I just want to go home." Behind her, the noise took on a different quality—a chilling animal howl that ended on a series of guttural broken stops. *God, you have no idea how much I just want to go* home. *Please help me.*

The lock on the back door chucked up. "Get in, lady. Don't stand around."

She clambered into the cab, slamming the door so hard she was amazed the window didn't shatter.

"You damn lucky," the cabbie said as he pulled away, excruciatingly slowly. "I usually tell people get out, they slam the door that hard. This thing's my livelihood, ya know."

*Jesus Christ, what the hell was that?* "I'm sorry," she managed. Her throat was on fire and her glasses were probably never going to be the same. Two hundred bucks she couldn't afford for the frames alone. "I guess I'm...I'm sorry." *Werewolves. And what the hell was that? Something came in the window, they were fighting. More werewolves?*

*Jesus Christ. I can't believe I'm even think-ing this. And I saw it and heard it all myself.* Cold air poured through the driver's window; it felt so good against her fevered cheeks and sweating hands. She gulped in the smells of exhaust, vinyl, the close muggy smell of other people who'd sat in this very seat.

Real people. Human people.

"Aw, don't worry about it. What happened to you, lady? You look awful scared."

*Scared* seemed too pale a word. So did *re-lieved.* She didn't twist around in the seat to look behind her only with a massive effort of will. If this guy got the idea she was maybe being followed, he might decide not to help at all.

"My ex-husband," she said, softly. *Lying, Sophie? But you're getting away from kidnap-ping werewolves, that's got to be a karmic pass.* And besides, she had the terrified-woman look down pat. "He's a real… He's—"

After a few moments, he felt around on the seat next to him and produced, of all things, a battered box of Kleenex, held up with one hand over the seat back. "Wipe your face, honey." He sounded much kinder now. "You leakin'."

* * *

Fifteen hours later, bone-tired, still barefoot, freezing, and so tired even her hair hurt, she locked her apartment door with shaking, weak fingers. The scab on her left palm crackled with pain. The warm scent of the apple-cinnamon candle Lucy had bought her as a housewarming gift on its small table near the door managed to penetrate her running nose.

*Christ, I'm a mess.* The thought drowned in a flood of relief so strong her knees actually went weak.

Sophie slumped against the door, wishing she had more than two dead bolts and a chain. A mad mental vision of nailing boards over the doorway like a cartoon character danced through her tired skull. Lucy's little jeweled purse dangled from her fingers.

Nobody knew she'd planned to go out with Luce. But there were her friend's car keys, big as life and twice as ugly. She should have dropped them off the train somewhere, except Luce had Sophie's house keys on her ring, and Sophie had left her own keys at home.

*Then throw them away. Just get them out of here.*

She wasn't sure if it was a good idea, or if it

was the kind of irrational impulse that might take hold of a woman after she'd been kidnapped by werewolves, seen vampires—and, oh yeah, witnessed the death of her best and only friend.

The pale gray carpeting was full of pearly morning light, the walls still bare of everything but a single print of van Gogh's *Starry Night,* another gift from Lucy. One bedroom, one bath, a living room, and a kitchen barely wide enough for two skinny women to stand in. She'd traded a luxurious house out in the Hammerheath suburb for this little slice of paper-thin walls and baseboard heating in what Mark always called "the blue-collar slum." But it was all *hers,* and she paid her rent a month ahead of time by living on ramen and frozen peas—and a generous helping of Lucy's cooking.

These were, after all, the types of places she'd grown up in. Big apartment blocks with tiny corner stores, trash bins overflowing outside the supers' doorways, kids playing in the streets, and the sounds of other people carrying on with their lives behind every door. She'd thought Mark was the prince, taking her away from the noise and the stink.

But he'd turned out to be something else

entirely. Everybody did. For example, she never would have thought flighty Lucy would be the friend to stick by her through that hell.

And now Lucy was gone. Sitting on a train gave you entirely too much time to think, and the inside of her brain felt moth-eaten and acid-dipped all at once.

*Oh, God.* She almost slid down the door and collapsed right there on the square of linoleum in front of the door. No welcome mat, even, but then, Sophie never felt particularly welcoming. She didn't want *anyone* to know where she lived.

Except Lucy.

*God. Oh, God.*

Her face crumpled, and she pushed herself away from the door. Her fingers cramped; she mechanically slid the keys back in the little jeweled purse and stuffed both on the counter next to her cheap black vinyl bag, placed precisely next to a stack of textbooks so she could take the ones she needed every morning.

"I have a Child Development final this week," she said, blankly, to her empty apartment. It was midmorning and the entire building was strangely deserted, for a weekend. Maybe everyone was sleeping, or hungover.

Another cab had let her off right in front of the building, and nobody—not even the conductor on the train—had said a word about her feet. She was going to starve a bit next month; she'd had barely enough to pay her way home and her savings were nonexistent.

She dragged herself into the bedroom. The blinds weren't down; she'd forgotten to pull them Friday night. It was Sunday, and she could sleep in her own bed—she had escaped werewolves and God only knew what else.

And Lucy was dead. And there was a little voice inside Sophie's head trying to tell her she was forgetting something, that she was the responsible one, and that it should have been her gasping and choking in that alleyway instead of beautiful, burning-bright Lucy.

She was scrubbing her hands on the clothes they'd given her, she realized. Scrubbing and scrubbing, like some mad Lady Macbeth.

With a short sob, she tore the flannel shirt off, stripped herself out of the jeans, and pulled off the thermal shirt. She left everything crumpled in a stinking pile right inside her bedroom door, took three steps to the mattress she called her bed, and managed to crawl under the covers.

At least these sheets and blankets didn't scrape her skin like sandpaper. And they smelled like comfort.

Like home.

She sobbed for a long time, curled around the one lonely pillow that had seen her tears in the battered women's shelter, and later, during the endless rounds of divorce hearings. When she fell asleep, it was a slumber so dark and dreamless the fluttering around her bedroom window, under the pale gray sky that promised snow, went unnoticed. She woke only once, as the sky shaded into the cold flat darkness of an early winter night, and fumbled for her alarm clock. With it turned on, she had no more responsibility for the rest of the day, and she immediately fled back into welcome unconsciousness.

## Chapter 10

Brun whimpered as Julia held his hand, the wet towel in her free fingers clamped to the side of his face.

"Oh, Jesus," Eric whispered. "Did they take her?"

"They couldn't have." Zach's shoulder ground with pain. One of the goddamn *upir* had bitten him, and its venom burned as his body neutralized it. *Focus, goddammit!* "I told her to stay down. She was between the beds—"

"I tripped over her," Julia said, calmly enough. "She was by the door."

His pulse was pounding so hard it threatened to push the top of his head off. "The door?"

*She couldn't have gotten far on her own.* "We'd've smelled it if she was brought down. She was triggered, it would have called us." *Any serious blood she shed would have been like a jet taking off—we would have dropped everything and clustered her.*

"You're sure she was triggered?" Eric wasn't challenging him; it was pure worry, wanting to be told everything would be all right.

"I'm sure." *I should be, I made it happen.* And she'd spent enough time with them all in the room, breathing their pheromones, to make her a Carcajou shaman. He was sure about that. Well, mostly sure, anyway.

Well, not as sure as he liked. But he couldn't tell them that. It would only worry them all, and he didn't want that. "Maybe she ran." *God, please tell me she's still alive. She has to be.*

In the van, fading but still present, was the smell of their shaman, who was unaccountably missing. It was a calming scent, but nothing like the real thing.

The real thing had vanished into thin air.

He hit the steering wheel again—but gently. The last thing he needed was to make their transportation unusable. "They didn't leave a guard. They expected whatever they were looking for to be *inside* the room. If there were *upir* outside we'd've smelled them."

"So she ran." Eric nodded. "Smart, very smart. Where would she go?"

*Jesus.* "We're *this close* to losing our shaman. If another Family finds her—" He stopped, aware he was saying something he shouldn't. He'd told them she was *theirs*. They had to believe that.

Silence crackled through the interior, broken only by the low hum of the engine. Brun made a small, helpless little noise, and Julia went back to soothing him. For once, she was in a giving mood—and her twin seemed to be the only person who could spark that gentleness in her anymore.

*Let it be. That's not your problem right now. Your problem is getting that shaman back.* "Where would she go?"

It wasn't hard to guess, really. He just needed a few minutes to think it out. And to calm the bubbling, blood-tinted fury burning behind his breastbone.

That would help. But he was so far from calm, he doubted he'd get there anytime soon.

Eric sighed, his fingertips worrying at his

cuff. "I don't know if she has any money. Maybe she has friends around here?"

*She said the only person who would pay a ransom for her is dead. There's something to do with her husband, and*—A blooming red rose of rage threatened to block his vision, and he had to take a deep breath and concentrate on the fading scent of ice and moonlight filling the van. *Not thinking clearly. Come on, Zach. It's up to you now.*

"Is it just me," Julia said, "or are we seeing a lot of bloodsuckers lately?"

*It's not just you. Something else is going on here. I knew we were being followed, even though I tried to write it off as just nerves and grief.* "I think we've stepped into something."

"With that little bleeder? Who the hell would want her? Other than us," Julia hastily amended, seeing Zach's eyes shift in the rearview mirror. "Shush." Her hair dropped forward as she bent over Brun, suddenly very interested in calming him down again.

Flashing lights boiled behind them. Zach checked the mirrors and moved over, and none of them spoke until the cop car had cruised by, its siren tearing a hole in the night. *Not looking for us, thank God. Maybe looking for something else.* Eric would have left a fake license-plate number and misdirection with the clerk at the front desk, and would have paid with cash and shown an ID that bore no relation to his real name.

Just another part of life on the run.

"What are we going to do?" Eric asked.

*Do? That's right. It's my job to figure out what to do. That's why I never wanted to be alpha; even if I was strong enough, I'm not smart enough for this.* "We go back. I leave you lot in a safe place with the van, I go find our shaman and bring her back."

"But if there's *upir*…" Eric glanced at him, gauging how far he could push the issue. It was what a second should do; it was what Zach had done for years with Kyle.

He wished with a sudden vengeance that he was doing it again, and someone else was deal-ing with this clusterfuck.

"I don't know just what's going on yet. I'll go and get the shaman. Won't be that hard." *I'll bet you anything she went home. And lucky me, peeking at her purse. I have an address to start at.* "And while I do, all of you will stay with the van and behave. Especially you, Julia."

Her head jerked up. "You think I want to get

anyone else killed?" she snapped. "And you're going to blame me for *this*, too?"

He winced inwardly. Outwardly he checked the gas gauge and began working his way toward the freeway. Either he stood by what he said and blamed Julia for losing the shaman, or he stepped up like an alpha and took the responsibility he'd been avoiding for a good thirty years.

What a choice. It'd be so damn easy to blame his sister, blame *anyone*. But a real alpha didn't do that. The real alpha stepped up and took responsibility.

"The *upir* aren't your fault, Julia." He kept his eyes on the road.

"But Kyle *was*. That was my fault." Her voice broke. "That's what you're saying, isn't it?"

"Kyle was alpha." The words were bitter; they tasted like the acrid reek of fear and grief. "He knew the risks, Julia." *And he let you run wild, didn't bother to teach you to control yourself. Not sure he could have, you might have unzipped his guts and saved the goddamn rabid bloodsucker the trouble. You wouldn't have meant to, but still. He was too weak.* "I need you to stay calm and help Eric while I'm bringing our shaman back, and I need you to not have one of your fits while I do it. Clear?"

Unmollified, she bent over Brun. "You're blaming me." Low, and her whole posture expressed submissiveness, but she was right on the edge. It was usually how her fits started. He could smell the anger on her, combat rage replacing itself with a low-level growl of irritation, working itself up to a whipsawing screech of fury.

"If you keep going, Julia, I'm going to pull this car over and put you in the restraints." He said it quietly, but his pheromone wash boiled with his own leashed rage. "You are not going to be the queen of this little drama. This one doesn't belong to you."

Amazingly, she subsided.

Eric slumped in the passenger's seat, making himself smaller, and Zach was suddenly aware of his own anger, musky deep red leaking out through his pores. He took a deep breath, and a freeway sign loomed up like a big green beacon of salvation. "Don't worry," he said to them, to Kyle's ghost, to the smell of his own failure. "I'll get our shaman back and we'll head south. It'll be nice and warm. We'll be a Family again, we'll be part of our Tribe and go to meets. We can settle down. Have a nice house out in the country and run whenever the moon's full—or whenever we feel like it."

"That'd be nice," Brun said quietly, surprising them all and muffled by the damp hotel towel clamped to his face. "Can we get a house with stairs? I always wanted to slide down a stair rail."

"That's up to the shaman. But I don't think she'd object." *If we get her back. If I can make her understand.* The on-ramp unreeled under them, Zach laid on the gas, and the trouble swirling through the van receded just a little bit.

Just that little bit was enough, though.

## Chapter 11

Morning came gray and fuzzy, and her alarm clock sent up one shrill shriek after another. Sophie pried one eye open and was faced with a choice: an extra fifteen minutes in bed, or a long, very hot shower to take the curse off the song of stiff pain her body had become.

She ended up hitting the snooze button, then decided a shower would be better and dragged herself off her mattress. It was a chore struggling to her feet, and she stood swaying for a few moments. The more she thought about it, the more just unplugging the alarm clock and climbing back under the covers seemed like a better idea than anything else.

But she had to make rent. If she didn't, her problems would be bigger than werewolves.

The bitter little laugh that called up bounced off her blank bedroom walls. What problems could be bigger than werewolves and vampires?

*Don't think of Unpleasant Things, Sophie. The next thing is taking a shower. Just do the next thing, and the next.* After all, she knew what the bigger problem would be. It would be homelessness, or getting thrown out of her degree program, or the police pounding on her door demanding to know what happened to Lucy.

So Sophie flicked her alarm clock off and shuffled in to take a shower. It was all she *could* do. And after that was dry toast for breakfast, and the usual hurry to catch the bus.

Her back ached, and the side of her head hurt even though the bruising had gone down a bit, helped by a good twelve hours of unconsciousness. She was muzzy-headed and scratchy-eyed from crying, and she kept her hair down to hide the swelling—an old trick, and one that rarely worked, but all she could do. Her left hand throbbed with pain whenever she answered the phone or input patient data.

And a very nice homicide detective named Andrews came by the office and asked to speak to her.

"Sophie?" Margo, her blue-tinged hair piled in a fantastic beehive held up with several coats of hair spray, appeared in her cubicle door. "There's a man here to see you." Marge didn't wiggle her eyebrows, but she did look concerned. "A *police officer*," she amended, mistaking Sophie's wide-eyed stare for fear. "I don't think it's about your ex-husband." Her stage whisper needed a little work.

"Oh, God." It wasn't work to sound tired. Sophie pushed herself up just as the phone rang again. "I don't know what else it could be about." The lie sat heavy in her mouth. Everything was too vivid today—lights too bright, smells too intense. She hadn't even been able to go into the bathroom, for Christ's sake. It was just too awful.

"He's in the conference room." Margo folded her thick arms across her ample chest. Today it was hot-pink scrubs, and her earrings were garish Carmen Miranda fruit bowls, tapping her red-apple cheeks. "I'll go in with you."

*Great. I'll have to fool two people at once.* "Okay." Sophie followed Margo, her fingers worrying at the pressure bandage on her left hand. Thank God she was in long sleeves today.

She'd spent a lot of time in long sleeves. The finger-size bruises on her arm where Zach had grabbed her in the alley were familiar, too. Even if he had been trying to get her away from that...*thing.*

A bolt of something hot went through her entire body. *Don't think about that. Don't think about him, either.*

There were actually bands of different smells in the halls. Passing Margo's office was like walking through cheesecloth veils of hairspray reek and old-candy smell from the dish of stale M&M's on the Battle-Ax's desk. The front office boiled with exhaled sickness, and Dr. Marcus hurried past, his deodorant barely covering a dusting of a billing specialist's perfume. They were a hot item, Dr. Marcus and Amy. Office gossip had it that Marcus's wife knew and didn't care, since she'd get half of everything, anyway.

Sophie almost wished she could shut her nose off. She'd always been sensitive, but this was ridiculous. And she was craving a French dip, *au jus* so hot it scorched—not that she could afford anything other than a batch of cheap fries to go with her ramen today, if the fast-food place two blocks away wasn't too jammed for her to grab something in the middle of the day.

*Pull yourself together, Sophie.* She blinked and tried to focus, put one foot in front of the other.

Margo paused, her hand on the conference-room door. Her small, faded blue eyes dark with worry. "Soph...you know, if you don't want to talk to this guy, if it's about your ex, we can always get Dr. Brunner to throw him out and take up a collection for bail."

Dr. Brunner was a big bear of a man, end-lessly patient with his pediatric patients but not so patient with anyone else. Sophie's heart gave a massive squeezing leap. "Thanks, Margo." *I take back every mean thing I ever thought about you.* "Let's just see what he has to ask."

"All right." Margo's chin came up and her beehive seemed to swell like a frilled lizard's warning signal. "You just remember you don't have to say a thing, honey."

"I know, Margo. Thanks." *Oh, believe me, I'm not planning on saying anything. I need to stay out of custody.* Sophie braced herself as the door opened. A wave of scent—small, brown and male—flooded out, and the image of a smallish man in a rumpled mackintosh took over the inside of her tired skull.

It was too much. *What is* happening *to me?*

The blinds were drawn, so the fluorescent light made everything pale. The table was clean, a sterile mirror-black surface; all the chairs were lined up except one. The man half rising from the table looked *exactly* like the image in Sophie's head, right down to his narrow nose, slumped shoulders and grubby raincoat. A battered leather attaché case stood to attention at his end of the table, and a blank, new manila folder was settled next to his right elbow. His hands were broad and short-fingered, and he was dwarfed beside Margo. His tie was wilted, the suit jacket under his mackintosh an indeterminate brown, and it was a good thing Sophie's stomach was empty. The conflicting odors of man, wet raincoat, paper, and hair spray made her queasy.

"Sophie, this is Detective Andrews." Margo had drawn herself up to her considerable, breast-jutting height, her arms folded. She had not, Sophie saw, offered him coffee. "I checked his ID. But you might want to see it yourself."

Her throat was dry. "That's okay," she

managed, and wondered if she sounded as sick and unsteady as she felt.

"Miz Harris." The man put his hand out, and Sophie was suddenly very sure that if she touched him she would break down crying. She tried to copy Margo's pose—head up, shoulders back, chin jutting proudly.

"It's Wilson," she heard herself say for what had to be the five hundredth time. "I'm no longer married." The words tasted like ash.

The detective's hand dropped. "Okay. Miss Wilson. I'm just going to be asking a few questions."

*Come on, Sophie.* Her face felt like a mask. "Is this about Mark? My ex-husband? I don't want anything to do with him."

The detective looked pained for a moment. "No, ma'am, it's not. It's about your friend Lucy Cavanaugh. At least, her coworkers said you were her best friend."

"Lucy?" It wasn't hard to sound stunned. All she had to do was think about the alley, the purple-faced thing, and the horrible gurgling noise as Lucy died. "Yes, she's...we're friends. She *is* my best friend. What's going on?"

His face didn't change, but a thread of urgency like a metallic wire slid through the warp of his fusty, frowsy smell. "When was the last time you talked to Miss Cavanaugh?"

"I…" *Do it like you practiced, Sophie.* "Friday afternoon, I think. She was going out dancing. I told her I had to study." Which was partly true—that had been her first excuse, but Luce had just rolled right over the top of it.

*"You're going to have some fun, Soph, if it's the last thing I do."*

Oh, Lucy.

His gaze was entirely too sharp. He indicated a chair, and she moved mechanically toward it. "Miss Wilson, something happened Friday night. Miss Cavanaugh—Lucy—was attacked."

The world swayed under Sophie's feet. A funny haze had begun on the mirrored surface of the table, streaks of mist like clouds. She tore her attention away, tried to focus on the detective. "Attacked? Is she all right? What happened?" *You're never going to guess what happened to her. Not in a million years. And I can't tell you, either.* She folded herself down gingerly in the chair he'd motioned her toward, guessing he wanted her there because he turned out to be the only thing she could look at unless she craned her neck and stared at the window.

Margo inhaled sharply. She swept the door closed and stood like a guard, almost bristling with protective indignation. As soon as the door shut, the smell of hair spray and unclean raincoat intensified.

"Miss Wilson, Lucy Cavanaugh is dead. I'm sorry." He sounded sorry, too. His mouth pulled down like he tasted something bitter as he dropped into his own chair and touched the folder. "I'm trying to find out all I can about her, so I can catch her attacker. Can I ask you some more questions?"

The clouds on the table's surface swirled together, and Sophie's empty stomach trembled as if she was going to throw up. The air in here was stifling, the walls suddenly shrinking, closing up on her. A rattling started in the center of her head—a buzzing, like copper-bottomed pans striking one another. "Dead?" she whispered.

Somehow, hearing him say it made everything too real. The all-too-familiar pressure of secrets to keep squeezed her entire chest until a black hole of panic opened up in front of her. She had to watch where she stepped, or she would fall off the narrow thread of safety.

Margo stepped close and put a beefy hand

on Sophie's shoulder. The clogging reek of hair spray crawled up her nose, and her eyes flooded.

*Oh, Jesus. What do I do now?* She looked up from the table's surface and found the detective watching her avidly, tense like a dog before the leash is unclipped. His fingers drummed once on the folder, and she could see paper stuffed inside it.

There were probably pictures, too.

Sophie did the only thing she could do. She burst into tears.

It wasn't too hard to break down crying and pretend to be confused. If Sophie was used to anything, it was cops asking her questions. Yes, Lucy was her best friend. No, she hadn't heard from Lucy all weekend, and what exactly was this about, anyway? Oh, my *God,* no, not Lucy. No, she had no enemies. Everyone loved Lucy. How could you *not* love her? Well, except for Mark, but he was angry because Luce had testified during the divorce hearings, and—

The pudgy detective listened, jotted notes on a little tiny steno pad, and patted her shoulder awkwardly once, before Sophie flinched away from the sudden wave of his smell. Margo

glowered, arms and legs crossed, in a chair just
to Sophie's left.

It wasn't that Sophie wanted to lie. But she
knew very well what would happen if she
started talking about being kidnapped and
ranting about vampires and werewolves. She'd
end up in the hospital, under "observation," and
Mark would find out and all sorts of Unpleasant
Things would happen.

No, if Sophie wanted to stay out of the psy-
chiatric ward and in her degree program, she
had to keep her mouth shut *hard*.

The instinct to hide things from the police
wasn't that far away even at the best of times.
She'd spent a long time hiding what Mark did to
her.

"Well," Andrews finally said, "that about
covers it. I'm sorry, Miss Wilson. Here's my
card."

Sophie stared at the rectangle of white paper
on the table's lacquered surface. It looked innocent and two-dimensional, compared to whatever trick of light was making the table run
with cloudy streaks. She was too goddamn exhausted to figure out why she was hallucinating.
It had to be something wrong with her glasses,
or something.

Margo leaned forward and scooped the business card up. "Thank you, *detective*. You can find your own way out."

"That I can, ma'am." He stood and swept the manila folder into a battered leather attaché case. She was suddenly beyond certain that folder had pictures in it, pictures of Lucy.

Fresh sharp grief welled up. The detective shuffled off, and as soon as he closed the door with a quiet click Margo started fussing at Sophie to "let it all out, and here's a tissue. My, he certainly won't win any prizes for tact, will he? Oh, sweetheart, you need some lunch. Here, I'll tell Amy to run down and grab you a sandwich—"

It was actually a relief to give in and let blue-haired Battle-Ax Margo have her way. Sophie finally escaped to the ladies' room, and the smell in there was almost enough to drive her back out again if she hadn't needed the sanctuary so badly. She locked a stall door behind her and cried until she threw up the toast she'd managed to force down for breakfast.

The grief keening inside her head was full of black, tar-thick guilt. It shouldn't have been Lucy on the floor of that alley. The rumpled little detective would never catch her killer. Life wasn't fair.

And the worst unfairness of all was that it wasn't a dream. Lucy was really dead.

Now Sophie was truly alone.

## Chapter 12

Night fell, cold and windy.

The first problem was the address. It was a strip mall. Or, more precisely, it was one of those little mail shops in a strip mall, the kind of place where you could pay a monthly fee and rent a box. It looked like a street address, and it was the sort of step a woman who needed privacy would take.

Which was interesting. And a dead end.

But he had another card up his sleeve.

*I've got night school, too. I'm studying to be a social worker.* Which meant all he had to do was find out about night classes. A city this size wouldn't have too many night-school programs, and all he had to do was start with the biggest and work down. Any place she was five nights a week would give him a trail.

He watched the mail stop from a pool of darker shadow across the street for a little while, though, wondering why she had *this* address on her driver's license. He hunched inside the denim jacket that had been Kyle's, always a little too big on his younger brother. It still smelled like him, though, a thorn of guilt spiking through Zach's chest every few inhales.

He suffered it. They hadn't had a chance to sing Kyle to the moon yet. He had to hope his brother would understand, that the *majir* had explained everything—and that Kyle had forgiven him.

He could hope, couldn't he?

Zach shook himself. *Come on. Concentrate on the problem at hand.* A maiden name, a mail drop, no friends to speak of, and flinching whenever a husband was mentioned. It added up to a picture, and not a pretty one.

*Still, could be wrong. Assumptions, you know. Fastest way to make a situation worse than it has to be.*

Yeah, right. He could be wrong like the moon was made of cheese and crackers.

His Family was safe as possible, in a motel at the edge of town with the van just in case. Waiting for him to bring the shaman back. This was the first time he'd been alone in years, and he didn't like it. There were crowds of prey around, and he had to think this was hostile *upir*-laden territory. Not to mention he had to keep his temper under control until he found her, but he had to do it without others of his kind around to keep him occupied and remind him he was human.

Most of all, though, he had too much time to brood when he was alone. Too much time to remember, and to think about mistakes.

It had been a cold, gray day of driving as fast as he dared, and the sound of city traffic had sharp edges, burrowing into his tired head. He could go for a couple more days without sleep, but he wanted to bring their shaman back before dawn. God only knew what would happen without him around to defend his Family.

Were the *upir* after them or after her? He just didn't know enough.

But why would *upir* be after her? It was just a random attack by a rabid sucker, right? So why would seven more of them, all too young to know what to do with their new reflexes, go after a group of Carcajou, even a small group with a shaman so new she didn't know what the hell to do with herself?

*It's a puzzle, and a nasty one. Work on it later. Find her now.*

The biggest campus with a night-school social worker program was a community college on the bus lines. The parking lots were huge, but there was no trace of her there or in any of the buildings. The second-largest was vaguely in the same part of town as the mail stop, another hour or two on the bus as the time ticked away, hopping off to find the campus was a good four-block walk away. She wouldn't be in any condition to go to class, but he'd be able to find a trail and her *real* address, and—

His head came up and he tested the wind. There it was. Ice, moonlight, brunette spice, and a sharp fresh note of weariness and pain. Strong, very strong.

The smell was a trail as wide as a highway to his sensitive nose, like a deer path in the woods. She'd walked this way less than three hours ago. He could almost taste each individual footprint, and he could track the scent *backward*, too, working along a flaring, fading drift of more pain and heaviness, and a pungent undertone of fear that prodded and teased at his already-fraying temper.

But the most important thing was the familiarity, and the musk spinning through the scent. She *had* been with his Family long enough to be theirs. The relief tasted like wine and fresh blood against his palate, a heady mix.

*Well,* he thought, *that's half the battle won. Now let's go see if we can find the war.*

## Chapter 13

The last flight of stairs up to her apartment was endless at about midnight. She was seriously dragging. On the other hand, she could sleep in tomorrow, since Margo had freaked out after the detective's visit. She had insisted that Sophie take a Paid Day Off, for Health Reasons.

Sophie couldn't even scrape up any thankfulness for that.

She reached the top of the stairs and stood for a moment, catching her breath. The hall smelled odd, musky, like it had this morning. But then, after the past two days, she was smelling weird things all *over,* like the dish of mummified M&M's on Margo's desk, or the smell of the seats in the classrooms—and classes had been an absolute waste, too. She couldn't concentrate worth a damn today, had left her books at home, and had swallowed tears when the Psych professor announced a pop quiz. Which she was sure she'd bombed, to top everything off.

She had to spend two and a half minutes jabbing keys at her door, because her eyes kept blurring. Her nose was full, but she could still smell *home,* and that weird musk was driving her out of her head. She needed to take another long hot shower, and for the first time she wished she kept some alcohol in the house. A nip of something hard would go down *really* nice right about now.

She flicked the light switches for the hall and living room without thinking about it. The door closed, shutting the world out, and she let out a long sobbing sigh, locking the dead bolts. It absolutely reeked of musk in here, and the smell reminded her of being pressed against the wall, Zach's face inches from hers, and his heat making it difficult to think straight.

A light breeze touched her hair, and she flinched, almost running straight into the door.

"Nice place," he said in her ear. "A bit small, but okay. Smells like you."

She hitched in enough air to scream, but his hand clamped over her mouth.

"None of that," Zach said softly. His breath was warm, and his other arm came around her waist, pulled her back from the door. Her vinyl purse hit the linoleum with a thump. "I'm not going to hurt you. But we *are* going to have a talk."

*Oh, holy shit, how did he* find *me?* Every muscle in her body had gone limp with shock. "Going to have a talk" was one of Mark's favorite phrases. It usually meant *I'm going to yell, and eventually you're going to cry, and if you're lucky maybe I'll only slap you a few times. But if you're not, by God, we're going to have a talk and before it's through Sophie is going to bleed.*

Her brain utterly failed, vapor-locking between memory and the terrible present. He dragged her into the living room, such as it was, and stood for a moment in the middle of the carpet, as if looking for a place to sit. There wasn't anything except one old ratty armchair from a downstairs apartment's moving sale, and he pushed her down in it, peeling his hand away from her mouth with a meaningful glare.

All her breath had dried up. He was unshaven, dark stubble on his cheeks, his eyes hot with anger and his hair still falling stubbornly across his forehead. He was even wearing the same clothes she'd last seen him in, plus a denim jacket spotted with rain, and he still moved with the same lynxlike grace. The jacket made his shoulders look absurdly broad.

He stood in the middle of her almost-empty living room, framed by the white wall, the print Lucy had given her up over his head like a halo. He was so *tall,* and his anger filled up the room until she couldn't breathe and started gasping, clutching at the chair arms and staring until her eyes threatened to bug out of her head completely.

"Christ." He made a swift movement and crouched down, looking up at her. The anger swirled away, like static draining out of empty space.

It was odd, but as soon as he did it he seemed exponentially less scary, and when he reached out to touch her knee and she flinched back he actually stopped cold, his hand hanging in midair. "That answers that question, I guess.

Breathe, honey. It goes easier if you take in some oxygen."

His tone—soft, conciliatory, like Mark's after a particularly bad beating, when he was in his repentant phase—surprised her. But what surprised her the most was his hand falling back down to his side, and he just cocked his head and regarded her, going completely, inhumanly still.

The gasps faded, little by little, and she stared at him. Air started to fill her lungs again. *Panic attack, and a bad one. No wonder.* She concentrated on breathing, pushing the air out, taking it in with small sipping sounds.

"I'm not going to hurt you." Quietly, his eyes holding hers. "I am not going to lay a hand on you unless it's to keep you from doing something silly, and I won't hurt you. Are we absolutely clear on that?"

Her wrists hurt, and her back, and the side of her head. The scab on her palm burned. He'd *already* hurt her. Still… *Agree with him. Let him think you're all right with this.* She nodded, tentatively. The phone was in the kitchen. If she could get to it somehow—

"As a matter of fact," he continued, "if your ex-husband—because I can tell from this apartment that he's ex, you know—or anyone else tries to lay a hand on you, I'll *feed* that hand back to them. In little bleeding pieces. Understand?"

*Jesus. How long has he been in here?* She managed another nod. The armchair creaked a little as she shifted, and she froze again. Her back gave a wrenching flare of pain, and her throat was so dry she doubted she *could* scream. All she could produce was a sort of croak.

"Now." He settled farther into his crouch, became motionless again. "Why don't we take it from the top. Why are there *upir* watching you?"

*What? He means the vampires, right?* She decided he had, indeed, said what she thought he'd said. "I don't—" Her voice was surprisingly steady, even if she did have to stop and clear her throat. "I don't know. I don't know what you want with me, either."

"Okay." He nodded, once, sharply. "Let's cover that. We need you. I'm sorry, but there wasn't…I couldn't explain before. You're special, Sophie. You don't know how special. Were things smelling strange to you today?"

*How did he—?* Her face must have betrayed her, because he nodded again. "And you're tired. Triggering does that, eats up a lot of the body's reserves. The biochemical changes are pretty intense." He moved a little, as if his own muscles were sore. "You're going to need at least a month or two to adjust."

*What?* "What are you going to do to me?" she whispered.

Amazingly, that made him smile. All the anger fled from his face, and his eyes actually lit up. It made him even more dangerously handsome, the stubble roughing up his cheeks and his mouth softening just a bit. "Well, first of all, I thought I'd feed you. You're probably hungry, aren't you?"

He sounded actually *cajoling,* and her heart gave an amazing thumping leap inside her chest. She was starving; she hadn't choked down more than toast and that had gone down the tubes this morning. "I—"

His head came up, tilting as if to catch a sound. It was a quick inquiring movement, like a cat's, and she flinched again. She couldn't help herself.

"Shit." The anger came back, settled over his face like an old friend, and chased the handsomeness away. "It never rains but it pours. Look, Sophie, can you trust me?"

*Trust you? Are you fucking insane? You* kidnapped *me, broke into my house, and you're… you're…* Words failed her. She just stared at him.

"Guess not." He slowly rose, and she noticed his boots were dusty and crushing the carpet. He made another one of those quick, inquiring moves, and swore under his breath again. "I hate to tell you this, honey, but there's *upir* in your building. There's no reason for them to be here unless they're after you. I'm going to ask you again, why the hell are they following you?"

"I don't *know.*" *How amazing. I actually sound irritated. Go figure.* Her brain began to work again. "How can you tell?"

"I can smell them." He turned in a tight circle, his gaze roving over every surface of the room and coming to rest on her again. "I wonder why they're so interested in you. Huh."

"Please don't hurt me." *How many times am I going to have to say that in my life?* she wondered, and not for the first time.

"I'm not going to hurt you." He took two quick steps and held out his hand, palm cupped. "But we're going to have to get out of here."

She shook her head. Loose curls fell in her

face. "I'm not going anywhere." She clutched at the chair arms like a drowning woman. "You can't kidnap me again."

"I'm not going to kidnap you, for Christ's sake. Can't you smell them?"

"All I can smell is whatever cologne you're wearing. Why don't you go find someone else to harass?" She couldn't believe the words had come out of her mouth.

It sounded more like something Lucy would say.

He gave her a smile too tight and thin to be an expression of good humor. "What if I like harassing you, sweetheart? You get all *cute* when you're mad."

*What the hell?* She stared at him. "You're insane."

"Nope." He moved his hand a little, urging her to take it. "How did you vanish the other night, by the way? We thought the *upir* had taken you. Were about to tear down the whole town looking for you."

*What the hell for?* She lifted her chin and scowled stubbornly at him. If he wanted an answer he was going to have to beat it out of her.

And if there was one thing Sophie Wilson

knew, it was how to take a punch and keep a secret.

His hand stayed where it was, hanging out in the air like it had nothing better to do. "Come on." He didn't look impatient or upset, just thoughtful and tense. "We need to get out of here. I smell bloodsuckers all over this building. I'd really prefer it if you came willingly."

"Go. To. Hell." She settled herself farther back in the chair, which squeaked again, and braced herself for an explosion.

Someone knocked sharply on her front door. Three hard, quick raps.

Sophie swallowed hard. *What now?*

"Huh." Zach spun in a tight half circle. "Male. Expecting a gentleman caller, sweets?"

Her heart gave a sickening thump, began pounding. *God. It's Mark. He's found me.* "Nobody knows where I live." *Except you, apparently. And now him. He's going to hit the roof if he sees a man in here.* It was the final straw.

And Zach was striding toward the door as Sophie, frozen, held on to the arms of the old chair with tense, aching fingers. He didn't pause, just swept her purse aside with his foot, tucking it out of sight over the kitchen threshold, flipped the dead bolts as if he lived here, and yanked the door open. "Hello?"

Sophie squeezed her eyes shut so hard fireworks slid behind her lids. Her breathing came in quick, shallow gasps, and her entire body was locked in a cube of ice. She could actually feel the wet cold against her skin, and a thin trace of sweat slid down the shallow channel of her spine.

The darkness behind her lids turned gray for a moment, as if a diaphanous scarf had wrapped itself over her head. A strange sense of comfort settled over her, warring with the lunacy she was trapped in, this nightmare that didn't want to end.

"Is Miss Wilson home?" It was a half-familiar voice. Not Mark's. Her breath whooshed out, gasped back in, and held itself again.

"May I ask who *you* are?" Zach asked, amiably enough. It was absolute insanity, and it wasn't about to end anytime soon.

She wondered if she *was* crazy. It would certainly explain a lot.

"Detective Andrews, CPD. I spoke to Miss Wilson this afternoon, about her friend Lucy Cavanaugh."

"She's really broken up, sir." How was it

possible for a werewolf who kidnapped her and dragged her hundreds of miles away, not to mention broke into her house, to sound so *calm?*

"I know. But I had a couple questions. You see, witnesses describe someone matching Miss Wilson's description entering the Paintbox with Miss Cavanaugh. You wouldn't happen to—"

"That would be what, Friday night?" Zach still sounded calm, and he paused. The detective must have nodded. "It couldn't have been Sophie. She was with me. We were at home."

"Here, in this apartment?" The detective sounded mildly surprised. "Miss Wilson didn't mention you this afternoon, Mr....?"

"Gabe. Gabe Sellers."

A faint, hopeless sound escaped Sophie's throat. *My God, is he even lying about his* name? There was the sound of cloth moving as men shifted weight, and her eyes flew open.

Zach filled up the door, towering over the pudgy little detective. She couldn't even *see* the man out in the hall. And that weird grayness didn't go away. It looked like the cloudy haze on the conference table earlier that day, swirling hypnotically.

She wondered if she was going into shock.

"Mr. Sellers." A floorboard creaked sharply under the detective's feet. "She didn't mention you. Can I come in?"

"Well, her ex-husband's kind of looking for reasons to make her life miserable. I guess she doesn't want me to be one of them." Zach leaned on the doorjamb. "And Sophie's crying her eyes out about Lucy. I don't think now's a good time."

"So, you're involved with Mrs. Harris?"

"It's Ms. *Wilson*." Zach's tone had turned chill. "And I'm not sure it's any of your business, Sir. Sophie was with me all weekend. Does that answer your question?"

"Where did you two spend the weekend, Mr. Sowers?" The detective's tone matched Zach's now, and Sophie let out another small hitching sound. Her nose was full, and tears had welled up. Two scorch-hot drops of water trickled down her cheeks. *Say something, you idiot. Yell. Scream. You wanted to call the police, there's one standing right there in the door! Do something!*

But if she did something, the inevitable questions would start—questions she didn't have good answers for. Or even believable, rational answers. *Where exactly were you*

*Friday night? If you were with Lucy, why didn't you report anything? Why did you lie? You say this guy kidnapped you? Why? Who is this guy, anyway?*

Zach leaned against the doorjamb, still blocking any view of the hall. The grayness resolved into streaks of fluttering transparency, easing around him. "It's *Sellers*. I thought you guys were good with names. As for where we spent the weekend, that's private. If you know what I mean. Now, if you don't have any other prying personal questions, I've got a crying girlfriend I need to feed and calm down. Have a nice night, Anderson."

"It's *Andrews*, Mr. Sellers. I'd like to speak to Miss Wilson, please."

"I don't think she's in any condition to talk to someone who can't even get her name straight." Zach half turned his head. "Sophie?" he called, as if she was in the bathroom. "Some cop's here. You want to talk to him?"

*Oh, Jesus. Dear God.* She made her arms work, pushed herself up out of the chair. It gave a protesting groan.

The gray things wouldn't go away no matter how many times she blinked.

She teetered, on old-woman legs, to the hall.

Andrews was making notations in his steno pad again. Zach's body language didn't change. Her knees almost gave out as she tried to figure out a way past him. If she could reach the hall she could run away from *both* of them, and everything else, as well.

Just keep running. Only she didn't have anywhere to go. The last time she'd run, she'd had a plan—a desperate one, but a plan nonetheless, and a friend to help carry it out.

*Oh, Lucy.* Her eyes brimmed with hot salt water.

Zach put out a hand as soon as she was within reaching distance, slid it over her shoulders, and pulled her into his side just like a protective boyfriend. "This the guy who told you about Lucy?" He tucked his chin to look down at her, and Sophie didn't flinch only through sheer willpower. He was very warm, a flood of heat closing around her. And that musk smell, which was beginning to be curiously comforting. The gray things pressed closer, floating as if the air was water.

She didn't trust her voice. She nodded. A horrible idea bolted through her head—she'd *seen* what Zach could do, the way his shape changed into something lean and wickedly clawed, covered in dark pelt.

What if the tubby little brown-eyed detective, who was still in the rumpled tan mackintosh, his tie a little askew, made Zach angry?

Her knees almost gave out. Which pitched her directly into Zach's side, and his arm tightened. Her heart crawled into her throat, and fresh hot tears slid down her cheeks. What had she done to deserve this? She'd only wanted to go out and have some fun, for God's sake.

"I'm sorry to disturb you." Andrews did look sorry, his muddy eyes as sad as they had been earlier. "You were with your fella here all weekend?"

*Well, technically that's true. And he's a werewolf. And pigs will fly.* She managed another nod, and Zach's arm tightened again. Maybe he even meant it to be comforting, but it felt like a warning.

Still, that musk smell was soothing. Something about it made her feel a little steadier. How was that for completely, totally insane?

"She usually comes to my place," Zach supplied. "But this weekend she wasn't feeling well, and I brought her takeout and tried to keep her in bed."

And Christ on a *crutch,* but his voice dropped, and he made that sentence sound... well, positively indecent. Her legs all but failed her, and now Zach was holding her up without any apparent effort. As if she needed a reminder of how freakishly, inhumanly *strong* he was.

"Where would your place be, Mr. Sellers?" The detective's eyes were suspiciously sharp behind their muddiness, and Sophie began to feel faint. Her head was full of rushing noise, and she had the urge to simply sink into the floor. If a huge cavern had opened up right then and there, she would have dropped in with only a grateful murmur.

"About four blocks away. Why?" He actually *sounded* innocent. It was hard to imagine him growling like a huge, very angry dog. Or holding her up against the wall, or pinning her to a bed.

But then, she knew all about men who could sound innocent when questioned, didn't she?

"Just curious." The detective examined Sophie for a long moment, and his face softened. "Sorry to disturb you, ma'am. You look worn out. Hope your fella here takes good care of you."

"I intend to." Zach loomed over both of them, suddenly seeming taller, and Sophie blinked. The lights in the hall were doing funny things, shadows weaving between them like gauze scarves. But that could have been the water in her eyes. Or the panic attack still reverberating in her nerves. Or— "Anything else we can help you with, Detective?"

"Not at the moment." Andrews was still watching Sophie's face.

Her cheek throbbed. Did she look like a beaten woman? She'd had plenty of practice. *I must look guilty. Oh, Lucy, I'm so sorry. It should have been me.*

A long, heart-stopping moment later, the detective tipped Zach a curious little salute and nodded at her. "Good night, then."

"Good night," she said faintly, and Zach pulled her back, sweeping the door shut as Andrews turned away. He locked both dead bolts, put the chain on, and took another two steps back, dragging her with him as if she weighed nothing. Paused, his head cocked again, as the heavy man's footsteps retreated down the hall.

"They'll probably let him pass," he murmured, and made a quick movement, letting go of her shoulders as he bent to pick up her purse. Sophie teetered, half fell against the wall, and let out a long breath she hadn't been aware of holding. "Not worth their time to kill a cop. But we've got to get out of here." His eyes swept down her body, a curiously impersonal glance, and Sophie braced her shoulder against the wall even harder. "Good work, by the way. The dewy-eyed innocent thing looks real nice on you."

"I thought you were…" *Going to kill him. Going to kill me. Going to do something awful.*

He thrust her purse into her hands. "I figured he was fishing for your alibi, sweets. He suspects something, he just doesn't know what. As long as you stick with that story—that you were with me and we were here—he can't do anything. Not like it matters—we have to get out."

"I'm not going anywhere with you." Instead of ringing and declarative, the words came out thin and tired. Her head swam. "I think I'm going to pass out."

"Pass out later." He grabbed her arm and

reached for the door again. "Right now we need to move."

The ceiling fixture in the hall began to dim, and the bulb in the living room began to make a strange fizzling sound.

## Chapter 14

*They'll be watching the fire escapes—it's what I would do.* His world of options was rapidly narrowing, and she wasn't making it any easier by becoming limp deadweight whenever he slowed down enough for her to lean against anything. The smell was rough and clotted in his mouth, an old-rust corruption of spilled blood and rotting spice that raised almost every hackle he had. Then there was *her* smell—ice and moonlight sharpened into the scent of a triggered shaman, *his* triggered shaman. With a wide wine-dark river of fear boiling underneath and rasping against his nerves until he didn't know whether to scream or hit something.

It didn't help that Sophie was pale, visibly trembling, and all the sharp intelligence had gone out of those lovely gray eyes. Her glasses were still shiny, her hair was a wild mass of electric, beautiful curls, and the gray pencil skirt and sheer nylons over those sweetly curved legs was enough to make a man's train of thought derail. But one glance at her pale, terrified face, fever spots of wild color high on her perfect cheeks—one of them slightly swollen, as if she'd been slapped—and the way she looked anywhere but at him, almost cowering if he made a sudden movement…

It was enough to make any man feel like tearing down a few brick walls to get at whatever had turned her into this.

Except he'd done a lot of it, by handling her in exactly the wrong way.

Her apartment spoke volumes. One armchair. A print of some painting that someone had probably taken pity on her with. One mattress and a pile of mismatched blankets, one pillow, five library books stacked next to the bed. Empty cupboards, two packages of ramen, four bags of frozen peas, one bag of bulk oatmeal. Nothing in her fridge but a quart of milk and a half-empty bottle of ketchup. There was some kind of froufrou scented candle on a small table next to the front door, half-burned and probably a gift, as well.

Five gray suits in her closet. A few pairs of sweats and one lone pair of jeans. He hadn't gone poking through her underwear drawer, but he'd be willing to bet it was as empty as the rest of her apartment.

He knew what poverty and fear smelled like, and the sad little place reeked of it. There were two boxes of papers in her closet, neatly labeled in a round Palmer script, and he'd taken a peek at the one that said *Divorce*.

The bloodless language of the law almost managed to cover up something capable of making him sick.

With the beast screaming in his blood, he had handled her exactly, completely wrong. Time to start remedying that—if, of course, he could get her out of this death trap of an apartment building.

There was only one way to go, and it was up. He had to half carry her up the maintenance stairs, both because he was using inhuman speed and because her legs kept giving out. She was in a pair of black heels he'd be willing to bet were her second and last pair, since her first were in the van, and he hadn't had time to get her into sneakers. God only knew where the outfit she'd had on a couple nights ago had come from.

*Keep your mind on your problems, and not on her clothes.* He paused, looking at an emergency exit and weighing his options. The building was five stories tall and they were on the fourth floor.

"God," she whispered, right before she collapsed again and he hauled her up. "You lied to him."

*Duh.* "Of course I did. What else was I supposed to do?"

"Is Zach really your name?"

Sharp girl. "It really is. The one I was born with, even." *Family name. We'll get around to that.*

"Why are the lights fuzzing out? And the… the things—" The only thing that alarmed him more than how pale she'd turned was the dreamy, disconnected way she was asking questions. "Like scarves."

*We hit the jackpot with you, honey, if you're already seeing that.* "You're seeing the spirits, the *majir*. And the *upir* make the lights go. They prefer to hunt in darkness."

"Hunt?"

"Us."

"Oh." She nodded, calmly enough, and drew a breath, as if to scream.

He couldn't take the chance and shoved her against the wall, covering her mouth. The fine tremor running through her infected him, as well. His fist curled, and he stopped himself from ramming it through whatever paste was masquerading as walls around here just in time. *"Listen."* A snarl ran under the words. Her throat-cut fear was teasing and taunting what little control he had left. "I need everything I've got to get us out of here. I'll keep fighting as long as you stay with me. Right here." He stared into her eyes, disregarding her glasses, pushed askew by his hand. "You *stay with me.* Understand?"

Something flared in her pupils. It was a spark, something struggling out from under the fear. He willed it to stay, but it was extinguished almost as soon as it came, and he heard the soft rotten drumming of their feet. *More of them. Jesus, what's going on here?*

"Okay," she whispered, when he peeled his fingers away. "Fine. Stay with you. All right."

Relief warred with fresh rage inside his chest.

She looked absolutely hopeless. "Good girl." He did something he'd wanted to do since he'd seen her—leaned forward and pressed his lips to her forehead, inhaled the smell of her hair. Clean, fresh, female—even with the sharp saw blade of fear underneath, it held the power to calm the animal inside him.

Goddammit, she smelled like she *belonged* to him, and he didn't have time to take it easy, ease her along. The lights were dimming rapidly as the *upir* came up, floor by floor, a pressure like an approaching storm.

She blinked up at him, surprised, and some of the sense had come back into her pale eyes. "What did you do that for?"

*Because I wanted to.* "Come on." Up the last flight of stairs, a locked door he kicked once and crumpled, metal tearing with a screech. Cold rainy air poured in as the lights failed completely, the night reaching into the building like spilled ink.

"They're *floating*," she whispered, in an awe-stricken little voice.

*Oh, yeah. Hit the jackpot. She's gonna be a live one if she's seeing that so soon. Need to feed her and get her settled somewhere she can shaman-sleep.* Wind cut across the rooftop, and he glanced out. The best bet was off across the flat expanse toward a likely corner. The three-story building over a narrow alley was the best route; it had cover and he'd be able to take that drop easily.

Still, he paused for a moment. There was nothing to be gained by running blindly. If *he* was hunting someone, he'd have a lookout on the roof.

*There.* A patch of foul-smelling shadow, drifting with the breeze, in the lee of an air-conditioning vent. Sophie shivered, actually moving closer to him and pulling her jacket close. He hadn't even given her time to change her clothes.

*Better start treating her nice, Zach. It's your responsibility.*

*Yeah, sure,* he told himself. *First let's get us out of here in one piece. Hard to treat her nice in the middle of a melee.* "Stay with me," he whispered. "Okay?"

She nodded, curls falling in her face, and he had the urge to brush at them, see if they were as soft as they looked.

Then he dragged her out into the rain, deliberately stumbling as if he was drunk or wounded, and the lookout took the bait—just like he'd hoped. It came streaking out of the darkness, disturbing the flung silver pellets of icy rain, and Sophie didn't even have time to scream before he shoved her down and away, grabbing two fistfuls of *upir* and letting the Change run inside him like glass daggers.

It answered one question, though. The blood-heavy parasite was a little older and more experienced than the rest, and it had come straight for Sophie, not even veering for Zach as the biggest threat.

They wanted *her.*

Its claws burned as it turned on itself, a rubbery snake of bloodlust; he took the hit without caring, low on the side, turning so it grated on ribs instead of opening up the vulnerable belly. In a normal fight this would be the time for noise, a roar to spur him on. But not now.

This was deadly serious, and deadly quiet, the only sounds Sophie's hurt little cry and hitching breaths, the patter of rain, and the *upir*'s high shallow breathing, air whistling past shark-sharp teeth. Scuff of boot soles and whisper of fabric as they closed again, the Change roiling down his side in a tide of thorny oil, closing the rips and fueling speed and strength with the pain.

His clawed fingers found the vulnerable soft throat and *wrenched;* there was a gout of foul noisome black blood, and the body of his enemy fell as Sophie let out another thin wordless cry of warning.

*I know,* he wanted to tell her, *don't worry,* but his mouth wasn't shaped for human words right now, and in any case, there was no time. He turned and leaped, every iota of force applied to fling himself back toward her, hitting the highest point of the arc just as the other two *upir* collided with him. He wanted to knock them away from her and succeeded, landing cat-footed on all fours and snarling just once, shoulders hunching as his claws snicked against the rooftop.

Once was all the warning they were going to get.

They spread out, then feinted in, trying to get past him at the shaman, who had scrabbled back against the wall near the kicked-open door. He snapped at them, stalemate for a moment while he worked the geography of the rooftop around in his head and tested the wind for more of them. Backed up a little to give himself room, his body between the shaman and the twisty-coiling things that smelled of death and spiced rotting rust, their faces twisted plum-colored obscenities because they had dropped the mask of breathing humanity they once wore.

They snarled, and he snarled back, teeth bared and a series of glottal clicks filling his throat. *This is mine,* the animal in him said without words, a wash of musk and blood-tinted determination.

The taller one leaped at him, and instinct took over, tucking his chin and twisting his body aside, his own claws tearing through reeking blood-fat flesh. The body thumped to the rooftop and the second, smaller *upir* fled screeching.

*Dammit. There goes my quiet exit.* He straightened, the Change melting from him, and felt the cold slap of rain. The rage folded down quietly, the animal watchful and angry in its corner at the very bottom of him.

The shaman hunched, hugging herself, her eyes huge and dark with terror. He held out his hand, noticing for the first time the cold sweep of the wind. "Come on. We'd better get out of here."

"Jesus," she whispered. "Those—they were—"

"We are going to have to have a talk. They're after you. We need to figure out why."

"I haven't *done* anything!" She was shivering, and in a little bit she'd be soaked. Her jacket was clinging over her blouse, and the way the wet cloth molded itself to her was not doing anything to help him concentrate.

"I know." *But maybe they don't know that.* "We've got to get away. Come on, Sophie."

She reached up blindly, and touched him willingly for the first time. Her fingers slid through his, and an acrid thread of smoke reached his nostrils. *Jesus. What the hell now?*

For a terrible second he was years ago and far away, smelling smoke and hearing the awful shattering unsound of a shaman's death. It took a deep breath he didn't have time for and a wrenching physical shudder to bring himself back to the present.

*Not this shaman. Not this time. This time, I'm going to do it right.*

A moment's worth of work got her to her feet, and he added up the rooftop again and arrived at the same answer. "You're not going to like this, but we're going to have to jump."

She didn't even protest, and that bothered him more than he wanted to admit. Instead, she just nodded wearily. "Yeah. Sure."

"It won't take long," he said, as if she *had* protested.

"You killed them." She sounded numb, and was shivering so hard his own teeth wanted to chatter.

"Of course I did. They weren't here to give you Christmas cards. No idea what they want?"

"None at all." She slumped helplessly as he hurried her across the rooftop, reached up to push her glasses up her nose with a fingertip. The little movement made his heart do something funny inside his chest. "We're jumping?"

"I'm jumping." He eyed the distance between the two buildings and decided he could do it even if she passed out, but he'd have to Change a little. His stomach spoke unhappily, and he told it to shut up. The smell of smoke grew stronger, drifting up through the open door. *Upir* hated fire, why would something be burning?

*I don't like this.* His stomach rumbled again, reminding him he needed to fuel the burn of the Change. He blinked away bad memories and the sick thumping of fear in his chest. Neither would help them.

First he'd get them the hell away from here.

*Then* he'd feed both of them, and everything would be fine.

"I'm jumping," he repeated, trying to reassure them both. "You just hold on."

## Chapter 15

He settled in a chair by the window, propping his wet, booted feet up on the sill. Sophie sat on the bed, staring at the blank screen of the television. The room was warm, and she wondered why the entire world still looked like it was wrapped in gauze.

The night was a confusing jumble. She remembered an all-night restaurant, a club sandwich he'd badgered her into eating, and the rain driving against the windows. A long street with lights burned out, and him pushing her against the side of a building and laying a warning finger on her lips, while something black and twisted slid past their hiding place—a slice of darkness that seemed suddenly far too small to hold them both.

This little room was warm, and the rain had decided to start pounding like it wanted to find a way in. The weird gauze covering the room was full of faces she didn't want to look too closely at. They moved, formed and re-formed, stared at her, some with goggles of astonishment, others gazing into the distance, some moving their mouths as if speaking. The ever-present smell of musk and male was comforting, and it seemed to hold the faces at bay.

He hadn't said anything since he pushed her inside the room. She didn't even remember where they were or if he'd paid for it; it *looked* like yet another hotel room.

Her nylons were sadly the worse for wear and her coat was soaked. And she had no goddamn idea what to do next.

Well, there was no harm in asking, was there? What was the worst he could do to her now?

*You know, I really don't want to know.* But she gathered herself. It took two tries before her voice would work.

"What do I do now?" she whispered, and braced herself.

He cocked his head. "You go ahead and sleep. I'll keep watch."

*Sleep? After all that?* "I don't think I can."

"Just lay down. The rest will take care of it-self." His hair was wet, curling a little, and if she hadn't seen him kill those…those *things,* she might not have believed it. Because he slumped in the chair as if he was tired, rolled his head back on his shoulders, and sighed. There was no sign of the thing he became, fur crackling from its skin, moving with a grace and speed that was far from human.

Sophie shivered. "I can't."

He didn't sound angry, only thoughtful. "Sure you can. Just lay down. It's almost dawn, we're safer during daylight. *Upir* don't come out much then."

*Much?* "I thought vampires couldn't stand daylight."

"The older ones can, but not much of it. It's fire they can't stand, direct open flame. Messy way to kill 'em, though. Best way is to take the throat out." He stopped, settled his boots more firmly on the windowsill. "You're safe. We weren't followed—I broke our trail and doubled back. You should sleep."

"But I…" Her feet ached and her back

twinged, too. Running in heels was *not* good. Her glasses were spotted with rain, but she hardly noticed because the gauzy things between her and the world were still moving, creeping closer and closer, pressing against the little sphere of normalcy her head ached to maintain.

He sighed, took his feet down from the sill, and rose fluidly. He shed his wet jacket, hanging it over the back of the cheap orange chair, and stepped over to the bed.

Sophie flinched, but he was faster, catching her face in his hands. His fingers were gentle, but she froze, feeling the strength running through them.

And the claws. She'd seen the claws. Her brain stuttered, turned this over, and gave up, shoving the memory away as an Unpleasant Thing.

He tilted her face up, examined it in the light of the bedside lamp. His eyes were so dark, and he looked worried—for once, his mouth drawn tight and the shadow of stubble on his cheeks contributing, the line between his eyebrows having the final say.

"You're triggered. It means your potential's been actualized, and you've been set as a Carcajou shaman. As *our* shaman." He said it gently, though it didn't mean a damn thing to her. "Right now you're seeing the spirits. The food will help, but you need to sleep. Your body'll finish changing while you sleep. I'll stand guard, make sure nothing gets to you. You just rest, and everything will be fine. Trust me. If you can."

*Jesus. He's serious.* She tried to pull away, but his hands were far too strong. "Let go." She sounded very tired, even to herself. "Why are you doing this to me?"

She expected him to be angry, but no hint of it crossed his face. Instead, he grinned, and the expression did wonders for his eyes. When he softened, he was handsomer. "What, saving your life? Maybe I like you."

*What?* She stared blankly at him.

"Maybe I like you a whole lot. Maybe I bumped into you and thought you smelled really good." A small shrug, his smile turning one-sided, a corner of his mouth lifting even further. "Maybe I like the way you walk, and I like your cute little librarian look. And maybe, just maybe, I like *you,* not just the fact that you're a shaman. How 'bout that for reasons?"

Vast, numbing incomprehension settled over her. None of this made any sense.

"For right now," he continued, "you need to rest. Not just any sleep, but shaman-sleep. I'll keep watch. When you wake up we'll feed you again, and we'll figure out what to do next. I'm all for finding out why the *upir* are so hot to put you six feet under, if we can do it without you getting hurt."

He let go of her face, but didn't leave her be. Instead, he slid her jacket off her shoulders like she was a little kid, tossed it aside, and half pushed, half guided her down to lie on the bed. He eased her shoes off, and the feeling was so wonderful she could have cried. He even, carefully and awkwardly, slid her glasses off, folded them up, and put them on the rickety little table next to the twin bed. "I've been handling you all wrong." The tone was soft, soothing. Like when Mark was in his rare happy moods, the ones that reminded her of why she'd married him in the first place. "I'm going to do better. But for right now, close your eyes and take a deep breath."

She didn't want to close her eyes. If she did, the gauzy faces might come closer, and if they touched her, she wasn't sure what she'd do. Go mad, maybe, if she wasn't already insane from all this. "There're faces. In the mist." *I sound about five years old.* Exhaustion weighed on her arms and legs.

He leaned down, brushed her hair back from her forehead, trailed his fingertips over her cheek. It was an oddly intimate touch, and should have made her blush. "They won't hurt you. I promise. Just trust me, and close your eyes."

*I don't trust you. You kidnapped me twice.* But the thought was very far away. Her eyelids were heavy, and he kept stroking her forehead. Her eyes closed without any conscious direction on her part, and the last thing she felt before slipping into complete darkness was one fingertip, calloused and warm, trailing down her cheek to touch her half-parted lips.

"Just sleep, shaman," he said. "I'll take care of everything else. No more worries for you."

*"Let's have a talk," Mark said, pleasantly.*
*Sophie's mouth went dry. She stood in the kitchen, sunlight pouring through the bay window with its neat collection of green herbs in pots. The dish towels on the rack were carefully folded, and she had dried every plate twice*

*before putting it away. She frantically reviewed everything she'd done today—if she could anticipate and apologize, he might take it easy on her.*

*Mark ran his hand back through his blond hair, the shark-charming smile showing his pearly whites. Everything about him was expensive, from the blue button-down to the immaculately pressed designer jeans; he was barefoot, his pedicure resting against the granite tiles he'd had installed the summer he almost broke her wrist and did break her rib. The same summer he'd almost drowned her. The granite had been his grand gesture—as if she wanted stone growing around the room where she spent most her time.*

*"Are you listening, Sophie?"*

*"Yes." She searched for the right answer, backing up in the angle between the corner sink and the counter to its left. The back door was eight feet away, and the kitchen island was between them. The copper-bottomed pans glowed, hung on a rack overhead.*

*Sometimes, even in the middle of the night, they would rattle and buzz, rubbing against one another like they were alive. Mark never heard them.*

"*I'm a little worried. Your friend Lucy called last night. She left a message on the voicemail.*" He paused. The sun gilded him, turned him into a statue, and he was wearing that most dangerous of smiles, the friendly one. Other people thought Mark was charismatic, but that smile always chilled Sophie's skin, sending a prickle of alarm down her back. His blue eyes were calm, thoughtful, and just a little bit amused. "*She seemed to think you were having coffee with her on Wednesday.*"

Of course she was, Wednesday was always her coffee day with Lucy. She was getting closer and closer to blurting something out, though; each time they met and the bruises twinged, she would tell herself to keep her mouth shut. It wasn't that bad, she would repeat to herself, over and over. Millions of women dealt with worse. And the house was so beautiful, and Mark was so rich—what right did she have to complain?

She said nothing. It was the safest course right now.

"*I think your time would probably be better spent volunteering. I've spoken to Delia Armitage at the Child Relief Fund, and she said they'd be glad to have you. You'll start*

*Wednesday, 3:00 to 5:00 p.m. I don't think I need to tell you to dress appropriately, do I?"*

*"No." The word escaped her, a breathless refusal.*

*"No, what?"*

*"No, Mark. Of course not." But that wasn't what she meant.*

*She meant,* No, I'm not going to put up with one of your mother's old-biddy friends who's always checking my clothes and reminding me you married beneath you. *She meant,* No, Lucy is my friend, my last friend, and you're not going to take her away from me.

*Mark heard what he wanted to hear. "That's settled, then. Good girl." But his eyes were the same, bright and paralyzing. "I don't think Lucy's a* proper *friend, Sophie. She seems a little...déclassé, if you know what I mean. You're flying with the eagles now, you shouldn't spend time with the sparrows."*

*Another one of his goddamn clichés. "Yes, Mark."*

*He slid around the corner of the kitchen island, and the copper-bottomed pans rattled warningly. They were polished each week by the maid service, and the sound of them strik-*

*ing one another was a rattlesnake's mouthless speaking.*

*"I can't see why you've allowed that to drag on so long." He sounded thoughtful, and Sophie braced herself. "You're a new person now, Sophie. You don't need your old life. Do you?"*

*He wouldn't stop until he'd made her say it. "No, Mark."*

*"All you need is me, and I'll take care of you. I'll tell you what to do." He was within five feet, and getting closer.*

*Her throat was dry. Her hands wanted to twist together; she kept them dangling by her sides only with an effort. If she flinched now, it would be waving a red flag in front of a bull. "Yes, Mark."*

*He took her shoulders. His hands were warm and manicured, and a fresh bruise on her right bicep ached as his thumb rubbed it. "Now, there's one other question. We know how...forgetful you are."*

*Oh, God. He wasn't going to let her go until he hurt her.*

*"How," he continued, his hands tightening slowly, "am I going to be sure you don't forget?" His fingers dug in until they rubbed*

*against her bones, and Sophie gasped. Next would come the slap, and the yelling—and she knew she was dreaming because this had already happened, she had escaped, she knew she had escaped, and this was a nightmare but it wasn't stopping, and Mark's face twisted into something plum-colored and twisted with rage, the pots rattled and the sunshine pouring through the window dimmed, became a flat darkness—*

—and she sat up, her mouth filling with a coppery rancid scream. Someone had her shoulders, light was filling the room, and for a moment she thought everything had been a hallucination, that Lucy was still alive and she was trapped, in the kitchen with Mark right before he knocked her to the ground and kicked her, shouting, the red explosion of pain in her belly enough to make her cry, at last.

"It's okay," someone said. "It's all right. You're safe, it's just a dream."

Sophie froze.

Zach's hair was damp and mussed, and he looked about as far away as it was possible to get from Mark's manicured blondness. He'd shaved, but he was still in the same rumpled navy-blue

T-shirt and jeans. Sophie stared, struggling for breath as the panic attack descended.

"Jesus." His hands were gentle, and she could shrug out of them if she wanted to. She didn't dare—who knew when his fingers would bite down, when he would start to yell? "Must've been a doozy. What was it, sweetheart?"

*God, just leave me alone.* Irritation warred with the need to breathe, her lungs closing down. She managed a short sharp inhale, a long gasping exhale, her body refusing to work. The shakes spilled through her, and he did a strange thing—he pulled her forward, folding his arms around her. The covers were all rucked up, cocooning her, and the slant of light against the cheap curtains made her think of late afternoon.

But the oddest thing happened. The heat of him soaked into her muscles, made it easier to breathe. Musk swirled around her, an almost-physical weight. She could smell the concern on him, clean and male, somehow healthy.

The panic eased. She took a deep breath. He was stroking her hair, murmuring something she couldn't quite hear because her ear was pressed against his chest and the thunder of his heartbeat drowned everything else out.

Slowly, very slowly, the shakes retreated. Now she could hear what he was saying— things like, "It's okay" and "I'm here" and "Just let it all out." Soothing, therapeutic things. It didn't matter. He *smelled* comforting, and that was another thing—how could she tell?

Her heartbeat eased. Her muscles loosened. When the panic finally stumbled and shivered to a halt, she found she was sweating a little, the light filling the room was pearly gray winter sunlight, and the man holding her was rubbing her back, his fingertips finding sore spots and working them gently through her rumpled suit jacket.

*God, I slept in my clothes. Ugh.* But she was warm, and for the first time in a long, long time, she felt…

Well, she felt safe.

It was ridiculous. He'd *kidnapped* her, for Christ's sake. But her brain kept running over the things on the rooftop, their eyes dripping hellfire, and the way he hadn't even hesitated, whatever he was, to throw himself at them. To get them *away* from her.

Still, would she be in this mess if it wasn't for him? He'd *done* something to her. The misty faces were still there, pale but swirling just below everything her eyes saw. *Spirits,* he called them.

A fast track to the psych ward and the ruination of everything she'd worked for since fleeing Mark was more like it.

"Better?" Zach asked, the word rumbling in his chest.

*I don't know. Still breathing, at least.* "I guess so." She had to clear her throat twice; she was dehydrated and her head hurt.

"Still seeing the *majir?*"

"Ma-zheer?" She blinked. He was very warm, and for a moment she wondered what it would be like to just relax there for a long time, leaning against someone. The moment passed, and she struggled away, her left palm sending a flare of pain up her arm as the scab scraped the sheets.

"The spirits. Faces, you said last night." He let her go, but didn't move off the bed. He should have looked awkward, half kneeling and watching her with unblinking dark eyes. But he didn't. He looked as self-contained as a cat, and as graceful, too.

She nodded, biting her lip. *This is so crazy. I'm pretty sure I'm still sane, though. He told*

*me I was. How could he know what I saw un-*
*less it's true?*

"Good." He slid off the bed, a short sharp movement. "Better get cleaned up. I'm not sure we should stay here much longer."

"Where are we?" Her nylons were ruined, and there was nothing else for her to wear. Her mouth tasted like the bottom of a cattle barn.

"Hotel." The sun gilded his hair as he crossed to the window, looked out, his shoulders stiffening a little. "I think it's called Happy Arms. What a name."

"Oh." *How could I sleep? I must have been exhausted*. She lifted her left hand, examined her palm. The scab was red and angry-looking, and she didn't have anything to bandage it with. "Ouch. Dammit."

That got his attention. "What?" Three long strides had him back at the edge of the bed; he seized her wrist and turned her hand up, examined the wound. "Jesus. When did you do this?"

"S-Saturday." *When I was getting away from all of you*. A sudden lump rose in her throat, and she sucked in a harsh breath as he manipulated her hand, squeezing the scab slightly.

"Must've bled. Probably how they tracked you, they're like sharks."

A bolt of pain went up her arm. She winced, and his eyes came up. He studied her face for a long moment, and she was suddenly sure there was something sticking in her eyes, or sleep-drool on her chin.

"You really don't have a clue about any of this, do you?" His fingers loosened.

She snatched her hand back. Sarcasm was probably the best response. "Is it *that* obvious?"

A shadow of irritation crossed his face, and he took a single step back. "Look, I've handled you badly. I'm sorry. I snatched you off the street because you were in danger and because you smelled good. It's not the best set of reasons in the world, but it saved your life. You think you could work with me here?"

"Because I smelled good?" *What the hell?*

"Yeah." One corner of his mouth lifted a little. "You smell even better now."

"I haven't even had a *shower*." The man was a lunatic, she decided. Her back ached, but overall she felt pretty good. Getting enough sleep was probably the answer to all the world's problems.

If she could sleep for a week, though, it wouldn't bring Lucy back to life. It wouldn't stop all this.

"Better hurry, then." He turned back to the window. A ripple passed through him, as if he was going to turn into that...the *thing* again. She froze, and huddled on the bed, blinking.

But he didn't. He just stood there, staring out the window like it was a movie screen. Silence stretched between them.

"So what happens now? I don't suppose you're going to take me home." *I sound strange.*

His broad shoulders rose, dropped. "I'm not so sure you have a home to go back to, Sophie. Is that short for Sophia?"

*You are so not the first person to ask me that.* "No, it's just Sophie. What do you mean, you're not so sure?"

"I smelled smoke. The more I think about it, I think the *upir* torched your building. Are you really sure there's no reason for them to be after you? Because it sure seems like they've got a grudge."

*Torched my building?* "Look, I've never seen anything like this before. As far as I knew, werewolves and...and vampires were only in movies. And not even very *good* movies. I don't know what any of you want from me. I just want to be left alone."

"To go back to starving to death? Look, you want to be a social worker? Great. We'll pay your way through school. We'll get you a place to stay, a nicer place than that little apartment. We'll protect you against anyone, including your ex-husband. All you have to do is be our shaman."

She stared at his wide back under the navy T-shirt. He was so...*big,* but it wasn't just his height or the muscle. It was the way he carried himself, with utter self-assurance. "What's the catch?"

His hair had red highlights in its darkness, and skin moved smoothly over the muscle of his forearms as he stuck his hands in his pockets. "You just have to put up with us being a little... different. I'll teach you everything you need to know. Look, Sophie, it's not just because you smell good. People like us, if we don't have a shaman, we can go a little...crazy."

*Crazy enough to start kidnapping people off the streets?* But she buttoned her lip over that one. It was what Lucy might have called Not Helpful.

Oh, but it hurt to think of Lucy.

"That's why others of our kind, other Tribes, won't even talk to us if we don't have a shaman. We're fugitives. Shamans help us stay controlled. Our last one…she died in a house fire, a long time ago. It was…" He sounded like he had something in his throat. "We need some help, Sophie. We need *your* help."

She licked her lips, wished for a toothbrush and a decent cup of coffee. "What if I say no?"

"That's not really an option." He said it so quietly she knew he meant it. "We can do it the easy way, or the hard way. I've got to make sure my Family survives."

A sinking feeling in the pit of her stomach. "Survives?"

"Without a shaman, we're vulnerable. You think I *like* doing this?"

"You certainly don't seem too broken up about it."

He turned on his heel, his chin dropped, and he regarded her with glowing-dark eyes. Sophie hugged her knees and wished she hadn't said it. He looked like Mark sometimes did when he was getting ready to yell, and she decided right now would be a really good time for her to start using some of that psych she was always studying.

Only, would it work on a werewolf?

He didn't yell. His tone continued, slow and even and very flat, as if he was choosing each word very carefully. "I would have liked it better if we could have trailed you, and if I could have met you, let you think it was coincidence. Asked you out on a date or two. Gradually eased you into it. We're not bad, Sophie. We're just different. And we *need* you, you can't imagine how much. I'm asking you to help us out, even though we haven't been exactly saints or anything."

"Why me?" *I'm just ordinary.* The rattle of copper-bottomed pans in her memory intensified.

"You're the first shaman we've found, the first person with any potential we've *ever* found. We can't wait around for another one—more of us will die. Probably Brun, he's weak. Or Julia, because she's been allowed to grow like a weed and she's too goddamn stubborn for her own good. Eric might hold out, but his animal…he might go over the edge any day. *I* might. And if that happens the other Tribes'll hunt us down and kill us like meat." He shrugged. "Against that—against more of them dying—I really have no trouble forcing you to stay put and getting to know us."

*Well, nice to know he's feeling no qualms.* "So what if I believe you? What if I agree? What happens next?"

The tension running through him didn't wane. He just stood there and *looked* at her, hands in pockets, shoulders drawn up, the weak sunlight bringing out red in his hair. "You get cleaned up. We get you some fresh clothes and something to eat. And we try to figure out what the *upir* want with you."

*Sounds like I don't have much of a choice. Story of my life.* "And you really don't have any trouble forcing me to do things?"

"Look, all I want is for my Family to survive. You're necessary for that. And I like you, Sophie. I like you a lot." His tone dropped from "friendly" to something else, and Sophie swallowed dryly.

"Because I smell good."

"You don't just smell good." One corner of his mouth lifted a little. "You smell *really* good."

*I wish he'd stop looking at me like that.* "Great." She pushed the covers down and slid over to the opposite side of the bed. He was looking at her *that way* again, as if she had something weird on her face. "I'm going to get cleaned up."

"There's a toothbrush in there, I brought it for you. Are you going to stay with us, Sophie? Keep us human?"

*I wasn't too great at keeping Mark human. But you guys are something else, aren't you?* If it was true, and they needed her…but did that excuse *kidnapping* someone?

Or saving her life?

She slid her legs off the bed, arranged her skirt, tried to smooth her jacket. "I want to go home." And she wanted to bandage her hand. "So I can pack, at least. There's things I have to take with me."

"All right. As long as it's during daylight, and we're careful." Did he sound *relieved,* of all things? "Thank you, Sophie."

She made it to the bathroom door, looked back over her shoulder, pushing her hair away. At this distance he was an indistinct blur, because her glasses were still on the small hutch next to the bed. "Don't thank me, Zach. I've been doing what people force me into all my life. This isn't any different."

He had no snappy comeback for that, and there was a definite feeling of satisfaction in shutting the bathroom door. Still, it was nice to have a fresh toothbrush, and she wondered about that while she tore it open. There was also a small travel tube of mint toothpaste. It wasn't like a kidnapper, was it?

And he'd protected her from those *things*. She still wasn't sure if he'd brought them to her apartment, though. But the first one had killed his brother. And then there was Lucy…and the detective. God, how could everything go so wrong?

*I just wanted to have a good time. I should have known. It should be me in the morgue now. They were after* me, *and they killed Lucy instead.*

*It's my fault.*

An even more horrible thought occurred and she halted, toothpaste in one hand, staring at the mirror.

*I'm not going to be able to go to Lucy's funeral. I don't even know when it is.*

Lucy was really, truly, irrevocably dead. All that brightness, all that life, poured out in a filthy alley. She'd been lured out there and—

Sophie made a small hurt sound, clutching

the toothbrush. The faces in the mist all around her sharpened, and she shut her eyes.

It was no use. She could see them even with her eyes closed. They were pale, nowhere near as clear as they'd been last night, but they were still there. It wasn't a dream. These things were *real*. They had killed Lucy, and they were happening to her.

"Sophie?" Zach was at the door. He sounded concerned.

She twisted the water on savagely. *I'm fine. Leave me alone.*

While the water ran, she cried, as quietly as she could. By the time she turned the shower on, wondering why she bothered because she would have to put her dirty clothes back on, the sobs had quieted a little. Just a little, and it was still hard to force herself to breathe, to stop being a sissy.

It was time to toughen up, like she had a year ago. Time to be a big girl and get some things done.

## Chapter 16

"Jesus," she whispered, and shivered. Zach had his arm over her shoulders, and was actually kind of liking the way she drew closer to him. A thin freezing rain, more like a mist with pretensions, kissed the blackened shell of her apartment building. "Jesus *Christ*."

*I told you, sweetheart. This isn't like* upir. *This is revenge.* "Who hates you this much?" He scanned the approaches. There were still a couple cop cars and fire trucks, so he kept them well out of sight. The entire area was cordoned off with yellow tape and orange traffic cones. Thin traceries of steam lifted into the morning air, and the stench of smoke was overpowering.

It was like the morning after the fire, when he'd gotten Kyle up on his feet and Kyle got all of them moving toward food and shelter.

Only this time, the shaman was next to him. For once, he hadn't failed. It was another thing to feel almost-good about.

"I don't... There's only one person who might." She shuddered again, and as much as he liked her leaning into him, he hated the sudden sharp drift of fear boiling from her.

"Let me guess. You were married to him." He gave a mirthless little laugh when she started and stared up at him, her eyes wide behind her glasses. She looked *just* like a librarian. A really hot one. "It's not that hard to figure out," he said, when he could keep a straight face. "How bad was it, with him?"

She was silent for a long moment, staring at the charred fingers of timber and blackened concrete. "Bad enough," she finally said, and tried to lean away from him. He didn't let her, pretending not to notice the little movement.

He decided to push it a little. "How bad is bad enough?"

"Bad enough that I left in the middle of the afternoon while he was due to be gone for two days. He got angry before he left. When I could stand again, I...I didn't take anything with me except what I was wearing and all the cash I could hide from him." She halted abruptly, licked her lips. He still didn't let go of her. "I went to the emergency room and insisted they take pictures. My—Lucy, she got me into a shelter. She didn't have much, but she managed to keep both of us fed and got me a job at a doctor's office. She..." This time, when she stopped, it was for good. She took a deep aching breath, and Zach's chest hurt for a moment.

*Goddamn.* It was one thing to see it in the divorce papers—the admissions statement from the hospital, copies of the digital photographs, the maneuvering of his high-priced lawyer and the torturous machinations of the justice system. It was another thing to feel the tension running through her, the flinch as if expecting another blow, and to smell the old hurt and fear under the ice and moonlight of a fully triggered shaman. The animal inside him turned over once, restlessly, searching for whatever was threatening her. *I'd like to talk to this ex-husband. Right up close and personal.*

"I'm sorry about your friend." *I'm glad it wasn't you, though.* "Come on. We'd better not hang around here."

She stared at the building. Little curls of steam mixed with the fine mist; the wind veered, heavy with the smell of sodden charred things. "It was raining so hard last night. Why did it burn so badly?"

He shrugged, careful to keep his arm lightly around her shoulders. "I don't know. *Upir* generally hate fires. Open flame's deadly for them."

"This was everything I had." She sounded sad, clutching her black leather purse to her chest. "*Everything.* And now it's gone. Again."

"I'm sorry." It was the only thing he could say, and it was completely inadequate. *But you're alive, aren't you? We're both alive. You're going to keep my Family alive, and we'll make sure you never have to lose anything you don't want to, ever again.*

"It's not your fault. I guess. Maybe." She sighed, and sagged hopelessly, leaning against him. "Yes, we'd better go. It was useless to come here."

"Not quite useless." He liked her leaning on him, and almost pretended it was for some other reason than the obvious—that she was exhausted, and she had literally nowhere else to go.

"You're right," she agreed, almost immediately. "Now I know I'm trapped. I *have* to go with you."

It should have felt like a victory. But she looked so lost, clutching her purse, her eyes too bright. She blinked angrily, denying herself tears, and that weird pain speared the inside of his chest. The animal in him turned uneasily, again, searching for the source of the hurt and not finding anything physically wrong.

"It's a mystery." He finally took a few experimental steps, pointing them down the street for the bus stop. "Why do they want you so badly?"

"I don't *know.* I never even knew you people existed. What the hell would they want from me?" She sounded calm enough, but the trembling stress in her hitched up another notch, and it began to be difficult to keep the animal under control.

"We'll find out, Sophie. I promise. And when we do, we'll settle it."

Instant wariness. "What do you mean, settle it?"

*What do you think I mean?* "Get them to stop chasing you. Find out what that one rabid *upir* was doing at the nightclub. Maybe he was someone important. Maybe they're after us, not you, but you're a tempting target. They can't take out shamans very often—they're too well-protected in most Families. The shaman's the most important person, you know. Maybe you just got mixed up with us at just the wrong time, I don't know. It could just be coincidence." *But I don't think it is.*

"But maybe not." She hunched her shoulders and stared down at the sidewalk, letting him steer her. Little crystal drops of rain clung to her curls, and he had to tear his attention away to watch where they were going. The sidewalk was cracked, and a sudden impulse to tighten his arm around her left him sweating. "There's no way to be sure, is there?"

"I can take you back to the Family. Then we can go visiting, and searching for information. If you want." *And if you'll cooperate.*

"Go visiting?"

It was like having a baby ask him questions. She knew *nothing*. But it was far better than her just staring off into the distance with those big eyes, refusing to even engage. "There're other Tribe around here. If we've got a shaman, we can ask them questions. Get some answers. If there's any of the Bear Tribe around, or the Felinii, we'll probably even have allies. Best would be other Carcajou, but they're rare. We haven't seen many." *And the ones we did scent we stayed downwind and far, far away from, without a shaman.* "There're just a few problems we'll have to solve before then. Like getting you some clothes and making you comfortable."

"Comfortable." She let out a bitter little laugh, and he instantly regretted opening his big fat mouth. Still, she wasn't screaming and struggling. It was looking up. "Yeah. So what other problems are there?"

"Well, you need a crash course in being a shaman." *And I need a couple days to show you I'm not so bad.* "We'll help you all the way, of course. And then we can find out who wants you dead so bad. Deal?"

The bus stop was a Plexiglas-and-metal cube, its benches littered with trash. Sophie sighed heavily, and hitched her purse up on her shoulder instead of clutching it to her chest. "All right." The words were almost lost under the sound of traffic, and Zach wished for a better van and a few thousands' worth of traveling money, to take her and his Family away from all this. "Deal."

He relaxed a little bit, smiled down at the top of her head. "Okay. Are you still seeing those faces?"

She gave a guilty little flinch. "I—yes. They're not as clear right now, though."

"Yup. First lesson: you've got to take care of yourself. When you have enough sleep and food in you, you're going to be able to control seeing the *majir* better. You've been triggered, which means you've changed. You're not going to Change like we do, but you're kind of halfway between us and the spirits—you can do a lot of things we can't. Make sense?"

"No." A humorless little laugh. "But I understand. I'm not stupid."

*I know that.* "So I'm going to be asking you how you feel, a *lot*. You might even get sick of that question, but I'm the alpha and it's my responsibility to take care of you so you can take care of talking to the spirits for us."

"Alpha?" She sounded curious, thank God, instead of angry or upset. Or that colorless little tone that somehow hurt him, the one that sounded like she'd given up.

"Yeah. That means I'm responsible." *I'm all that's left.* "The only other choice is Eric and he won't take it. So it's up to me."

"And it's up to me to talk to the spirits. What if I don't want to?"

He worked this around in his head for a few moments, trying to see things her way. "It's the *majir*. Why wouldn't you want to?"

"Maybe I want to be normal."

*Jesus Christ, honey, who would want that?* "You mean like a bleeder? A nine-to-fiver, one of those sheep? What the hell *for?*"

She withdrew. It was an almost-physical movement; he could literally *see* her pulling away, into herself. Walls going up, doors slamming, the essential Sophie retreating behind a blank screen. She gave him a mistrustful glance, her eyes darkening and that cute little mouth turning into a thin line before drawing down, and she looked away.

But she didn't demur when he kept his arm around her.

The right bus—the 48—came lumbering along, and he cursed his big mouth again. She didn't say a word after that, no matter how much he tried to engage her in conversation. He ended up just giving her random bits of information, nothing very useful, watching other passengers around them as the bus ground on and on toward his Family and the mist thickened into an actual rain. The temperature was dropping fast, and he had never wished so hard for a brick wall to beat his head against.

*Screwed up again,* he kept thinking. *You'll be lucky if she doesn't run again too, you idiot. How could you be so stupid?*

## Chapter 17

It was a Doze Inn, in a section of town Sophie had never dared to enter before—south of downtown, just on the edge of the core of housing projects that were always in the news. The concrete building slumped, tired and dispirited, under a gray sky, and the room had two beds, a kitchenette, and the hopeless smell of burned food and desperation.

"It was a productive morning," Eric said, with a meaningful glance in Sophie's direction. "We went channel-surfing."

"Good." Zach shrugged out of his wet coat. It had started to pour again, as if the sky wanted to wash the city clean. "See any other Tribe since we split up?"

"Not yet." Eric looked like he wanted to say something else.

Sophie pushed past him, heading for the bed that wasn't piled with a mound of clothes. Her feet were *killing* her, and she was soaked clear through. Her purse was heavier than she could ever remember it being; her shoes were full of water and, she was sure, half a street's worth of gravel. She sank down, shivering, and kicked the heels off. Immediately her groaning feet felt wrinkled and slightly soiled from the cheap carpet.

"Holy *shit,*" someone said in the kitchen, and the girl—Julia—appeared, holding a steaming, industrial-white china mug. "I don't believe it."

"Believe it." Zach relaxed, his shoulders dropping and a grin flashing across his dark-stubbled face. He filled up the room, and a wave of relief spilled through the air. It smelled like warm cookies, and Sophie found her own shoulders loosening, tension sliding out of her. She sighed.

*What is that?* She had to examine the feeling before she figured out it was *safety,* again, that weird sense that things were going to be all right. Julia shoved the mug into her hands, and Sophie found it contained blessed, fragrant coffee.

"You brought her back." Brun sat in front of the room's puny little television, cross-legged on the floor, a large piece of leather across his lap. A shy smile lit his young face. "Hello, shaman."

Sophie blew across the top of the coffee. She felt a little faint. Her lower back was cramping up, waves of pain tightening the muscles.

"I figured out your sizes and got you some clothes. Oh, and you can use my shampoo." Julia's dark eyes were wide and pleading. She looked a lot younger than she had, and the way she hunched down, glancing at Sophie only peripherally, was a little…troubling. The pale streak in her hair almost trembled as she hunched, easily, as if it was perfectly normal to crouch at someone's feet.

"Thanks." Sophie wrapped her aching hands around the mug, welcome heat soaking into her bones. Her hair dripped. "You wouldn't happen to have a towel handy, would you?"

"I'll get it!" Brun bolted to his feet and leaped for the bathroom. Julia collided with him halfway there, and they crashed into the door. Sophie flinched, and Eric swept the room door shut and rolled his eyes.

"They've been like this the whole time. Goddamn pups."

"They're young." Zach actually grinned for a moment, but quickly sobered. "Any oddness around?"

"Not that I can smell. I've kept us in here all rutting day. Bored out of our minds, but we caught the soaps. Brenda finally ditched that SOB." Eric shrugged, his leather jacket creaking.

"No shit?" Zach's smile came back briefly. "Because he slept with Susan?"

"No, she doesn't know that yet. It's because she's carrying that other guy's baby. Or she thinks she is, because someone switched the pregnancy tests. I think it was her roommate— the blonde girl."

"Huh." Zach scratched his cheek, ran his hand back through his dripping hair. Water darkened the pale streak, slicked it back from his strong-boned face. "Wow. No kidding."

*They watch soap operas?* For a moment, Sophie had the exquisitely weird sensation of being in a world where normal rules didn't apply. *I can't even* afford *a television. And here I am with a bunch of striped, soap-opera-watching werewolves. Jeez.*

A swell of laughter hit right under her stomach, rose to her lips with a burp. She took a scalding gulp of coffee, and Brun leaped out of the bathroom, bounding up to the bed with two quick strides. He presented her with a towel as Julia burst out of the bathroom, as well, her face a thundercloud and her entire body rippling.

Sophie didn't even see Zach move. One moment he was by the door, one hand in his pocket and the other combing his hair back. The next, he had the girl by the throat, and the impact rattled against the flimsy wall. She kicked, but he avoided her foot and slammed her against the wall again—not as hard as he could, Sophie could tell, but hard enough to make everything rattle again.

"Calm down." The touch of a growl under the words made the window—looking out on a sorry weed-strewn parking lot, the maroon van parked right in front of the room—flex and clatter. Sophie's jaw dropped and she almost dropped the mug, as well. There was no place to hide herself. "We're not going to have any of that."

Sophie braced herself, waiting for the

explosion, but Julia seemed to shrink. She made a curious noise, half-whining way back in her throat, and Sophie was reminded of a nature special she'd seen about wolf packs way back in high school. Fights in a wolf pack rarely turned deadly, because the submissive wolf would surrender in some way and the other, more dominant wolf would take the submission as a signal to stop fighting.

Now she wondered if Mark just hadn't been able to get that signal, if that was the reason why he had kept going until he *really* hurt her. Made her cry, or scream…or bleed. Her hands shook.

What was she going to do if Zach started yelling and punching? There was nothing she *could* do. She was as helpless as ever.

The misty faces sharpened, laying over the real world in a gossamer sheet. She tried pushing them away; they crowded around Zach and Julia, watching. Some of them reached out thin, insubstantial hands, smoothing them over the girl's body without quite touching her.

And just as soon as it had started, the violence in the air…disappeared.

Zach let go of Julia, who landed on her feet and shook her hair back, the pale streak flashing. "Bully." Her lip curled, but some essential unsteadiness had vanished, and she slid away. The faces retreated just a little bit.

She didn't seem afraid or upset in the least.

*What the hell just happened?* Sophie's eyes darted across the room, searching the different faces.

Eric let out a short breath, his shoulders dropping. He glanced at her, and she could have sworn he looked...grateful? Was that it?

Brun had dropped the towel and now stood watching this, his eyebrows drawn together. His face went through several changes, emotions flickering too fast for Sophie to decipher, and finally settled on deep relief.

"Yeah, right." Zach sighed. "I think we'd better get out of here. We've got work to do. Got to find our shaman a new place to live—the *upir* torched her apartment building last night. She's not too happy about that."

*Boy, is that the understatement of the year.* A completely inappropriate urge to giggle shrilly bubbled up inside her, right next to the unsteady, panicked feeling she used to get when Mark came home angry and silent.

"Don't they hate fire?" Brun had dropped down into a half crouch, watching Sophie's face.

She firmed her mouth into a usual expression, or what might pass for one. Her face didn't feel like it wanted to cooperate, so she dropped her gaze and focused on the coffee's brown-black swirls. The liquid sloshed; she tried to steady her hands.

"Yeah. Which is why we're going to be keeping a low profile for the time being. Since we have a shaman, though, there's no need for us to be Tribe-quiet, and we've got to find out who wants her dead. Julia, Brun, start packing. Eric, get the van ready." Zach's gaze swung over the room once, taking notes, and met hers. "Sophie. Want to get cleaned up, get some fresh clothes?"

She didn't miss the way all of them suddenly focused on her. Their attention was heavy weight, settling against her shoulders. She *hated* being looked at. Cold rainwater dripped down the back of her neck, her hair was a mess, and her entire body ached so bad she wasn't sure she'd be able to stand. "Sure," she said into the mug, coffee trembling as her breath touched it. "Love to. You wouldn't happen to have any aspirin, would you? My head's killing me."

"Find her some aspirin, Julia." Zach didn't

miss a beat. They all whirled into motion except him—he just stood by the bathroom door looking at her, both hands stuffed in his pockets now, wet hair hanging over his dark eyes.

*I must look like a bag lady.* Her clothes were sticking to her skin, her glasses were fogging, and she felt suddenly shapeless and very vulnerable.

The coffee smelled good, though. It was warm, it wasn't raining on her, and there was nothing to worry about right this second.

Unless it was her entire apartment building, gutted. Or Zach's eyes on her. Or the ghostly, gauzy faces even now clustering around her, their mouths moving. Under the sounds of the real world—Julia asking a question, Eric humming to himself, Brun rolling up the leather he'd been working on—was a reedy little mumble, like crickets.

And now she was wondering if she might see *Lucy's* face, and the prospect was enough to make a little shiver of dread slide down her spine. What exactly were these spirits? Was she going crazy? Zach said she was sane, and he knew what she was talking about. It didn't seem like a joke.

No, this was all too real. And Lucy was gone.

"Sophie." Zach's hand touched her face, cupped her chin. His fingers were far too warm, almost scorching, and that smell of warm safety was coming off him in waves. "How are you feeling?"

*Dizzy. Aching. Half-crazy.* "Fine," she mumbled, trying to avoid his eyes. *Why am I not terrified of him? I just saw him...what* was *that?*

He leaned down, his nose a few inches from hers. "You look pale."

"I'm fine." She tried to scoot back on the bed, failed. Coffee slopped inside the mug. "Just a little tired, that's all."

"And probably hungry." His eyes were kind, she realized. Deep, and dark, and very soft. The water on his tanned skin looked like a decoration, and the slight curl in his hair made it drop stubbornly over his eyebrow again. Her heart made a funny lurching movement, and she wished he didn't look so concerned.

"Aspirin, your highness," Julia said behind him. He held out his free hand, she dropped two tablets in, and went on her merry way. She didn't seem fazed in the least about being held down and threatened.

The sense of motion intensified, the door opened, and a burst of chill rain-washed air cut through the musk.

He handed her the aspirin. "Here you are. We'll get you something to eat, too. For right now, how about you get dried off? I can't get cleaned up until you do. There's only one bathroom."

*Why don't you use it, then?* But her clothes seemed suddenly, incredibly sodden and irritating, and the idea of a hot shower became just short of heavenly. "All right." *Let go of me, and I will.*

But he didn't. He still cupped her chin, his fingers warm on one cheek, his thumb touching just under her bottom lip. Her skin was still wet, and she could feel every single ridge of his fingerprints. She clutched the aspirin in one hand, the coffee in the other, and suddenly felt like a huge idiot.

"You're going to have to let go of me." *Why do I sound breathless?*

He nodded slightly, still staring at her. It was the same look, like he saw something green on her face, or something. "Yeah. I guess so." But he didn't move.

"I mean it." She blinked. The faces were

clustering behind him, their lips moving, and that reedy cricket sound became the rattling of copper-bottomed pans.

Sophie flinched, and he let go of her as if burned. He straightened and stepped away, shaking his fingers, and gave her a scorching, unreadable look. She slid to the edge of the bed and had to try twice before her body would let her stand upright. Julia was suddenly there, with a handful of clothes. "God, Zach, give her a minute. She's soaked. You don't have to—"

"Shut up, Julia." But there was no heat to it. He simply stood there, watching her, as Sophie palmed the aspirin up to her mouth and took a throat-scouring mouthful of coffee to get them down.

"Jeans. A T-shirt. I found a pair of Keds that might fit you, too. I even got underwear." Julia tucked her dark hair behind one ear. "About the only thing I didn't get was a bra, since I didn't know your cup size. But nobody ever died from going braless. Let's get you dried off and cleaned up and warmed up, and then we'll—"

"I'm fine." Sophie grabbed blindly for the clothes and beat a retreat to the bathroom door while she could. Halfway there she had to brush past Zach, so she looked over her shoulder. Julia looked crestfallen, and in that moment Sophie saw how young she really was.

*I feel old.* "Thank you." The words were ashes in Sophie's mouth, but Julia brightened. And then Sophie was past Zach, who stood very still. She swept the bathroom door closed, locked it, and took a deep breath.

The mirror held a very pale, half-drowned Sophie, dark circles under her eyes and every scrap of feeling okay she'd had that morning drained away. She took another gulp of the too-hot coffee, and found a furious heat rising to her cheeks.

*Why was he looking at me like that?*

And another, more troubling pair of questions. *Why did he hold her up against the wall? And why didn't he hit her afterward? I was sure he was going to.*

She didn't know. She didn't know their rules, and she had to learn quickly.

# Chapter 18

He supposed he might've felt lucky if she'd wanted to sit next to him, but he hadn't given her much of a choice. He'd dropped down in the semicircular booth next to her, and with Julia squeezed in on her other side, she didn't have a say in the matter.

"You mean you *steal?*" Her pretty eyebrows drew together, and she pushed a few stray curls out of her face. At least she was taking an interest in things, instead of just going all pale and glaze-eyed. Some food in her perked her right up, thank God.

Julia gave a contemptuous little laugh. "We're scavengers, honey." His sister took a giant bite of her cheeseburger, and Zach suppressed the desire to strangle her. "We pick up the bits and leavings. How do you think we live? Nothing's *free.*"

Brun signaled the harried waitress and asked for another side of fries. The bleached blonde looked about to protest until Brun gave her puppy-dog eyes, and the woman melted. Sophie's quick eyes took this in, and she hurriedly took a sip of Diet Coke. Zach tried not to hit her with his elbow, but it was close quarters with all of them crowded into the diner's biggest booth.

It was good to feel a shaman in the Family again, good to see Eric stop twitching and Brun open up a little bit, the ice and moonlight smell calming both of them. Julia was on her best behavior, making girl talk and acting world-weary. The only thing missing was Kyle's quick grin and sharp good humor.

Kyle would have liked this woman. The thought was a hurtful jab.

*She won't see a hunting run for a while. Let's be happy about that.* "Enough." He decided to stop trying to give her some space, and leaned a little closer. "We don't just fleece, Sophie. We do leatherworking, Julia's a fair seamstress, too, and I've fixed cars before. We're jacks-of-all-trades."

"Oh." Sophie nibbled at a French fry. "Like Gypsies."

*Djombrani are different, and there's no love lost between us and the Rom.* "Kind of. And now that you're with us, we can settle down and get real jobs." He almost smiled when she shifted her weight, almost tipping herself into Julia's lap, and settled back down next to him, her arm brushing his. Her hip bumped against his, and the flush that went through him was pleasant and frustrating in equal measure. She just smelled too good, and he was finding out that he liked her.

Every once in a while she would stop, look over the top of those glasses, and take a deep breath, as if readjusting the world. Each time, the ice and moonlight intensified, a powerfully soothing pulse spreading through them all.

When she did that, he wondered what it would be like to taste her breath. As it was, he got a drenching wave of her scent whenever she moved—healthy, brunette spice with that silver thread of *shaman* running through.

It was enough to drive a man crazy. Especially with one of those curvy little hips touching him. And when she picked up her turkey sandwich, her elbow brushed his again and she gave him a quick glance of apology.

*Jesus.* He was actually *sweating*. Not much, but enough to drive home the fact that she smelled too good to be left wandering around alone. She'd already blooded him, so that was all right—not that he thought Eric would try to muscle in, and Brun was far too submissive for her. She needed someone who could bully her into taking care of herself, someone who—

*Wait a second. Bullying her around is the worst thing to do.* He listened with half an ear as Julia chattered at her, Sophie's soft interested responses like music. *Slow and easy, Zach.*

He almost wished Kyle was around to give him some advice. Women liked Ky—it was the little-boy smile and the stubble when he was wearing his rough face.

Zach's hands tensed. There was that, too—revenge for Kyle. A way for them to all avenge their brother, their alpha, one of their own.

The *upir* were working in concert, had killed his brother, and were after his mate. Never mind that she didn't know she was his. Yet.

He turned it over inside his head for the rest of the meal, watching the restaurant and keeping vague track of the conversation. Eric paid and tipped the waitress, Julia dragged Sophie off to the restroom, and Brun took one last, long pull at his milk shake. "You're awful quiet." His face hadn't lost its baby look yet, smooth-cheeked and with only a suggestion of the strong jaw he'd eventually have. The paleness beginning over his left temple marked him as young, too.

Zach could remember the kid in diapers, with his open sunny smile. "Thinking."

"About Kyle." Brun nodded. "Julia thinks it's her fault."

*It was. But it wasn't—if I hadn't let Kyle take the alpha, he might still be alive. Goddammit.* "It's not. *Upir* are nobody's fault. They're just carrion."

"I know. But *she* doesn't." Brun slid for the edge of the booth. "I like the shaman. She's nice."

*And she's got no choice, she admitted it herself.* "She's seen reason, I guess."

"Or something." Brun grinned, and was gone before Zach could ask him what the hell *that* meant.

Zach made his way up to the front counter, and eyed the newspapers in their little metal hutches. He was contemplating getting a toothpick when something snagged his attention.

*What the hell?*

The headlines were screaming in thick black ink. MILLIONAIRE'S ESTRANGED EX-WIFE DEAD IN FIRE, ARSON SUPECTED.

And right under the headline, next to a block of dense text, was a spotty black-and-white picture of a younger Sophie, probably a wedding picture since a small band of white held a veil on her head. She was smiling, and it had obviously been cropped out of a larger photo.

He dug in his pocket for quarters, found none, and took a quick look around. Nobody was watching—the place was packed for dinner, waitresses hopping to and fro but nobody at the front just now. There was a clatter from the kitchen, and one of the cooks cursed as steam hissed.

Zach curled his fingers around the top of the door and gave a quick downward yank. There was a popping *zing!* lost under all the other noise, and it burst open pretty as you please. He grabbed a paper and shoved it closed.

It was righteously purple prose, especially since the millionaire in question—Mark Harris, who didn't rate a picture for some reason—owned a good chunk of the town. A few more pieces of the puzzle that was their new shaman snapped into place. It was a "bitter divorce," but the accusations of domestic violence and stalking apparently weren't news.

*Why didn't she move further away?* But then he thought of her bare apartment, and how it took money to stay on the run. And just how jealously a rich man would guard his money during a divorce. Sophie probably hadn't had a choice. She was damn lucky to have had a friend to help her escape.

Her dead friend. Another thing to hold the *upir* to account for.

He scanned the rest of the article. They'd recovered a body identified as hers, but Sophie was alive and well.

*You know, that just about screams "coverup."* He mulled over this for a few seconds, a shape he didn't much like turning inside his head.

They needed a defensible place to stay, and they needed to make contact with any other Tribe in town. There had to be more. With other Tribe backing them and a place to stay, they could handle *upir* and make their shaman comfortable.

*Think quick, Zach.*

Julia's voice floated across the restaurant. "He's right there. Let's ask."

"I don't—" Sophie began, and he hurriedly folded up the newspaper, sticking it under his arm just as Julia bounced up.

"I want a cinnamon roll. There's a place down the street. Can I take the shaman?" His sister bounced on her toes, her hair swinging. She sounded about twelve years old again, and for a moment he wished they'd found the shaman sooner.

*Wishes don't feed your Family, though. Or protect them.*

Sophie's shoulders slumped, and she looked away, out the plate-glass window of the diner. Rain spattered dully, and Eric arrived, picking at his teeth with a mint toothpick and looking supremely unconcerned.

"Can I?" Julia persisted.

"Later." His eyes met Eric's. "Take Brun. You three need to find a place for our shaman to live. Fleece a crowd if you have to. Get us a house. Somewhere in the suburbs, okay?"

Eric nodded. His eyes narrowed a little, but he wasn't about to ask questions.

"But I want—" Julia subsided as he eyed

her. *She's giving up way too easily, you know. Storing up trouble for later.*

"Later," he repeated. "Pick us up downtown, near the fountain, at eight sharp. Got it?"

"Eight sharp. Where are you headed?" Eric dropped his eyes in case Zach didn't want to say. Sophie pulled her new jacket—one of Kyle's, actually, and far too big for her—up on her shoulder. Her black vinyl purse was still damp.

"We're going to ask a few questions. I'm taking our shaman with me and looking for Tribe."

"But why? What's the—" Julia shut her mouth so fast she almost lost a chunk of her tongue.

The growl retreated under Zach's skin. Sophie was hugging herself now, her pale eyes wide as plates, staring at him. He wanted to reassure her, tell her she wasn't alone anymore, calm the rabbit-thumping of her pulse and the fear that was so much a part of her scent it almost canceled out the calm a shaman could bring. "Come with me, Sophie." He didn't phrase it as a request, which was wrong—the alpha didn't give a shaman orders.

Still, she nodded, a curl falling in her face. It

hurt to see how she almost-flinched, her shoulders coming up, when he stepped close to her.

Well, he knew one thing for certain now. Someone wanted her dead. Maybe it was the *upir,* maybe not; it didn't make a goddamn bit of difference. What mattered now was protecting her, not just to keep his Family alive but also because of the way she glanced up at him—her eyes stuttering to his face to read the emotional weather there, bracing herself for God alone knew what.

She shouldn't have to look like that.

He was inside her personal space before he realized it. She almost backed into Julia, who stepped smartly away. Zach caught Sophie's arm, his fingers closing gently but irresistibly, and he realized what he was about to do only when his mouth met hers.

It was a brief pressure of lips, tasting of spearmint gum—how had she gotten hold of that? It didn't matter, because the contact burned right through him, the smell of her filling his nostrils and the animal in him circling once, a fierce sweet pain running through the center of his bones.

He inhaled just as she let out a soft, shapeless, shocked sound; her breath touched his mouth and for a moment he was drowning in it. The rest of the world—diner, Family, the sound of the rain and traffic a formless hum outside—vanished in a white glare, and he wouldn't have cared if the whole world had gone up in flames just that moment. He inhaled again as she breathed, the air touching his skin laden with *her,* an unfamiliar weakness spilling through him.

She was shaking like a rabbit. He blinked, loosening his fingers one by one and straightening. It took him two tries to find words.

"Everything's okay, Sophie." He wanted to rub his cheek against hers, bury his nose in her hair; the conflicting desires shook him before he clapped a lid on both of them.

She blinked. Her mouth slightly open, she looked dazed and adorable. Those eyes of hers behind the glasses were velvet winter sky, with fine threads of gold in the iris. If he looked closely he could see a very, very light feathering of paler hairs at her right temple. She'd have a streak before long, when her body finished settling into the balanced chemistry of a shaman's.

Just looking at her this close made him want to kiss her properly, but she wouldn't be ready for *that*. He heard, very dimly, Brun saying something and the diner's door closing behind his Family.

They were alone now, just him and his shaman, standing in front of the cash register and the broken newspaper hutch. "We're going to go visiting. I'll ask the questions, you just sit and look pretty. Okay?"

Sophie blinked again, losing that dreamy look. She didn't smell like fear now, which was a blessing. "I…I guess so. Why on earth did you do *that?*"

*What, you can't guess?* His smile widened. He didn't quite let go of her arm, and she didn't resist as he pulled her toward the door, the newspaper tucked safely away. "Maybe I like you, shaman."

"Maybe?"

*You sound so surprised.* "Definitely. Try to get used to it."

She muttered something vaguely uncomplimentary, and he was surprised into a laugh. He really *did* like her. And there was an edge of something else creeping through her scent now, replacing that maddening tang of fear. Something warm and familiar, the first thread of a Carcajou's musk.

All in all, Zach reflected, things were looking up. Though he still had to figure out who was trying to kill her.

## Chapter 19

*If I have to sit in another seedy bar, I'm going to tell him to take his shaman job and shove it right up his—*Sophie shook the water out of her hair. If she had to put up with more cigarette fug, the smell of stale beer, sticky floors, or filthy bathrooms, she was going to say to *hell* with this.

But she couldn't very well say that, could she. Her home was burned down, and she was depending on Zach for everything. She didn't much like it, either. They'd told her at the shelter how an abusive relationship started—and how a man could isolate you from your friends and family, so you lost all sense of proportion and ended up thinking whatever he wanted to do to you was right and normal.

*How do I know he didn't bring those...those vampire things, too?* She followed him, most of her attention taken up with worrying, until Zach stopped short and a low thrumming sound alerted her to the fact that the outside world was going on without her.

Sophie looked up.

This bar looked the same as every other puke-palace she'd seen this afternoon. It was long, and low, and dim even in the middle of the day, and the only thing separating this bar from the others was the number of shapes inside it. Who knew so many people drank during the day?

The only bright lights were over three pool tables in back, and Sophie shook yet more water out of her hair. *Why did he do that?* He'd leaned in and pressed his lips against hers, then done something odd—*smelled* her, an intimate little movement paired with an inhalation so deep she was surprised his ribs didn't crack.

"Carcajou," someone said, a low smoky male voice. "Well met."

"Ursu." The thrum under Zach's tone didn't go away. It wasn't quite a growl. "Well met."

The man clasping Zach's forearm was *big*. He had wide shoulders under a wine-colored rugby shirt, stubble over his strong-jawed face, and dark eyes that gleamed like coals. Feathers were tied into his hair, fluttering on a draft from the door Sophie was holding open, and he loomed, slump-shouldered, over both of them.

The smell of the place hit the back of her throat like a shot of burning whiskey, and she coughed. It smelled like animals in here—healthy animals, under the pale ghost of cigarette smoke. The confusion was immediate, her newly sensitive nose picking out at least a hundred different odors at once and connecting them to strange images of fur and teeth, muscular sleek sides and broad paws bearing claws. The rush of mental pictures was so intense she actually rocked back on her heels, shaking her wet hair.

"That's a new shaman. Congratulations." The huge man was looking at her, unblinking. "Welcome, sister. The spirits speak well of you."

*What am I supposed to say to that?* "Hello," she managed, faintly. He was just so *big*. And he looked dangerous—not in the sleek, supple way Zach did.

She was suddenly very, very glad Zach was between her and this man.

They let go of each other's forearms, and as her eyes adjusted to the gloom she saw others, all with that air of zinging vitality and danger. There were a few women, mostly playing pool, that smelled like cats—slightly oily, dry and healthy. A few of the men smelled like the one who had greeted Zach, the others smelled like different kinds of fur and wildness. One tipped a shot glass of something far back, slammed it down, and gave her an odd salute. He had little bones tied in his hair that clicked and clacked as he moved.

*Toto, I don't think we're in Kansas anymore.* Sophie swallowed a lunatic laugh and moved closer to Zach. He was the only one who smelled familiar, and the musk he carried wrapped around her like a warm blanket.

Zach actually looked tremendously relieved. "I've got a bit of a problem—I'm hoping I might be able to find something out."

"You mean about the price on your shaman's head?" The big guy grinned. "I'm Cullen, by the way."

"Zach." They grinned at each other, toothy

white grins that didn't look very friendly. "I hadn't heard there was a price."

"Nobody in the Tribes would take it. But… well, why don't you come in and sit down?" Cullen's eyes wandered away from Zach, and Sophie let go of the door. It eased shut, latching with a small click. Her eyes finished adapting to the dark.

"Wait a second." Her throat didn't want to work properly. "A price on—"

"Just relax, Sophie." Zach sounded, of all things, bored. "You're on Tribe turf. This is pretty much the safest place for you in the whole city."

"You got *that* right." The big guy's grin turned more genuine and widened, his lips coming down to cover most of his teeth. A rush of noise like crickets on a summer night filled her skull for a moment, and her vision did a funny double-trick.

Where Cullen had been standing was a pile of fur that resolved itself into a hump-shouldered bear, standing on its hind legs and testing the air, looking at her sidelong. And *grinning* at her, its tongue lolling fat, wet, and pink.

She backed up, moving so fast she barely felt it when her shoulders hit the door, and suddenly

Zach was there, his hands on her shoulders. "Easy there," he said softly, and there was movement behind him. The image of a bear had turned back into a man, and was staring at her, his chin lifted and his nostrils flaring. "Sophie. *Sophie.*"

She tore her gaze away from the other man with a physical effort, found herself staring at Zach. His eyes were dark and deep, fixed on her face, and his hands were gentle. That odd, heavy musk filled her nose, and her heart gave a pounding leap.

"I need you to be calm," he murmured. "Otherwise we're going to have a situation here."

"She all right?" the bear-man asked, and the new tension in the air kicked up a notch.

"Just peachy." Zach's eyes never left hers. "Come on, Soph. Help me out here."

*It's not Soph. It's Sophie, goddamn you.* Her lungs were refusing to work right, and another one of the panic attacks threatened, her muscles on the verge of locking down.

"I thought you said this was safe," she managed, in a breathy whisper.

"It *is* safe." He didn't roll his eyes, but it was close. "You're with *me*."

*Oh, well, that's all right, then.* She swallowed another weird hysterical laugh. But oddly enough, it was. She'd seen him change on a rooftop and take on three *vampires,* for God's sake. A man who looked like a bear—who *was* a bear—was no sweat. Zero perspiration, as Lucy used to say.

She hitched in a breath, found her lungs were working. *I can deal with this. I've got to deal with this.* "Oh." She searched for something to say. "Yeah. I'd forgotten that bit."

"Is she all right?" the bear-man asked again.

Zach's face didn't change. But she could *feel* him, in some odd way, willing her to buck up. To help him out. She didn't know quite what would happen if she said she wasn't okay, but it probably wasn't anything nice. "I'm fine." The words came out confident, if a bit breathless. "It just…a price on my head?" *That's news.*

Zach winced slightly. "I'll explain." It was merely a breath of sound, and she found herself staring at his lips now. He'd *kissed* her—never mind that it was just a chaste press of closed lips. If she could handle that, and handle the way he was moving in on her now, his body inching closer and closer into her personal space, she could certainly deal with a man turning into a bear, right? "There's something going on, Sophie. I'm getting to the bottom of it. Just hang loose, okay?"

He was *pleading* with her, she realized, and her head felt a little too light suddenly, and full of more cricket noise. "Okay," her mouth said without her prompting. "But we're going to have to talk about this."

"In a little bit. I promise." His chin dipped a little, that soft curve of hair falling over his eyes, and she suddenly longed to push it away. Wondered what it would feel like.

She nodded. Her shoulders peeled away from the door, and he let go, finger by finger.

"You sure she's okay?" The bear-man was still alert, every hair quivering. She could *smell* the readiness on him, and a queer coldness that managed to be soothing. The coldness was like a snowy night, peace laying over every edge with a blanket of soft white.

"I'm all right," she repeated, more loudly, for his benefit. Zach's mouth firmed, and she dropped her eyes. It didn't seem polite to keep staring. A flush rose to her cheeks, and a fresh swell of low sound rolled through the room, like whispers.

"Christ, she's raw. Come in and have a drink, Carcajou. Just keep her calm. I've got a whole barful of Tribe here, they won't take kindly to a shaman losing her cool."

*Losing my cool? I lost that a few days ago when Lucy bled to death. I'm not sure I'll ever get it back, either. Jesus.* "I'm okay," she repeated, numbly. "Why don't you believe me?"

"They can smell it on you." Zach half turned, glanced across the bar. Everyone had gone still, even the women at the pool tables. "Just like I can. How much is she worth, Cullen?"

"Quite a lot, actually, but only if she's dead." The bear-man shrugged. "Some interested party is dangling a prize for a hit. Then something went wrong a few nights ago. Some sort of rumor about downtown and a Puppet ripped to shreds—"

"A Puppet?" Zach perked up. "I thought…"

"Where have you been living? Probably on the rough, if that's your only shaman." Cullen backed up a few steps, and Zach moved, too. It was as if they were dancing, neither one of them really giving ground. She followed in Zach's wake, trying not to feel clumsy.

"We're new in town." Danger lay under

Zach's words, like he was daring the man to comment further.

"I guess so." Cullen laughed, and turned on his heel, presenting them with his broad back. The tension snapped like a rubber band stretched too far. Zach took a seat at the bar like he belonged there, and Sophie hitched herself up awkwardly on the one next to him. The clacking of pool balls and low murmur of conversation resumed. The bear-man poured them both a shot of Johnny Walker Red and settled behind the bar, one eyebrow hitched expectantly.

Zach tossed his shot back, cracked the glass against the counter like an expert, and brought out the newspaper he'd been carrying around and fiddling with all day. "Look at this." He spread it out on the counter, and Sophie leaned over, not daring to touch her own shot glass. There was…*My God, that's from my wedding picture. The one hanging in the hall.* She remembered that day, the taste of the cake and the heavy yards and yards of white satin, the way the veil blinded her—and how Mark had dug his fingers into her arm right before she threw the bouquet, because she hadn't been paying attention to him.

She'd had finger-shaped bruises for two

weeks afterward. And on the honeymoon, he'd been so charming and repentant, until the night she'd accidentally slammed a door and he'd bitten her—

*That's in the Past, and it's an Unpleasant Thing. Don't dwell on it, Sophie.*

She focused on the columns of text, and felt the world slide a few more degrees over into unreality. *Wait a second.* "But I'm not dead," she heard herself say.

"I know that, and you know that." Zach's fingers touched the damp, smudged newsprint, sliding over the curve of her cheek and leaving a black mark. "But they found a body that someone's identified as yours. That means cover-up."

"Christ." Cullen set another shot glass out, poured himself a jolt of Walker. "Is it *open* war on our shamans now?"

"Since when do the Tribes fear *upir* so much?" Zach sounded honestly puzzled, and dangerously calm.

"You forget most of us aren't Carcajou. If they band together they can make it difficult for us. And here...well, the *upir* have worked their way into high society. They own the town. We keep a low profile for fifty miles in every direction. This is like a hunting preserve, and the head bloodsucker is a piece of work. Name's Armitage."

*What?* "Armitage?" Disbelief tinted her tone. "But—"

"Harold Armitage." Cullen shrugged. "Big name in town, I guess. You want some club soda or something, shaman?"

"No." She shook her head, curls falling in her face. "I—Jesus, I know his *wife*. Harold's a stockbroker. Old money, they do the country-club Christmas each year." She realized how idiotic that sounded. "You're saying he's a vampire?"

"He's *upir*. Has been for the past forty years. He hands out the Change in return for favors, and for other services rendered." Cullen gave her a narrow look, and she leaned back, the bar stool creaking as her weight shifted.

"Accept something to drink, Soph. It's polite." Zach gave her a tight smile.

*Great. Yeah. Sure. Fine.* She picked up the shot glass, downed the whiskey, and coughed as it stung her throat and exploded in her stomach. The gauzy faces hanging over the world sharpened briefly—some of them were clustering around Cullen, whispering in his ears. He tilted his head briefly, and one solidified, its lips moving.

*Oh, God. I'm going crazy, no matter what Zach says.* Her eyes watered, she blinked furiously, and Zach's smile turned absolutely genuine. He even *winked* at her.

"So they have a body, and they're calling it hers. When exactly was she triggered?" Cullen laid his hands carefully on the counter. Broad, blunt hands—if she looked closely, would they turn into paws?

"Couple days ago. We found her during an *upir* attack. We thought it was rabid since it was hunting in the middle of a bunch of bright lights and crowded prey. It took a friend of hers outside and ripped her throat open." The smile was gone as if it had never existed. "Then, just as we got our shaman out of town, seven young suckers broke into our nightly den. And there were more of them at her apartment last night. They fired the building."

"*Upir* using fire?" Cullen's eyebrows drew together. He uncapped the bottle, and Sophie hoped he wasn't going to offer her more. He didn't, just poured himself another shot. "Just who is she, anyway?" He leaned down, his mouth moving a little as he stared at the newspaper.

"She's our shaman." Zach watched the bear-man read the article.

"She's *Harris's* ex-wife?" Cullen glanced up. "Holy *shit*. I heard that there was a sacrifice gone wrong, and someone was paying big money, and then we started to hear about *upir* chasing down a shaman. But—"

"A sacrifice?" Zach wanted to know, but she had a different question.

Sophie grabbed the edge of the counter. The world was still spinning off course. "How do you hear all this?"

"Oh, you know. The air talks, we listen."

"No. I don't know." Sophie shut her mouth, took a deep breath. Zach's knee bumped hers. A wave of heat slid up her neck, filled her cheeks. "I don't know at all." *I know nuh-thing,* a mad voice from childhood reruns of *Hogan's Heroes* crowed in her head. Lucy had done a great Sergeant Schultz impression. It had cracked them both up to no end.

Tears crowded her eyes, blurred the whole bar. She blinked furiously, forcing them back.

"Well." Cullen didn't take offense. "You'll

find out soon. When you're ready, the air will talk to you."

*You know, that really isn't comforting at all.* "Like the faces?" she hazarded. "The ghost faces?"

"Exactly." He nodded. "The *majir.*"

"Right." *I am handling this very well.* She stole a glance at Zach. He was looking at her like she'd just won a prize, and there was something else about that smile that made her breath refuse to come properly. Something warm and interested, adding to the musk threading through his scent. *I am handling this very, very well. Even if it's weird as fuck.*

"Well, if you're seeing them now and you were just triggered a couple days ago, you're going to be one hell of a shaman. I'll bet you've always heard weird things, seen things out of the corner of your eye. You were a big daydreamer when you were a kid, right?" Cullen outright grinned, though it wasn't the feral baring of teeth he'd shown to Zach.

She gave a half-guilty start. "How did you—?" *Well, that's a useless question, Sophie.*

"I was the same way. It about knocked me sideways when the old shaman from our sleuth—that's a group of bears, a sleuth—found me. It was kind of a relief to find out I wasn't crazy." He tapped his fingers on the bar's surface, meditatively.

"So you were normal? Before?" This was the most information she'd gotten from *anyone*.

"Yeah, sort of. Nobody's really normal. Being a shaman, though, it's a lot of fun. Wait until you take a run."

*Take a run? Is that like taking a bowel movement?* "A run?"

"I hate to interrupt." Zach's knee bumped hers again. "So that first *upir* we killed was a Puppet? Armitage's? And there was a—"

"Right. He was spitting mad about it, too. Or so I heard. I guess there was something about the target not being hit."

"Wait." Sophie clutched at the edge of the bar. "Target. The *target* means me, right? The vampire wanted to kill *me?*"

"It's certainly looking that way." Zach tried to shift closer, his knee hitting hers again, and Sophie hopped off her bar stool. "Hey. Sophie—"

She took two quick, nervous steps back. "No. It was after me, right? And it killed Lucy. That means—"

"I'm not *sure* yet, and there's other questions

to answer." Zach slid around on the bar stool, leaned back against the bar, and eyed her. "I'm guessing you didn't spend a lot of time out partying, right?"

"I...no. It was the first time I'd gone out in ages. Lucy said I needed to have some fun." *She said she was going to get me to have fun if it killed her. I guess it did.*

"So maybe they were watching your friend— the only friend you had—and waiting for you to show up someplace out of daylight. And the—"

"Hold on," Cullen said. "Can I get a word in edgewise? The target wasn't hit. Only one of the two people they were looking to kill ended up dead. Then a shaman got mixed up in it. That's what I heard."

Zach tensed, muscle by muscle. "What exactly are you saying?"

Sophie stared at the bear-man. He held her eyes, and his expression was kind. Her mouth closed with a snap, and she found her voice right afterward. "He means someone wanted *both* me and Lucy dead, and they just waited until we were together." *It means it's my fault. I knew it.*

"Maybe it was efficiency." Zach nodded.

"You were pretty hard to find. I'll bet you were even registered under a different name at school."

"My mother's maiden name," she whispered. "The degree would have been issued in my name, though, when I finished. Because of the domestic, ah, the divorce." *Because of the police reports and the pictures. Lucy went in with me, and the Dean said they saw so many others like me, that things could be done. And that once I got my degree I could get a job and move, and I'd be safe.*

*Safe. Oh, God.*

Zach let out a sharp breath. "Your phone was probably unlisted, and the address on your driver's license was that mail drop. You were smart, and hiding probably saved your life."

"I was over at her place all the time, all they had to do was wait." The urge to just lie down on the floor and let the world go on without her was overwhelming. *If I hadn't given in, if we hadn't gone out dancing...God.*

"It's not your fault," Cullen said softly.

How the hell did he know whose fault it was? She squeezed her mouth shut. The entire place had gone very quiet. She would have bet money, if she'd had any, that they were all looking at her, and she *hated* that. She hated being the center of attention.

The only thing to do was look at Zach, who had a line between his eyebrows and a firmness to his mouth suggesting that he knew what she was thinking. Whether or not it was true, it was comforting. He was the only thing she *had,* now.

"What do we do?" She hitched her purse higher up on her shoulder and hugged herself, palms cupping her elbows.

"Can we count on the support of the Ursa?" Zach didn't look away, but she had the idea the question wasn't directed at her.

"Well, you're Carcajou. And they're trying to kill a shaman. Maybe." Cullen scratched at his neck and sighed. "At least, the Bear Tribe won't stand idly by if it gets any worse. But my advice? Take your shaman and run. Train her up and keep her safe. You don't want to fuck with Armitage. He's not just *upir,* he has the means to make a lot of people uncomfortable enough to come looking for you. Weight of numbers— and weight of cash—tells."

Zach looked puzzled again. "Huh. The Tribes around here, they all feel like this?"

"Don't get cute. The Tribes here have lost

two shamans to Armitage. I, for one, don't want to lose more."

"Lost two shamans? And you're just *sitting around?*" Zach slid back around, like a kid on a malt-shop stool, and leaned on the counter. "What the hell is going on here?"

"We're *not Carcajou*. We're just Tribe. They have numbers on us and Armitage has cops with long-distance assault rifles. We step out of line and it's open season in the whole city."

Zach shook his head. "Jesus."

"Take my advice and get her out of town." Cullen set the bottle on the counter. "Sooner or later Armitage will self-destruct. It's what they do. He'll get a batch of bad blood, or one of his little goons—like Harris—will take him out."

"Excuse me." She felt like an idiot for even speaking, but both of them went still. "Mark's not a vampire. I lived with him. He's just…" What words could she pick? The old instinct to lie rose under her skin, and she shut her mouth with an effort. Better to just be quiet if she couldn't tell the truth.

"Harris has been his regular daylight hatchet man for a couple years, but he just took the Change. He was supposed to offer a sacrifice, but I gather he's in Dutch because he didn't."

"A sacrifice?" *What does that mean?*

Cullen now looked acutely uncomfortable. "That's how Armitage runs it. It's an old *upir* trick. In order to buy the Change into bloodsucker, you've got to sacrifice a member of your family."

"Now we get to it." Zach hopped off the bar stool, his hair falling over his eyes. He looked furious, his mouth a tight line and his eyes alight. "Killing two women with one stone. God*damn,* but I hate that type of man. It doesn't even deserve the name."

"Wait. So he was supposed to kill me, so he could get turned into a *vampire?*" *Well, if I can believe in werewolves and vampires, I should have no trouble believing this. And it's just like Mark, too. God.*

Zach halted right in front of her. "That's what a sacrifice is. I'm just surprised nobody's done it on this large a scale before, in a city."

*Well, I guess that makes them trendsetters, doesn't it.* "What do we do now?" *Because I don't have a stinking clue.*

"We take you back to the Family and we have a discussion about running or staying. I'm in favor of teaching this Armitage bastard not to mess with Tribe." His lip lifted, and she was reminded of the long, lean, graceful lines of the thing he could become. *And* of the hard weight of him against her, the way he leaned in close and touched his lips to hers, inhaling as if she were perfume.

*Maybe I like you, shaman.*

"But." He stuffed his hands in his pockets, his shoulders slumping, and though he was much bigger than her, he seemed to be trying to make himself smaller. "This is your town, and they've killed your friend, and I haven't made things any easier on you. So I guess it's up to you what we do."

*Oh, God, not another decision. Who made me responsible for you?*

He must have read her face. "Come on. We should get to the pickup point just in time."

"Carcajou." Cullen looked like he was ready to say something else, but Zach just turned his head, not quite looking back over his shoulder. "She needs training, and you—"

"If the Tribes won't deal with this, why should we stay and risk her?" He pitched his voice just loud enough to carry. "She'll decide what to do. In the meantime, you can tell the air—and Armitage—that if he comes after her

I'm going to personally reach down his throat and tear his diseased little heart out. *Nobody* messes with her from now on."

## Chapter 20

It wasn't much, just a two-story fake Tudor on a quiet, depressed street, but Eric was visibly proud of himself for scrambling a rental on short notice. "It's good," Zach said, and hoped Sophie would catch the hint. She'd been quiet since the bar, the kind of quiet he was beginning to think spelled trouble.

And he didn't want to break the news that all the trouble might've been wasted if they had to get her out of town because the *upir* here were getting too big for their britches.

"It's nice." She stood in the empty living room, looking at the fake fireplace; the gas wouldn't be turned on until Brun or Eric could get down to pay a deposit, but there was electricity, the place came with a fridge and a stove, and Julia had already hung up her clothes in one of the bedrooms—*not* the biggest one, for once.

That one belonged to the shaman. And, not so incidentally, to Zach. But he'd cross that bridge when he came to it.

Assuming they stayed here.

"It's *really* nice," she said, pushing her hair back. A thin thread of her musk reached him. She even smelled pleased, and Eric drew himself up a little straighter, grinning. "You did all this just in a few hours?"

His leather jacket creaked as he shrugged. Was he actually *blushing?* Wonders never ceased. "The hardest part was finding mattresses. But we're champion scroungers."

She was actually *smiling,* her eyes damn near sparkling and the corners of her mouth pulling up. The smile did something funny to Zach's head, even though he thought he was pretty prepared for how goddamn attractive she was.

That smile made him want to do something, anything, to keep it on her face. Maybe make her laugh. She didn't just smell good, she was smart and capable and soft in all the right places, and—

The smile waned. She gave the living room another critical glance, and slid her purse off her shoulder. "We might not be here for long, though. We found some things out."

Which brought Eric's eyes around to rest on him, speculatively, and he found himself wondering if his cousin was having second thoughts.

There was going to be a short, sharp fight if *that* was happening.

"Like what?" Eric made a restless movement, the pale stripe in his hair gleaming under the ceiling fixture's flood of gold.

Zach kept his hands loose with an effort. "Like why the *upir* are after our shaman. What's for dinner?"

"Julia and Brun are at the store, should be back in a little while. Julia said she'd do steaks." Eric studied Zach's face, his forehead wrinkling. He looked younger when he did that, a ghost of the gangly kid he used to be. "What's up?"

"Steak? Wow." Sophie looked relieved. That smile peeped out again, a shadow of its former self.

Still, he almost lost track of what he needed to say, looking at that shadow. "Seems like our shaman's ex-husband wants her as a sacrifice. And the *upir* in these parts are getting uppity, in bed with the police and the local gentry. Met a shaman of the Bear Tribe who doesn't think anyone will stand up to them."

"So it's simple." Eric folded his arms, his leather jacket creaking. "We slap them around a bit, show them who's boss, crack 'em like a nut, and be home in time for breakfast. Right?"

*If something so simple can fix it, I'll be relieved.* "It's up to the shaman." Zach clumped over to the window, his boots squelching. He'd be lucky if she didn't catch a cold after being dragged around through the rain all day. No wonder the Tribes were so hard to find in this city, if they were lying low, scared of *upir.*

Scared of *upir.* What next? They were dangerous, true, but Tribe—especially Carcajou—were well-equipped to handle them. Right?

*Unless there's so many of them they can swarm a Family and take out a shaman.* It was an uncomfortable thought. *Cullen said they'd already lost two. Are pigs gonna start flying next? Jesus.*

The street lay under a heavy gray pall, night

already mostly fallen. Streetlamps struggled into life, pale yellow dots on the canvas of winter dusk. The house was full of disused stale air, but the musk was already beginning to seep in and make it smell like home.

"What are we going to do?" Eric sounded as young as Brun, and for a moment Zach was glad nobody was asking him. He was having a difficult time keeping his temper down, thinking of *upir* stalking a helpless woman.

Stalking *this* helpless woman.

"I don't know." There was a sound of movement, and a sudden drift of her almost-perfume. "You're angry." Soft, tentative.

He forced himself to stand still. "Of course I'm angry." *They're threatening our shaman. My mate. But you don't have a clue, do you?*

"Well, what should we do?" Still, that cautious tone, as if she wasn't sure if he was going to explode.

He just might. Even the ice and moonlight hanging on her wasn't enough to smooth his nerves. "What I *want* to do is go find this motherfucker and tear his spleen out. Because I can smell how afraid you are every time you think about him. Then I want to find his happy little handler, this Armitage, and tear *him* apart, too. And all their little helpers."

The touch startled him. She had her hand on his shoulder, a light pressure through his damp jacket. Both of them had been rained on all day, and for what? To find out the *upir* had a lock on this town so tight the other Tribes were afraid instead of proud.

"Why are they afraid of Carcajou?" She pronounced the name slightly wrong, but he thought he detected a little bit of high-school French. "And what does that mean, anyway?"

"They're afraid of us because that's our specialization, hunting *upir*. And because we don't back down—that's why there're so few of us. We breed slow and we fight hard." *Our Family was an exception, but Dad had three mates. The first left him after two stillborn, the second had me and died giving birth to Kyle. Then the shaman threw twins, and that was a Big Event. Every Tribe Dad knew came to pay their regards.*

His hands had turned into fists. He felt more than heard Eric withdrawing, probably spooked by the high-level bloodlust pouring out of his glands.

"Well. That answers *that*." Did she sound

*amused?* Did she not have any idea what was going on?

He glanced down at her. Yes, that was her hand on his shoulder. Yes, she was smiling. It was an odd, wry smile, and her glasses glinted wickedly at him. She'd unbuttoned Kyle's jacket, and the rain had slid in, plastering a triangle of shirt to her chest.

Yup. Curves to make a racetrack die of envy, and she was standing right next to him, the closest she'd ever willingly been. Close enough that he could feel the heat from her, even through her soaked clothing.

*What the hell?*

"I guess you saved my life." She was looking at the window, not at him. "Though we're going to have to talk about that kidnapping thing."

"I didn't have a *choice*." The growl rattled the window, and he fought to keep the anger down.

"I know. I said we'd talk about it. Just calm down."

He could *smell* the fear on her, but she stayed right where she was. He wondered what it cost her, and how much practice she'd had. "It's hard to be calm when you smell frightened, shaman." *You don't know how hard.*

"I can't remember not being scared. Isn't that funny?" Her expression suggested she didn't find anything amusing about it. "I know I must've been, maybe before I married Mark. But not anymore."

*Jesus.* "I'm sorry." *And I'm something you should be afraid of, too. Dammit. Of all the things to happen.*

"I was terrified when I left him. I was scared nobody would believe me, or he'd find me and drag me back, or the outside world really was too huge for me to handle on my own. That he was *right* somehow, you know? That I was weak and he was justified every time he…" Maddeningly, she stopped.

*Every time he hurt you.* "But you did it, anyway, right?"

"I did." Her hand fell away from his shoulder, but she didn't move away from him. "Just like I'm scared of you and your family, but I'm going to stay with you, anyway. Being frightened isn't a reason *not* to do something. Lucy always tried to tell me that."

*Lucy? Her friend.* "I'm sorry about her." *And sorry about Kyle. And sorry about you, too. Sorry I've frightened you. Why couldn't this have been easier?*

"Me, too. I just… Why would Mark want *her* dead, too? I can't figure it out."

*You can't guess?* But of course she couldn't. It was utterly alien to her, probably, the things some men were capable of. *And they call us beasts.* "I'd bet it was because she helped you get away. Didn't she?"

*Because when that type of man thinks he owns something, he'll kill everything around it just to prove he does.*

She was silent for a long span of moments, staring out the window. When he looked closer, he found out her cheeks were wet, not just with the endless, stupid rain. Big gemlike tears made her pretty eyes sparkle, and she was biting her lower lip gently, worrying at it.

"Then it *is* my fault," she finally whispered. "It should've been me."

"Oh, Christ." He had her shoulders before he realized it, restrained himself from shaking her only by sheer willpower. "Don't. It's not your fault and not hers, either. It's *him*. He's the—"

She reached up, awkward because his hands were around her upper arms, and pulled his head down, gently but irresistibly. His mouth met hers, and he forgot everything but the taste of her, flavored with the ghost of spearmint gum, her lips opening shyly. His body pushed against hers, searching for resistance, and found none until her back met the living-room wall near the dead fireplace. His hands slid down to describe her waist, those hips he'd been longing to touch unreeling just like a roller coaster.

It wasn't a gentle kiss, but he tried to make it gentler. He pressed himself against her, seeking comfort and trying to give it all at once. His hands found the edge of her shirt and slid under, and her skin was so warm and smooth underneath wet cloth that he made a low sound of approval deep in his throat. The sound transformed halfway into an inquiry, because he was describing the cathedral arches of her ribs with his fingers and aching to touch more—like the soft hot underside of her breasts, just made for cupping his hands around.

She broke away, gasping in a short deep breath. He kissed the corner of her mouth, her cheek, even the wet edge of her jaw, flavored with salt and rain. And a part of him wanted to drag her down to the floor right there, get rid of all the irritating sodden cloth in the way, and show her just how much he appreciated each curving inch of her softness.

And how much closer he wanted to get to *her*.

"Stop," she whispered, and he was almost out of his mind enough not to care. Her hands were on *his* shoulders now, pushing ineffectually, and he went rigid for a long moment, almost trembling with the urge to kiss her again so she couldn't repeat it. "Please."

He let her push him away, slowly. Arousal was a lead bar with roots sunk in his belly, and the animal in him was not satisfied with just rubbing his scent all over her and a tiny bit of foreplay. It wanted a few hours to mark her thoroughly as his, and a few more hours to begin learning how to enjoy her.

And for once, he and his animal wanted the same thing. But it wasn't time yet, and he wasn't a savage. He was Carcajou, and she was drawing in deep flaring breaths, staring at him like he'd lost his mind.

"You *stopped*." Her hair was tangled, a glory of damp sandalwood curls. He wanted to bury his face in it and inhale, and let his hands discover that beautiful little curve below her ribs and above her hips, just made for his fingers to do a little skimming and skating on.

*No shit.* "You told me to." He swallowed

dryly, imposed control. "I'm not going to force you, Sophie." *You've been forced enough.*

"Just kidnap me?" But she smiled when she said it, a private little curve of her pretty lips, and he about lost all his good sense right there. High color bloomed on her cheeks.

"I'll kidnap you as many times as you like," his mouth said, independently of his brain. *Shit. Dammit. What's wrong with me?*

Amazingly, her smile broadened. She actually looked *amused*. "Did you just make a joke? I think that's the first one I've heard."

"Step a little closer. Or let me go back to what I was doing about thirty seconds ago." What was it about her that could make him smart off like a teenager? Maybe it was the way she was blushing, or the way she tipped her head down and looked over the top of those cute little steel-rimmed glasses. It made her mouth look nice and soft, and it gave him all sorts of ideas about getting her to take them off and—

The front door rattled and he whirled, his head coming up and new tension snapping through him. Sophie sucked in a breath at the sound.

But it was only the twins. "Raining *buckets* out there," Julia announced. "What? Oh. Whoops."

The air was full of musk, his and the shaman's. Good thing she was completely triggered, or he might not have had any luck stopping. He relaxed and swung back to face her.

The smile had dropped from Sophie's face. She hugged herself, cupping her elbows in her palms. Her eyes were huge, and he smelled the instant jump of fear, her pulse turned hard and hammering.

*Even a door opening did that to her. Jesus.*

They stared at each other for a long moment, Zach ignoring Julia's snigger and Brun's low whispering. There was a crackle of plastic— grocery bags. Both of the young ones smelled like rain and high healthy spirits. They were both more relaxed now, and she'd officially been their shaman for less than a day. She was theirs. The longer she spent with them, the more she would grow into them. No other Tribe could take her away now.

Not unless she went willingly, and was willing to undergo the discomfort of getting used to another Tribe. It didn't happen often.

*Then why am I so afraid she might vanish?*

Sophie inhaled, closing her eyes. The fear from her glands didn't recede entirely, but she did manage to mute it. She raised her chin a little, her shoulders coming up, too, and finally looked at him. "Is that better?" The words trembled just a little.

He wondered what it cost her to struggle with that fear, to live with it just under the surface of every day. "It's just fine." The idea of doing something, anything, to lift that burden sounded equally ridiculous and irresistible. "Look, Sophie—"

She was past him so fast he almost suspected superhuman speed, except a shaman couldn't use it. "I'm going to help," she said over her shoulder, and left him standing there in the living room, frustrated as a kitten tied up with a yarn snarl and aching with the need to hold her. Just hold her, instead of pinning her to a wall and sucking half her face off.

But she'd initiated it, hadn't she?

Conflicting desires caught the animal living inside him, made it snarl, and turned it into a serious ache below the belt.

"Damn." It was the only thing he could say. How the hell could a man have wanted to hit her instead of holding her?

And how could a man get a volcanic kiss like that without wanting more?

## Chapter 21

Sophie lay on her side, staring at the mutated rectangle of streetlamp shine reflected against the wall. The house smelled like caramelized onions and steak, musk and warmth. It took so little to make a place into a home.

Or a trap.

She closed her eyes. The Hammerheath mansion rose up behind her eyelids—granite-floored kitchen, God help you if you dropped an egg. The receiving room and parlor, the sweeping staircase. The bedroom with the huge princess bed she'd retreated to once every few months, after Mark beat her so bad she couldn't stand. The maids, gliding on noiseless slippers—they went home every afternoon, and as soon as the prying eyes were out of the house Mark could come home and find fault with everything Sophie had done during the day. The land-scapers constantly clipping, mowing, watering, spreading bark.

The parties, worrying over the caterers and avoiding Mark's drunken fists afterward. The sense of being in a pressure cooker, the heat rising and the tension building, each moment a potential land mine waiting to go off.

Those goddamn copper pans, buzzing and rattling against one another. Sounding just like a lazy rattlesnake.

*I'll bet you've always heard weird things, seen things out of the corner of your eye. You were a daydreamer when you were a kid, right?*

That didn't prove anything. But the vampires did. And the faces in the mist—and the crack-ling that went through all of them before they changed into lean graceful figures, nothing like werewolves in the movies.

She sighed, turned over, rested her head on her arm. She hadn't wanted to use someone else's pillow, though Zach probably wouldn't have minded. He'd watched her all evening, quiet except for when Julia got a little too rowdy, his dark eyes following every move Sophie made.

Not like Mark's eyes, assessing, judging, weighing. No, Zach looked at her like he was hungry, but too mannerly to insist on eating. Just like a stray cat, careful not to wear out his welcome. Though she didn't think of cats when she smelled them. That musk, for one thing.

*I wonder what Carcajou means? He never said.*

Did it matter?

Someone was right outside her door. She'd heard him settle down about a half hour after retreating to this room—the biggest one in the house, upstairs and along a short hall. The shaman's room. They really wanted to please her. Even Julia, who kept shooting her sly little glances. Checking to make sure she was watching, just like a kid.

Julia wasn't afraid of Zach at all. Each time she got a little overexcited, Zach would corral her. It didn't escalate, and it was strange to see.

The someone shifted right outside her door. *Oh, let's be honest, we know it's him.* She was helpless to stop imagining Zach leaning against the jamb, or maybe settled down with his long legs across the hall, that one stubborn curl falling across his forehead. Was he standing guard, or making sure she wasn't going to escape?

Her back ached. The scab on her hand throbbed. She had the peculiar head-stuffed feeling of having spent all day tramping around in the rain, following Zach's broad back. The side of her face hurt a little, too, dully. Her eyes drifted closed, and the faces drew closer. The reedy cricket sound was faraway, but definitely louder than it had been.

He tasted like wildness. Like pure sugared heat on a summer night.

*That* was the thought she'd been avoiding. Sophie almost groaned, pulled the blankets— all smelling of musk and detergent—up a little farther. She was exhausted. Why couldn't she sleep?

Because something was bothering her. Why would Mark sacrifice her? He didn't care if she lived or died, right? That was what *divorce* meant. Still, there were the precautions she'd taken, because he was damn near unstoppable when he decided he wanted something.

He was quite capable of killing her, if he was enraged enough. She knew that now. Not just strangling her or drowning her in a fit of rage, but planning and lying in wait and striking, like a venomous snake.

But why would he want Lucy dead? Unless it was pure revenge. He had to have suspected Lucy helped her. But she'd been so careful, planned for every eventuality to cover their tracks.…

Still, he wasn't stupid. He had to have guessed, especially since Luce had showed up in the courtroom. Lucy was the only friend she *had*. Other than all the old-money wives, but none of them were in the least friendly.

And Delia Armitage, always watching, queen of the social scene, her beady little eyes fixed on Sophie as if she was always doing something wrong. *That* was one thing she didn't miss— all those eyes, watching and weighing and judging.

But Zach was something different, and she could still feel his hands on her, calluses rasping against her skin. A gentle touch, as if she was precious, caressing fingers instead of hard biting knuckles.

*Will you stop, Sophie?*

The cricket voices got louder. She pushed them away, a warm lump of food in her belly. Finally, a meal that wasn't all industrial grease.

Julia was a good cook, if impatient. And Sophie had obsessed over every meal even before the chef was fired for burning Mark's potatoes. Between the two of them, everything had turned out fine.

She was warm enough, and so tired. Every inch of her was weighed down.

The streetlamp shine faded a bit. Maybe her eyes were playing tricks on her. They closed, and when she opened them again the room seemed darker.

There was a sound of brushing cloth. Zach was outside her door, and he was moving. The cricket voices rose, then fell away as she concentrated on making them shut *up* so she could get some sleep. It was like a radio playing in a next-door room, too soft to discern the words but too loud just to tune out. And highly, highly annoying.

The mutating rectangle of streetlamp light blinked and fuzzed. The sense of someone breathing outside her door leached away, the hall floor squeaking slightly as he moved. There were other quick little sounds, too, as if others had gotten up.

*What's going on?* She rolled over again, irritated, and rested her head on her arm again. *God, can't I just sleep? Please?*

The room darkened. The wind picked up outside, and a bitter taste invaded her tongue. Sophie sighed. Maybe it was indigestion.

But it didn't *taste* like indigestion. It tasted like dirt. Something dangerous, ugly, and covered with grimy slime.

She pushed herself up on her hands, her left palm sending a bolt of red pain up her arm. *Ow. I hope that's not getting infected, that would just cap the whole damn—*

*Crash!*

The window exploded inward, glass raining down. Sophie cried out, her arms jerking up to protect her head. There was a staticky half-breath sense of a thunderstorm building, the hair-lifting moment before the first lightning strike cracks the night like an egg.

They poured into the room, a tide of half-seen, jerky shapes. There wasn't even time to scream before they were on her, cold hands gripping like iron vises, their eyes dripping bleeding hellfire. They breathed on her, a tidal wave of rank foulness. The blankets tangled around her like a shroud before she thrashed, striking out with hands and feet, realizing she was, after all, screaming.

The last thing she heard were crashing howls and Zach yelling her name before darkness closed over her head.

She lay on her side. It was utterly black in here, and it felt like a very, very small space. Hardness under her, it felt cold as concrete. Something was dripping, and there was an odd cacophony—screeching, clicking, a sound like thick dark meat pulled from a recalcitrant bone.

"That's just fine," a woman said, and she recognized the voice just as she realized she was tied up, thick coils of rope cocooning her body. "We'll make an example."

*Oh, God.*

"She's *my* sacrifice," Mark said petulantly. He actually lisped over the sibilants, and Sophie had a sudden, horrible vision of malformed teeth, canines long and sharp, curving in and affecting the way the tongue moved.

It was so *dark*. She couldn't tell if her eyes were open or closed; she only knew that she could see the ghostly faces. They pressed close, and the cricket sound of their voices as their lips moved had a hard time getting through the squealing and ripping.

"She'll suffer later. We're going to send a little message to those animals. That's enough, children." Delia Armitage sounded normal, at least. Except for the cruel glee in her voice, as if she was leaning over a table at a charity dinner, gossiping. Sophie had heard *that* particular tone many times, usually just before Delia fixed her with a gaze dark and cold as leftover coffee. "Be mannerly, now."

Sophie strained to see. Her entire body ached, and it smelled so horrible she thought she was about to faint again. The crunching, slurping noises tapered away, and in the pregnant silence afterward the reedy cricket sounds became clearer. They almost, almost became real words. The faces pressed close, some of them contorted with worry. Others looked sad, and a few of them had sharp teeth, looking like the lean graceful forms Zach and his family took.

*Zach.* Had they hurt him?

Another question rose, foggy at first through the various noises competing for her attention. *Why didn't they kill me? I thought that was what they wanted, right?*

She was already dead as far as the newspapers were concerned. Logic dictated that Mark had something bad in store for her. *Really* bad, not just a shot to the kidneys or a bloody nose, or the sudden blow to her stomach that made her lose all her air, or—

*Did they kill Zach?*

The faces crowded around. They whispered to each other, the cricket sounds growing louder.

No, it was the other sounds that were growing fainter. "Come along, children. You too, Harris."

"What if she's awake?" Mark, petulant again. And with the edge of bafflement that meant he hadn't gotten something he wanted. The edge that used to make her mouth dry and her heart pound.

He sounded so petty. So spoiled. Had he always sounded that way?

"Leave the little mouse in the dark, we'll deal with her soon enough." Delia Armitage laughed, a giggling little titter like razors drawn through broken glass. There was one final wet sound, a hungry little moan, and Sophie had a sudden, vivid mental image of Delia, her eyes bright with liquid crimson, pulling Mark's blond head down, her tongue sliding snake-like into his mouth, and the heavy smacking of a deep, violent kiss echoing in a small space. It was dark, and a single dim bulb hung from a cord over the two. The walls were splashed with black liquid, and the light flickered out as Sophie tried to shake her head.

The unwelcome vision vanished.

Her head dropped, her temple hitting the concrete floor as if she'd been punched, and she saw stars threading through the wall of foggy faces pressing close, closer, closer to her.

Silence, now, except for the cricket song. It almost made words.

Hot tears filled Sophie's eyes. *Oh, God. All I wanted was a night out.* She wriggled a little bit, testing the ropes. Nothing. No give.

As if she'd know how to wriggle out of this, anyway.

The ghosts—spirits, *majir,* whatever they were—drew closer. They brushed her with spectral fingers, their voices the soft rushing of wind and water now. Each touch was insubstantial as smoke, and yet left a strange sort of calm in its wake. They ruffled her hair, brushed her wet cheeks, drew the pain out of her fingers and soothed the burning in her legs. One of them drifted closer—a girl's face, wide shadowy eyes full of terrible knowledge, her small mouth moving soundlessly.

*I'm going crazy.* Sophie lay still, petrified, and wished the darkness would take her again.

*Chapter 22*

He put his fist through the bar's heavy wood surface, disregarding the splinters and the way the skin over his knuckles broke and briefly bled. The lacerations closed almost instantly, but the jolt of pain up his arm was worth it for the clarity it brought in its wake.

*Control, Zach. You're not a savage.*

The short, sharp movement brought all motion in Cullen's bar to a halt. The assembled Tribe—most of them had been there when he arrived, and more were showing up all the time—turned still and silent, watching him. Julia clamped a sodden, bright-red towel to her arm. Brun slumped against her, dark rings under his eyes and the acrid tang of worry hanging on him. The smell of blood added a teasing note to the stew of anger riding the air.

"Listen," Zach said, quietly and reasonably, in the silence that followed. "I did not come here to sit and listen to you idiots whinge and moan. They've taken our shaman. And you're sitting here wondering what the fuck to *do?*"

Cullen sighed, folded his arms. The bar was full of snarling, a river of bloodlust running right under the surface of the air, and most of it was coming from Zach. Eric shifted restlessly, and one of the Bear Tribe—Cullen's alpha, a female with the wide shoulders and studied, careful movements of their kind—stared unblinkingly at him.

"They'll crucion her for sure," one of the Felinii said softly.

"Crucion?" Eric started forward, but Zach put his arm out to stop him. Getting to the bar could have been hazardous; but the *upir* had vanished.

They had what they came for.

Zach's decision to find other Tribe had been instant. There were more *upir* than he'd ever seen in one place before, enough to litter the entire house with bloody rotting matter and overwhelm four Carcajou desperate to reach their shaman for the small, critical time necessary to spirit her out of the house.

She had to still be alive. *Had* to be.

The *majir* would know that a shaman was in trouble, and still alive. The shamans—two from the Bear Tribe, one from the Felinii, and a slim-hipped kohl-eyed woman of the Tanuki Tribe—all had the glaze-eyed look of listening to the spirits, but not the look of devouring sadness that would mean Sophie had joined the earthbound wisps.

"Since when do we just let *upir* take and kill our shamans?" Zach asked quietly. Julia let out a sobbing breath. She was healing, but painfully slowly, *upir* venom working in the claw marks.

And Sophie might already be dead. But she was triggered, the *majir* would know. Wouldn't they? Unless she hadn't been triggered enough, maybe, despite everything. Or if something was wrong, or if—

He told that rabbit-jumping part of himself to shut up. They were all looking at him. As if he was some sort of new animal, one they weren't quite sure they liked.

Of course, without a shaman, he and his Family were only here on borrowed grace.

"Carcajou." One of the Felinii made a swift, abortive movement, stopped when he glared at her. "There're so *many* of them."

"Fine." Zach folded his arms, his hand hurting briefly, one final red grinding of pain as the animal turned over briefly inside his bones, finishing the job of healing. "Where are they likely to be holding her?"

Cullen finally spoke up. "You're not seriously thinking—"

"She's our *shaman*." *And my mate. Though she doesn't know it yet.* "What do you not understand about this? Where are they likely to hold her?"

"Zach." Eric surged forward again, was held back again. "You're not going without me."

"Or me," Julia piped up. Brun muttered something that might have been assent or "Here we go again."

Zach ignored it. "Where?"

Cullen shrugged. The bones in his hair shifted a little, clicking. "Armitage has estates. Harris has a house out in Hammerheath—the tony section of town, a suburb. It's crawling with *upir*. One of our sleuth did pool cleaning up there, and he says it smells like death all over, especially in the past six months. But—"

"Addresses. I'll start at Harris's house." *Probably the same place listed in the divorce papers. Wish I'd thought to write it down.*

"You're not seriously considering—" The door opened, a few more Tribe trickling in. They could smell something happening, of course—and the night outside was probably crying with Sophie's distress.

Zach took a firmer hold on his temper. "If she's still alive, they're probably not going to kill her tonight. Especially if they're using the crucion, they'll want from dusk to dawn to do it right." A little shudder of distaste and fear ran through him. Thinking of Sophie strapped to an X-shaped frame while the wheel turned and bones splintered—

*Stop it. The* majir *would know. They always know. It's their job.*

"We can't let him go alone." A Felinii, her hands clasped together like a schoolgirl's, straightened as a ripple ran through the assembled Tribe. "They outnumber us, yes. But we have several advantages."

"It's that kind of thinking that got our other two shamans killed," the Tanuki shaman said, her narrow nose lifting.

"Small teams headed by a shaman don't

work," the Bear alpha said, quietly, but with a great deal of rumbling force behind her words. "What if we emptied out the city? Got every Tribe and every shaman involved?"

"Coordinating Tribe is like herding cats," one of the Tanuki muttered, and quickly ducked his head when a Felinii gave him a meaningful look. "Sorry."

"I don't have time for consensus building." Zach's fists ached to batter something else. "I need to find my shaman, and I need to find her *now*. Either help me or not, I don't fucking care. Either way, I need those addresses, and I'm going to teach those bastards not to hunt Tribe. And *especially* not to hunt a Carcajou shaman." *I'm not too picky about how I teach them that lesson, either.*

"It *might* be possible." The Tanuki shaman's clever dark eyes sparkled. Her fingers twitched. "Think of it. We could take our city back."

"If we could have done that, we would have done it ages ago." Cullen sighed, rubbed at his eyes. Exhaustion sat heavily on his big frame, darkened the rings under his eyes until he looked almost like the Tanuki. "I know it's rough, Carcajou, but—"

His hands ached to grab the Bear shaman

and throttle him. "Fine. I'll track her my own way." He turned on his heel, and surveyed his Family.

Eric, his prized leather jacket shredding. Julia, peeling the blood-sodden towel away from her arm. Brun, who looked steadily back at his older brother.

A ripple ran through the assembled Tribe. "I think we're all equally sick of taking crap from *upir*," said a very soft, deceptively gentle female voice.

It was the other Bear shaman, the one who hadn't spoken yet. She was slim for a Bear, but wide-shouldered and generously hipped. Little bits of copper wire were strung in her hair, and her voice held such a wealth of calm power every Tribe in the room took a deep breath.

Except Zach. The anger was growing inside him, a rage even Sophie might be hard-pressed to soothe. *If we lose her...* He took a good look at them, at how Julia's face was thin with pain and hunger, Brun cringing at the slightest sound, and Eric quivering like a leashed greyhound. She hadn't had any time to start smoothing their rough edges and welding them together. But she was still their shaman, their one shot at belonging again. Being a part of the Tribes instead of jackals at the edge of the world, falling off a bit at a time.

And then there was Kyle. Those fuckers had killed his little brother. Never mind that Kyle had been too weak to carry the alpha, and Zach had *known*. Ever since the fire, when Zach had been driven back by the heat and grabbed Kyle, keeping him from throwing himself into the flames, he had known Kyle was too weak—and he let him carry it, anyway.

Now he'd screwed up their only chance of keeping a shaman. They'd been depending on him, and he'd let them down again. He'd let his mate down, too—even if she didn't know she smelled like she belonged to him. He would never have the chance to maybe coax her into considering the idea that he was worth her.

Because he'd failed. Again.

*Not this time,* he told himself. *Not now.*

"The *majir* have told us to be patient. The *majir* have told us to wait, and now they do not." The Bear shaman moved slightly, copper bangles sliding on her wrist and making a chiming sound. "It is time. Come dawn, we can have every Tribe in the city aware of what we intend. Those that will help us, will help us. The *majir* will aid us, as well."

"Ilona." Cullen sighed, spread his hands. "I don't want to lose another shaman, either. But think about what you're saying."

"Cullen." The other Bear shaman fixed him with a steely glare. "Ask the *majir* for us. Cast the bones. But I'm telling you right now, any except the cubs who want to go are free to go with my blessing. This has gone far enough. And with Carcajou with us—"

"There's only *four* of them!" Cullen objected.

"Four's more than enough," the Tanuki shaman replied. "We'll help. We'll unlock any doors and steal any shinies." Her nose twitched again.

Cullen stared at Ilona, who returned the stare with interest. It wasn't quite a struggle for dominance, but there was a general move backward, anyway. If the two decided to tangle, nobody wanted to be in the way.

Zach saw his moment and slipped back. The Tanuki shaman gave him an odd look as he passed, her kohl-smudged eyes bright and intelligent, and the low thrumming growl in the air mounted another few notches.

There was a crowd by the door, but they parted for him. "Zach—" Eric sounded breathless.

"Stay with the Tribes." His tongue felt too thick for his mouth.

"Zach—" Julia, this time.

*"Stay with the Tribes."* The Change ran inside him like glass wires. His failure, his responsibility, goaded the animal living under the surface of his skin.

The animal stretched, finding that he would not chain it this time. There was a meaningless babble of noise, ignored like everything other than what the animal understood. Food. Shelter.

And *possession*.

The rain outside was flung silver needles, soaking through his hair and useless clothing. The blood in him burned, his nose lifted, tasting the night. Wet concrete, burning exhaust, the jungle of a city like every other wilderness. Only this one had a clear crystalline ringing under each raindrop, a distress call muted by concrete and inimical metal.

It was the call of a shaman in danger.

The human part of him couldn't have heard it. But the animal knew, and it responded with a throaty howl that ended with a series of clicks. The rage was sweet fuel to them both, a golden thread he would follow until it ended at what he sought.

Something that belonged to them had been taken.

And he would not rest until he had taken it *back*.

## Chapter 23

The dark was total. Sophie lay in a small space on concrete, though near her feet was a wooden door. At least, she thought it was a door—it moved slightly when her feet found it. And she was vaguely aware of needing to pee, though it wasn't critical yet.

She had other problems.

It smelled too horrible to be believed in here, and the thin thread of musk rising from her skin didn't help. It only accentuated the reek coating the back of her throat. Her mind kept pairing images to the smell—terrible, soul-destroying images of rotten flesh, skeletons grinning through veils of slime, bones and worms, and—

It was better not to think about it, the cricket voices said. Sometimes their words were coming through, reedy little sounds shaping comprehensible syllables. The faces pressed close to hers, insubstantial smoke warming for just a moment until it felt like flesh, but they never stayed.

She lay there and thought about it. If she was crazy—

No. Zach swore she wasn't crazy. And there *were* vampires, she'd seen them. Which was more insane, seeing crazy shit or denying the crazy shit right in front of your own eyes?

She tried to breathe deeply, working through the incipient panic attack. Her nose was full, and her muscles were cramping despite the way the faces crowded around, ghostly hands stroking along her limbs, easing them, drugging the pain. Tears leaked hot and soundless down to her temple, dripped over the bridge of her nose.

She'd huddled on the floor so many times, trying to breathe through the sobs, her body on fire with pain. It never got easier to deal with.

It never became *routine*.

At first she'd tried to predict him, tried to be more pliant, more perfect. She'd tried to find what was irritating him so much, find ways to soothe him, make him happy. Back when she still thought he loved her. Back when she still thought love was pain, or pain was all right if you could just love enough.

Then came the survival phase, where everything began to seem like a dream. Just keeping her head above water was hard enough. Actually *thinking* about what was happening lost out to just trying to get through the next explosion.

After that was the most horrifying thing of all—being so trapped, so hopeless, that she began to think she deserved it. The world skewed itself a few degrees off, and she began to lose parts of herself.

If she had to get right down to it, she wasn't actually in school to become a social worker. She just wanted to understand how she worked, how *people* worked, so she could put herself back together again. And quit looking over her shoulder.

It was no use. The ropes were too tight, and the faces were contorting, some of them crying soundlessly.

Thank God Lucy's face wasn't there. Which

brought up an interesting line of thought—were these dead spirits, or something else? Zach hadn't said, and she hadn't thought to ask.

Another sound intruded. A squeak, a thump. Footsteps. Distinctive footsteps, the heels jabbing hard.

Sophie realized she was making a small whining sound, swallowed hard. The reek filled her throat, the footsteps grew closer. The faces whispered, and she caught enough of their reedy little syllables to guess who was down here, wherever "here" was.

*Oh, God. I really didn't ever want to see him again.*

There was a scraping sound, and weak light fell into the closet. It *was* a closet, she saw, and its dimensions looked vaguely familiar. He grabbed her ankles and pulled, his fingers biting in cruelly, and if the spirits hadn't been clustering around her, somehow easing the soreness from her muscles, she probably would have screamed in pain.

She lay on her side, still on hard concrete, blinking furiously as her eyes ran with hot tears. He walked behind her, heels landing hard on the concrete, and she suddenly realized why he did.

He wanted her afraid.

*Well, I am.* But after the past few days of whipsawing terror and comfort, her fear-meter seemed to have busted.

And God, she was so *tired* of being afraid.

"Hello, Sophie," he breathed in her ear. The hot, meaty smell grew ranker, if that was possible. She had a sudden mental vision of canine teeth grown long, lips thinned out and flushed with deadly cherry-red.

She found her voice. At least they hadn't gagged her. "Hello, Mark." *Now that I've got a really sensitive nose, I just have to be stuck around hideously stinky stuff. Great.*

"You've been a very bad girl, my dear." He kept breathing on her ear. Three days ago Sophie would have cringed.

Now she just wanted a bathroom and some more of Julia's steak with caramelized onions. So she just kept quiet. He was going to talk for a little while, she knew that tone. The falsely conciliatory cheerfulness.

"Bad enough that you embarrass me with legal difficulties. But then you hide from me, as if I'm some sort of common criminal. And you take up with such undesirable elements. My dear, you have no *couth*."

*And you've been hanging out with the Happy Vampires. Really, Mark, lecturing me is so passé. Why don't you find something else to do?* But that was a sure way to make him angry, so she concentrated on blinking away the tears. The room gradually began to take shape.

It was a basement. Or more precisely, the wine cellar. She'd been down here hundreds of times, obsessing over which bottle to choose, knowing the wrong one would bring a patronizing grin and a promise of punishment.

The racks of bottles had been taken out. Dark, nameless liquid splashed the walls, and the heavy wainscoting over concrete was splattered, as well. The lighting was always dim down here, and she'd been in the small temperature-controlled closet for the brandies and cognacs.

*Dear God. He's emptied out the wine cellar?* For a moment she was confused, then she remembered the heavy insulated doors, both on the closet and on the cellar itself. This was an ideal place for someone to scream their lungs out without being heard—and if the splashes on the wall were any indication, a lot of screaming went on down here.

She should have been more surprised. But

her surprise-meter was like her fear-meter, completely busted by now. She knew where she was, she'd escaped this house once before.

It wasn't looking like she'd escape again, though.

"There's something called a crucion, Sophie. It's shaped like an *X*, and when we catch one of those animals we like to strap them onto it and play. It's not a nice kind of playing. First the arms break, then the legs. And if we keep turning the wheel, other bones break, too. Doesn't that sound painful?"

*You've been hanging around with nasty people, Mark. Not me.* She tensed, her bare throat feeling very exposed. Very vulnerable. Especially with him breathing that horrible smell all over her.

He nudged her. Her flesh shrank at the idea of him actually *touching* her. "Are you listening? I want you to listen very closely, darling."

*Just shut up and go away. How could I ever have thought I loved you?* She took a long shallow breath in, trying not to taste it.

"I asked if you were *listening*, Sophie." Another nudge, rougher than the first. After Zach's leashed strength, Mark didn't feel so horribly, hurtfully strong. But she remembered the thing in the alley and how it twisted on itself, how quick it moved, and poor Lucy's pale face—

The most amazing thing happened.

A pinprick of something hot dilated behind Sophie's sternum.

Her mouth opened. "You are such a moron, Mark." Flat, matter-of-fact, as if she was telling him about the weather. "I'm tied up on the floor. What else do I have to listen to?"

She couldn't believe she'd said it. But the burning itch in her chest *demanded* she speak. It had been so long since she'd dared to feel any anger at all, and this wasn't just anger. It was too red, too acid, too *hot,* to be anything but pure rage.

He was silent for almost thirty seconds. Probably shocked that she'd dared to talk to him at all. Quiet little mouse Sophie, scared of her own shadow.

*Not anymore,* she thought. There were other things to be scared of now. Things like vampires and werewolves and—

But she wasn't scared of Zach, was she? Not anymore.

When had that happened?

"Sophie." Mark's fingers threaded through

her hair and tightened, making a fist. "Where did you learn to talk like this? From your plebeian little friend?"

"The one you wanted killed, you mean? Her name was Lucy, and I *hope you rot in hell.*"

The blow came out of nowhere, an open-handed slap that glanced off her cheek and smacked her head back, bouncing it off the floor. Stars exploded behind her eyelids, but she didn't cry out. He hit her twice more, bracing her head with the fist in her hair, a terrible yanking pain each time. Her lip split, and the hot streak of blood in her mouth was cleaner than the terrible smell filling the room.

He pulled her head back, her throat exposed and neck craning, and leaned close enough that she could feel meat-hot breath on her cheek. Stinging warmth dripped into her eyes, and she blinked.

Mark's face was a caricature, flushed almost purple. The fangs were wickedly curved, needle-sharp and bone-white. They dug into his chin and thin lines of black ooze slid down from the punctures. His eyes ran with orange wetness, a dripping metallic sheen she'd mistaken for fire. It shifted, running down his cheeks and leaving an opalescent slug trail behind, as if he was weeping hellfire.

"You *bitch*," he said thickly, but his tongue wouldn't work quite right. The fangs were in the way.

She knew that tone. He was about to beat her senseless. But instead of the cowering, complete fear and confusion, the still-hot point of rage behind her breastbone became a flood, pouring through her body.

"You were never any good in bed, either," she said, loud and clear. "All that grunting and whining."

He made an inarticulate noise, half roar, half wounded cry, and erupted into motion. Sophie curled away—and the second miracle happened.

The cricket voices rose around her in a swirling tide, insubstantial hands clutching and ripping. Mark's fist glanced off her cheekbone; he leaped to his feet and kicked her, a red explosion of pain spearing through her ribs.

Something inside Sophie turned, shifted… and *woke up*. The feeling poured through her, like a gulp of too-hot coffee, exploding in her middle. It was so unfamiliar she couldn't think of what it was for a long taffy-stretching second, before the realization hit her like thunder after lightning.

It was *power.* And it was hers. The *majir* borrowed from her, slid through her as if she was an open door. Now that she had ceased resisting, they filled her like water. And she wondered if the other shamans ever felt like this.

She would probably never find out, now.

The ropes *loosened.* They slithered like fat snakes, rasping against flesh rubbed raw. The second kick caught her in the back—she was rolling away, her muscles on fire from a long time lying on concrete, unable even to shift her weight. He screamed, the torrent of obscenities and beast sounds splashing inside her head and making it difficult to think. He was always so goddamn *loud* when he started in on her.

Her head hit something soft and a shower of foulness splatted over her hair. She kept rolling, squirming away—his foot caught her under the ribs again. He screamed and kicked, catching her just under the jaw. A red explosion smashed through her head; she scrambled blindly and got her feet under her.

*He wants to kill me,* she thought, dazed. *Of course. I've known that for a long time.* She hit the wall, the spirits crowding around her, and her legs almost failed. Cramped and bruised, she found herself hitting the wall again, her back thudding against it as Mark crouched, one hand on the floor like he was part of some crazy football game.

"You *bitch*," he said, again, thickly. Or the thing that had been her husband said it with a mouth full of sharp teeth and clotted scum.

The heat and power inside her crested, her entire body shaking and buzzing. Warm salt ran in her eyes. She was bleeding, her hands held up fruitlessly, the swirling ghostlike faces crawling up her arms. Their touch was warm and forgiving, and she no longer tried to hold them at arm's length. The rattling intensified, became a rattlesnake buzz.

Mark gave a sound halfway between a wet lip smacking and a throaty growl. His entire body bunched up, and Sophie knew she was going to die. He was going to kill her the same way another vampire had killed Lucy. She was going to die down here in a stinking wine cellar.

Three days ago she might have screamed.

Sophie opened her arms. The spirits streamed through her, whispering. *Don't worry*, they said. *Everything is going to be all right. Not long now.*

And the world…exploded.

No, not the world. The door to the wine cellar, driven in with megaton force, broken bits of wood whickering through air gone suddenly hard and viscous. The spirits streamed away from her, a tide of quicksilver and smoke, bright eyes and claws glittering. They splattered against Mark's face like Silly String, steam rising as they bit and clawed at him. A completely inappropriate desire to laugh bubbled up inside Sophie's chest, right next to the simmering crimson rage. *Go ahead! Burn him! Hurt him any way you can!*

The thing came through the shattered door, pouring like liquid and resolving into a low shape running with fur, smoking with black blood along one side, a white stripe sliding down its length. It landed in a compact ball, a sound of claws snicking against the concrete, and its growl trailed off in a series of clicks.

She sagged against the wall, staring, as Mark whirled, flying wood smacking him with obscene little chucking sounds.

And Mark, the monster, the huge, terrifying thing that haunted her, actually screamed. It was a high girlish sound, all the more absurd because she *recognized* the striped thing that uncoiled, stalking forward with graceful eerie authority.

She would know him anywhere now, with the spirits crawling under her skin, the rattle of the copper-bottomed pans buzzing in her veins. The feeling was delightful, new strength that laughed at the deep drilling pain in her side whenever she took a breath, snickered at the way blood kept dripping in her eyes, and snarled at the way her legs kept trembling, threatening to spill her on the concrete.

The thing that had been her ex-husband let out a screech and jumped for Zach, who faded aside with scary grace, striking out with one elegant-clawed hand. His form blurred like ink in running water, never pausing, fur shifting along its lines. He was sleek and deadly, and she recognized the crackling in the air around him because it invaded her own veins.

It was the rage. And it was *good*.

The spirits knew. They whispered that he was too far gone, that the anger had taken him and he was just as likely to kill her as Mark. They whispered that he was over the edge, and that she should back away, make herself small and quiet so they didn't notice her.

For the first time in her life, Sophie didn't want to hide.

She launched herself forward, the spirits crackling around her, their faces turned to pictures of astonishment, and landed on Mark's back, barely aware she was screaming. Her blood-slippery fists pounded, something tore in her side again and a red sheet of pain fed the thing roaring inside and outside of her skin.

He threw her. She was weightless for a long second, the spirits pouring around her in a confusion of long hair and open, awestruck mouths. The wall loomed; she hit it with a sick thump, her head snapping back and something else breaking.

The rage ate the pain and turned into a thunder crack. The noise was incredible. The shapes in front of her eyes refused to make sense for a moment, hazed with red.

Zach and the thing that had been Mark circled. The vampire was making a sound like horny nails dragged over concrete, its throat swelling and its clothes ripped up one side. Zach hunched down on all fours, moving fluidly, still making that odd clicking noise. His muzzle lifted, white teeth showing, and they closed in a welter of noise and tearing.

Darkness fuzzed around the edges of her vision. She tried to push it away, taking in hitching little breaths. The faces were closer now, taking on weight. They looked so, so sad.

The vampire jetted forward with that scary, liquid speed, and Zach froze for a split second, his eyes flicking past the threat to Sophie. *Don't worry about me!* she wanted to scream. *Pay attention to him! He's coming right at you!*

Zach faded aside, somehow not there as the thing that had been Mark let out a short sharp victorious cry. The lean furred shape twisted amazingly, the ribbons of his slashed T-shirt fluttering like pennants, and made a movement almost too quick to be seen. His hands lengthened into claws, light shearing off each of them, and foul blackness exploded. The noise trickled away into shocked silence, and Sophie heard her own breathing again, bubbling, each gasp a hitching agony.

The body thudded down.

Zach crouched over him, the clicking growl fading bit by bit. His fur moved restlessly, motion sharply controlled. His eyes were wide, dark, and there was no trace of the man she'd kissed in them.

There was just an animal, its hide twitching,

favoring its left front paw. The white streak down its side was slicked with blood and darker fluids. It paused, the clicking settling into a sort of chuffing.

Sophie stared. *Oh, God. He just killed Mark.* The red pain jabbing in her ribs cranked up a notch, darkness closing around the edges of her vision like a camera shutter closing. The faces moved between them, gossamer-thin now, and so sad. They were crying, crystal droplet tears vanishing as they fell.

The animal sniffed. It turned, a loose fluid movement, and faced the door. Sophie tried to get up, but her body wasn't having any of it. The pain was fuzzy, and very far away now. The darkness was closing in.

The clicks and chuffing shifted. It occurred to her, in a sideways leap that might have been intuition or might have been the spirits whispering, that he was trying to say her name.

The single bulb in its glass shield grew dimmer. Or was it that her eyelids wouldn't stay up? A bubble of heat burst on her lips.

Just before complete blackness crawled through her, she saw the shadows at the wine cellar door. They were moving jerkily, their eyes glowing and dripping.

They were the vampires. There were plenty of them.

And down here Zach was all alone.

Sophie fell away from consciousness, still trying to scream.

## Chapter 24

It was a joy to kill.

Carcajou were so few. They, among all the Tribes, did not know what it was to retreat or surrender. Their battle rage, when it truly took hold, didn't stop until muscle was pulled from bone, blood vessels popped, and the brain was shattered.

Even facing a good twenty *upir,* the idea of disengaging from the battle didn't even cross the sea of bloodlust serving him for a mind now. The animal in him was unchained, unloosed, and the mate that belonged to them both lay behind him, wounded. Her blood and musk and terror filled this small space, maddening him even further.

He slunk back a few feet, the blood-trill filling his throat. The movement was only to make certain of his footing. The enemies were near, things of foulness and rancid death, more and more of them pressing through the small door.

He could hold them for a long time here, since only a few could fit down the stairs. If they wanted to advance into this room, it would cost them dearly. He had already thinned their numbers above, following the fading, flaring drift of light musk and silver distress.

Of *her*. She was here, and behind him. His mate was bleeding, and *they* had made her bleed. Had *hurt* her.

One of the *upir*—a female—appeared in the door. "*Another* one of these things? You'd think they would learn."

His lip lifted a little. It was all meaningless noise. His growl was not. It resounded from the sides of this little hole.

One of the *upir* darted in. A young one, and stupid. It was a moment's work to tear his claws through the sweet-sick rotten skin and spill out the rancidness inside. He growled again, a warning.

"Kill it, you imbeciles!" the female shrieked. She smelled old, and she smelled sick. Not the sickness of a bad batch of blood burning up an *upir* from the inside, but a clotted smell of pale wriggling things bursting when sunlight hit them, leaving a thin scum on everything they touched.

The *upir* surged forward, and he showed his teeth. The animal roared. Behind him, his mate had gone silent, even the thin shallow gasps missing. The tortured air was hot and close, his nose stinging, blood slicking his fur down and a sharp, sweet pain spurring him on. It was like wine in his blood, that pain. Strength and invincibility.

They moved forward. He smelled the fear on them. It teased at his nose, smarting and sting-ing from the thick miasma of death held close and hot in this little bolt hole.

He waited for them to come and die, his lip lifting in a snarl.

A sound like a drum being struck resounded through the bones of the house above, a mon-strous reeking burrow. The animal knew what it was as soon as it sounded.

Tribe. Others of his kind, coming here. Perhaps they came to kill the prey. He heard their footsteps, their cries, a clash of bodies. There were so many *upir,* the sickness had been allowed to spread here without the Tribes cleansing it.

He could not, now, remember why they had not cleansed this place. It didn't matter.

The *upir* milled about in confusion, and he waited. He cared very little what they did, as long as they left his mate alone.

She was so still, so quiet. He couldn't hear her breathing. The crystalline call, the thread of musk that had led him through the cold slanting rain and successive waves of *upir,* was fading, as if she had moved.

He didn't dare glance over his shoulder. Not with the enemies drawing so near. He growled at them again.

A mass of them surged toward him, the female who seemed to be in charge screaming in a high piping voice, her white head-fur rising and falling in thick tendrils, hellfire dripping from her eyes.

He killed two with one sweep and the red rage took him. They surged forward, champing and slavering, and he knew he was going to die. It didn't matter. What mattered was standing fast, keeping them away from his mate as long as possible.

There were too many; he went down under the weight, clawing desperately, a last roar of pure defiance shattering what remained of the human in him. The useless *weakness*. It vanished, and nothing was left but the pain as their claws tore at him—

—and the world *stopped*.

The enemy scattered like quicksilver as Tribe poured into the bolt hole, Changing and leaping, their howls and cries cleaner than the twisting groans of the bloodsuckers. Confusion reigned. He lay on the floor, trying to rise, his skin running with crimson pain that spurred him even as it drained his will.

The *upir* died. Shrieking, cursing, howling, running or standing to fight, they *died*. One of the Tribe—a Bear, his hulking shoulders hunched—halted behind him. He lay on the floor, knowing the Bear was near his mate.

She belonged to *him*. He would keep everything and everyone *away* from her. He had to. It was what he had set himself to do, and he was Carcajou.

But his body would not hold him up. The rage intensified, beating inside his brain. The rage would keep going until his heart gave out or his brain burst. He knew it—and struggled harder.

Ice and moonlight filled his nose, a soothing smell. "He's far gone." The words meant nothing, but the female who said them was Tribe. "Ilona! Help me!"

The smell reached back into memory, tinged with smoke and terrible grief. He had stopped someone else from plunging into the flames to save that smell, because the cold determination of animal survival told him to.

The human in him, all but buried under a landslide of rage, gave one powerful, agonized scream—and vanished again.

He struggled, but they were too strong. Fingers like vises, the cold drugging smell like chloroform, and he was dragged under a breaker of darkness. Still struggling. Still trying to scream a name that had lost all meaning but still had to be repeated, over and over again, the name that had been beating under his heart since he had slipped the chain and gone running into the cold night. Even as his muzzle was clamped shut and hands smoothed

along his flayed sides, the name gonged in his
head, over and over again.

*Sophie!*

## Chapter 25

Warmth. And softness.

She lay in the dark, cradled by the spirits. They spoke to her, in reedy little voices, no longer cricketlike but the soft murmur of a whispered secret. They told her things.

*We are the* majir, they whispered. *And you are one of us. Let us heal you.*

They drew the hurt out of her body while she rested, unthinking, in the darkness. This was a forgiving darkness, like the small closet in the cellar where—

*Don't think on that,* they said. *Not yet.*

It was right. That was an Unpleasant Thing,

and she'd had enough Unpleasant Things to last a lifetime.

But something did nag at her. Something she needed to remember. Something important.

Someone.

Was it Lucy? No, Lucy was dead. When the tears came, they were a balm. Her grief leaked out, made the pillow wet, and the voices whispered her into a sleeplike trance while they worked, insubstantial fingers plucking at her flesh.

Gradually, other voices became audible. She listened from the darkness.

"She'll be all right." A big, gruff voice, a man somehow familiar. He smelled like fur and honey, ice and silver light. "Don't worry. The *majir* say she'll be just fine."

"She'd better be." Julia, her teeth snapping in every word. "She's our shaman."

"Nobody's disputing that." *Cullen,* that was his name. She could see him now, standing near a window, rain-washed light coming through. The feathers in his hair fluttered. His breath fogged the glass.

Julia was next to a bed where a small pale shape lay. It was odd, but Sophie could see the tangled mop of dark, limp curls, and she knew they were hers. It was as if she was standing at the foot of the single bed, watching the gray light play across a quilt covering her slowly rising and falling chest.

The face under the limp, unwashed hair was thin and terribly bruised. The *majir* covered it in a fine network of ghostly silver light, their faces turned in, long, insubstantial fingers stroking. The fingers were coaxing out something from inside the body, a kind of light and heat, encouraging it to grow across the skin and bind everything together.

A shadow fell across the door, and Julia glanced up. She looked worried, dark rings under her eyes and the pale streak in her hair glaring. "How is he?"

"Hard to tell." Eric hunched his shoulders, touching the door frame with two fingers. He looked worried, too. "He doesn't shift back, even while tranquilized. It takes two shamans and Brun to hold him down. Brun's the only one he won't kill."

"I wish she'd wake up." Julia sighed. "She could bring him out."

"I dunno." Eric scratched at his cheek. "I haven't seen anything go through *upir* like that since…"

"Since Dad." Julia's tone softened. "He still thinks it's his fault."

"It's Zach. Of course he does." Eric's gaze rose, touched Cullen's broad back. "How much longer?"

"As long as it takes." The other shaman turned away from the window. "She had six broken ribs, a broken arm, a concussion, skull fracture—should I go on? She's shaman, so the *majir* are healing her directly. It takes time."

"He doesn't have much time left." But Eric sighed, his shoulders slumping.

Itching spread along Sophie's not-body. She was standing *outside* herself, and she realized she should be faintly alarmed by this.

"I know." Cullen's broad face set itself, the feathers in his hair fluttering slightly. "But if it comes down to losing him or losing a shaman…"

"God." Julia hunched. She touched Sophie's fingers, and the not-Sophie standing at the end of the bed felt a faint tingling warmth in her not-fingers. "Just get better, Sophie. We need you."

"They're doing all they can." Eric turned. "I'm going back down. Maybe if I cook something, he'll eat."

Sophie watched as the bruising on her slack, unconscious face retreated, the swelling easing as if by magic.

Maybe it was magic, she thought, slowly. With werewolves, vampires, spirits, shamans—magic couldn't be far behind, could it?

Zach. They were talking about Zach. Something had happened to him. She strained to remember, the room going fuzzy and distant.

It was an Unpleasant Thing. She waited for the *majir* to tell her she didn't want to see, waited for her own brain to shiver away from a bad memory.

It didn't happen.

*Zach.* He'd found her somehow. And she remembered him—it was funny, the memory kept slipping and sliding inside her, as if it hadn't found its proper place yet—crouching in front of the rest of the vampires, hunching down defensively. It probably hadn't occurred to him to leave her to Mark's tender mercies.

No. She knew it hadn't occurred to him.

Had he gotten her out of there? *How?*

And now he was in trouble. Something was wrong with him.

The *majir* crowded close.

*We cannot force you,* they said. *You can*

*accept our help, and be truly a shaman. We will aid you, and you will hear us. You will be part of the Tribes. There is no going back.*

Well, that was a laugh, wasn't it? There had never been any going back, for her. Not since she'd married Mark, thinking he was Prince Charming instead of a beast. Everything followed from that one mistake.

The room solidified around her. The spirits had stilled, their quicksilver smoke hanging over her body, oddly frozen. Bruises retreated visibly, swelling receding, and the body on the bed stirred slightly.

*How strange,* she thought. *I don't feel that at all.*

It was odder still to think she could take two steps backward, and leave the room. There might be somewhere else to go, after all. Werewolves, vampires, shamans—why not heaven? Or hell?

She could be done with the whole thing, with a life spent cowering in fear. It didn't seem like it would be difficult.

But there was Zach. He'd kidnapped her, and saved her life. He'd found her, and it sounded like he'd killed a lot of vampires to do it, too.

What else had he done? How had he gotten her out of that cellar? Was he hurt? Dying, maybe?

She hesitated. The spirits said nothing. Just when she'd gotten used to their chirping all the time.

How on earth was she supposed to get back in her body?

Just as she thought it, the *majir* turned away from the form on the bed. They streamed toward her, and Sophie found herself reaching out with her own insubstantial hands to clasp theirs. They felt warm and tangible, just like real skin, and for a moment all their faces flushed with warmth, their mouths becoming little *O*s of surprise.

There was a moment of soft confusion, heat folding around her like the blooming of an orchid, and she sank into a hot darkness full of thudding.

For a moment she panicked, thinking she was back in the cellar again. But her eyelids snapped up, the light striking into the center of her head, and she realized the pounding was her own pulse, marking off time.

Her throat burned. Her body ached, her head and ribs most of all. The sheets rasped against her skin like heat on a fresh sunburn. Her scalp crawled, and she could *smell* herself, sick and unwashed under a rush of musk and queer silver.

Dizziness poured through her. Then someone was there, lifting her up with a gentle arm under her shoulders. A cup hit her lips, liquid filled her mouth, and she was so thirsty she drank until the burning sourness of whatever it was reached her stomach and made her eyes water. Deep retching coughs pulled at her tender ribs; she flinched and tried to cut them off.

It didn't work.

"Easy there," Cullen rumbled.

"God*damn*." Julia was the one holding her up, and Cullen kept pouring whatever was in the cup down despite Sophie's spluttering. "That smells *foul*."

It did. And it *burned*.

"It's good for you." Cullen's eyes twinkled. "Want some?"

"No, thanks." Julia's clean hair brushed her face. "Shaman brews. Worse than distemper."

"What would you know, cub?" The bear-man grinned. "Hello, Sophie. Glad to see you among us again."

Whatever he was pouring down her throat burned and smelled like rocket fuel and wet seaweed, with a healthy dose of damp fur and nose-stinging mint. It was like gasoline toothpaste, for God's sake, and he kept pouring until she spluttered again and lost half of it over her face.

"Don't *drown* her, you moron!" Julia snatched her away. Sophie's body was limp as a rag doll's. Her muscles were all unstrung, the heat of the drink filling her belly and exploding outward. It filled her arms and legs with unsteady warmth, as if a wire had run through the middle of her bones and started glowing. The girl held her up, hugging her close. She was warm, and her musk was oddly familiar. And comforting.

Sophie coughed. The *majir* gathered, watching solemnly. They had done what they could for now.

The rest was up to her.

Her lips were chapped. She licked them, a residue of bitterness coating her tongue. Her mouth wouldn't work right for a moment.

"You need more." Cullen leaned in.

"For Christ's sake—" Julia didn't think much of this notion.

"Quiet, cubling." The bear-man rumbled deep in his chest.

Sophie found her voice. "Z-Zach. Where's Zach?"

They both went completely still.

"Just relax," Julia finally said, steadying her. "Shaman-healing's hard on the body. You were in bad shape."

"Zach." It was hard to sound firm instead of querulous. "Where is he?"

"In a safe place." Cullen set the mug down on the nightstand. "Where he can't hurt anyone or himself."

"Aren't you going to tell her the rest of it?" The words burst out, and Julia didn't look even faintly daunted by the glance the big man gave her. "He can't shift back. He's gone into the rage. We have to—"

"That's enough." Cullen actually *glowered*. "We have to make sure this shaman doesn't die of shock and join the earthbound spirits, that's what we have to do. If you can't shut your mouth, Carcajou, I'll—"

"Leave her alone." Even to herself Sophie sounded tired. "Where's Zach? I need to see him."

"You can't even stand up," the bear-man pointed out. "The *majir* have done what they can. You need food, and rest, and—"

*You know, I have had it up to* here *with other people running my life.* "I want to get cleaned up." She enunciated each word clearly. "Julia can help me."

"Right on. I'll get everything." The girl laid her back down, gently, and Sophie found herself sinking into pillows again. Julia bolted for the doorway, almost hit the side of it, kicked the door itself, and was gone into a white-painted hall outside in a trice.

That left Sophie looking up at Cullen, who was even bigger and broader seen from this angle. "Zach." She moistened her dry lips again. "What's wrong with him?"

"You don't know anything about Carcajou." He didn't even bother to make it a question. His eyes were very blue, and circled with dark rings. "Of all the Tribes, they're best at killing *upir*. But that's not what they're famous for."

She lay there, wishing she could look at the ceiling or out the window.

"They don't stop," Cullen said quietly. "They never back down once they've picked a fight. It gets them killed a lot. But it's the rage in them. All of us have it, but they've got double, and doused in diesel, too." He sighed, heavily, shoulders slumping. "He went after you while we were all still arguing over what to do. Cut a path right through a colony of *upir* and took on Armitage's wife. Turned out she'd been running her own little playground on the side, right under her hubby's nose."

He turned away, paced back to the window. The *majir* turned thin, retreating into insubstantial air.

"How do you know—"

"Armitage sent a peace envoy. Turned out we were wrong—he hadn't offered your ex-husband the Change. His wife did. She was grooming him to be a successor, I'd guess. But that's not our problem right now. Our problem is Zach's still caught in his Tribe form. He's turning into an animal without any human in him at all. He won't eat, we have to keep him tranquilized and tied down—"

"Tied *down?*" The words were a dry croak.

"Otherwise, he'll hurt himself. Or someone else. He's still trying to rescue you."

*Oh, God.* Sophie struggled to push herself up on her elbows. Made it, just barely. The unhealthy heat in her bones crested. Her stomach revolted. "Are you saying he's—"

"That's enough." Julia bashed back in through the door, her arms full of towels, clothing, and—of all things—a squirt bottle. "Get the fuck out. I'm going to clean our shaman up and she'll fix Zach, and then we'll see who does what around here." She dumped her cargo on the single bed and put her hands to her hips, dark eyes flashing. "You can't have her. She's *our* shaman. Our alpha rescued her. Go suck on a beehive or something."

"She can't even get out of bed." Cullen sidled for the door, anyway. "You lose us this shaman, Carcajou, and your little Family will regret it."

*If they lose me, what happens?* Sophie didn't want to find out. She also didn't want to be "lost." It sounded a little more serious than taking the wrong bus, and if the way she felt was any indication, she'd probably been close to taking the wrong bus in a big way.

And never seeing Zach again.

"You know," Julia said to the air over his head, "I'm really not liking this whole *veiled threat* thing you've got going on. This is our shaman. She's not going anywhere."

"That's right." Sophie surprised herself. The words came out stronger than she would have thought possible. "And I'd like a little privacy while I get cleaned up, Cullen. Thank you."

He inclined his head at her and was gone,

pulling the door shut with a muffled thump she suspected would have been a rattling bang if he hadn't pulled it at the last second.

"Bear Tribe." Julia made a small snorting sound. "Always so careful and cautious and stupid and boring. And that one's got a head made out of concrete."

*You must like him.* She didn't even have the energy to say it, but Julia cocked her head as if Sophie had spoken.

"I'm sorry. You must feel awful, all covered in that crud. I'm going to fix you up, right? Then you'll fix Zach up. Right?" She suddenly looked very young, and not at all determined. The pale streak in her hair glittered in the gray light.

As a matter of fact, with her eyes huge and round and her mouth all but trembling, Julia looked about three years old.

A weight of responsibility settled on Sophie's aching body. They were depending on her. And she really didn't even think she could make it to the bathroom without falling down in a heap.

*Buck up, Sophie. This isn't the first impossible thing you've done.*

She set her jaw and lifted her chin. "Right." It came out sounding like she actually believed it, even though it was more of a whispering croak than anything else. "You bet. But first I have to pee."

The house was larger than she would have guessed from the narrow upstairs room, and smelled of floor wax, fabric softener, and clean healthy animals. A whole "sleuth" of Bear Tribe lived here, and the house was full of them.

And they were all nervous. Sophie got the idea it was because they weren't quite sure what Zach would do.

Her scalp still itched. Julia had helped her to the bathroom, where Sophie stared longingly at the shower before getting rid of some serious bladder pressure. Then it was the laborious process of scrubbing off dirt and dried blood. It was curiously like having a mother scrub a child—Julia evinced no embarrassment whatsoever, and it was hard for Sophie to even blush when she was concentrating so hard on staying upright.

There were stairs, which Julia half carried her down, Sophie's arm over her slim shoulders. Two bear-people were in the hall—a stocky woman who nodded at Sophie and a smaller, wider young man with beads braided into his long dishwater hair. He smelled somehow pale, and when a low sound ran through the house's walls he actually flinched.

"That's Zach," Julia whispered. "If he gets free the sleuth will have to stop him."

*Stop him.* Sophie concentrated on one foot in front of the other. Her arms and legs were as weak as a newborn kitten's. The drink was still burning in her, heat running through her bones, but she didn't like the unsteady queasy feeling following in its wake. *I don't think they'll be baking him cupcakes. I think she means "kill him" but doesn't want to say it.*

The hall passed a living room, three bear-people clustered around a television, playing a video game. One of them glanced up, sniffing, and stared at Sophie. Two more bear-people were on the couch, sleeping snuggled together like cats. An older man hunched in front of the window, watching the street. He held a shotgun easily, and yawned without blinking. More pale light fell through the window and picked out the wiry coarseness of his hair.

The entrance to the basement was in the kitchen. The kitchen was packed with people, all smelling of fur, a few of them with the cold silver smell Sophie was emitting now, too. One of them, a woman with so much eyeliner on she looked bruised, was perched on the counter next to the sink, turning a foil pie plate around in her clever little hands.

They all froze when Sophie appeared.

"You shouldn't be out of bed," the bruise-eyed woman with the pie pan said.

"I want to see Zach." Sophie lifted her chin.

"That one can't go with you." The pie pan made a crinkling noise. "She's too dominant. Timbo, where's the sub-Carcajou?"

"Downstairs." This was another eyeliner-painted girl, but without the authority of the one on the counter. "I'll get him."

The woman nodded. Something about her quick hands and her ringed eyes was oddly familiar, as well. "Be careful."

"Brun will take you down," Julia said in Sophie's ear. There was a low thrumming sound from below the floor, and everyone in the room tensed again. "Anyone else would smell too dominant."

"This is his mate?" A young man, a bear by the look of him, leaned against a door that must lead out to the backyard.

*Mate?* Sophie blinked. *What?*

"Yup." Julia sounded proud. "Fell in love

with her right away. That's why he went and rescued her while *you* idiots were all running around in yapping circles."

"Better put a leash on that girl's mouth, shaman." The raccoon-eyed woman on the counter rattled the pie pan. Her nose wrinkled. "She's not making any friends."

Somehow Sophie doubted making friends was high on Julia's agenda. She decided to distract her. "Mate? Does that mean what I think it means?"

A ripple of amusement ran through the assembly just as the cellar door opened and Brun appeared.

He looked tired, and like he'd lost a few pounds. His clothes were disheveled and painted with dirt, and there was a massive, fantastic bruise up the side of his face. His hair hung lank and greasy, and his eyes were wet and red-rimmed.

But he brightened when he saw Sophie. "Oh, thank *God*." The instant relief was kind of scary. What was even scarier was that she could *smell* it, through a wash of musk that was eerily familiar—and just as comforting as Julia's scent.

"Hold her up." Julia straightened, and Brun

pushed through the crowded room. He looked even more thin and tired up close.

Sophie's arm was over his shoulder in a trice. "He's getting more and more upset." Brun's entire body vibrated nervously, trembling. "And it looks a little…well…"

"It's okay." Sophie gathered what little strength she had left. The burning in her bones was fading fast. Whatever Cullen had dosed her with, it was doing its job—but it was wearing off. "Just get me down there."

"Okay." Brun's trembling eased. "Thank God you're here. I was beginning to get worried."

The crowd parted. How could so many people fit into one kitchen? Or did the smell of them make them seem bigger than they were?

"That's me," Sophie said weakly. "Showing up in the nick of time." *Or rather, that's Zach. He saved my life.*

There were rickety wooden stairs. She hung on to Brun and got a faceful of strong musk, and a red smell. It was probably a good thing she was too tired to be afraid, because the red smell reminded her of fists meeting flesh, of screaming, of contorted faces and pain.

It was the aroma of rage.

A shape moved on the stairs. It was another

shaman; her nose told her it was a male bear before her eyes deciphered long hair and a strong jaw. The ice-and-silver smell came off him in waves, and Sophie took a deep breath. Unfamiliar relaxation washed through her, and she suddenly understood a whole lot more about this entire thing.

"Good Christ," the bear-shaman said. "Look at you. You should be in bed."

"That's what they keep telling me." Sophie's eyes struggled to adjust to the darkness. Brun carried her past the man, letting out a slight hiss as he stumbled.

Sophie had a sudden vision of falling down into the cellar and would have winced, if she could. *That would just top everything off, wouldn't it?*

A loud, low growl filled the air, rattling her entire body. She recognized it even as Brun flinched, his scent curiously masked by the deeper musk in the room.

Another shape loomed in the dimness. It was Cullen; her nose identified him with no help from her eyes. "Are you sure this is a good idea?"

"Positive," Sophie lied. "Point me at him."

"He's tied. Right over there." Brun pointed,

and her eyes adjusted a little more. "Against the wall, and—"

"I see him." Her heart gave a painful leap. She *did* see him. The long, lean shape, sliding with fur, his eyes flat shining discs. There was a flash of white teeth, and the nose lifted, sniffing.

The low thunder of the growl stopped.

Until that moment Sophie hadn't realized just how loud it had been. It had been running through the house like the vibration of a subway, and the sudden cessation was ominous.

Cullen drifted back toward the stairs, so quietly Sophie barely noticed him moving.

"What do I do?" she whispered.

The furred shape against the wall sniffed again. She could see the ropes now—several of them were broken and messily slopped over with fresh ones. He must have been struggling for a long time.

"I have no idea," Brun whispered back. His pale aroma almost vanished under the welter of confusing smells in the basement. "Can you get close to him? I'm…"

He was afraid to get any closer. Sophie summoned every last scrap of strength. "I think I can." *I might fall flat on my face. What will happen then?*

"I'd try talking to him first," Cullen offered.

At the sound of his voice the growl came back, a warning.

"Now stop that," Sophie said, sharply.

The rumbling died, spiraling slightly up at the end like a question.

She braced herself, pushed away from Brun, and took two weaving, faltering steps. "Zach? I know it's you. I'm right here, I'm okay. I kind of need to talk to you."

No sound. The furred shape hunched on itself, and she thought she saw it shiver. It was a challenge to stay upright. She tacked out over the uneven concrete floor, and the similarity to the wine cellar would have made her shudder if she hadn't been concentrating so hard on not falling on her face.

"Zach?" Her voice sounded very small. "I really would like to talk to you."

The shape erupted into wild motion. Sophie let out a short, surprised cry, tipping over, as ropes snapped. Her knees failed, her eyes shut tight, and she had enough time to think *I'm going to hit, it's going to hurt, dammit—*

—before something broke her fall. Something

hairy, very warm, smelling of musk, and growling loudly enough to shake the foundations.

The noise stuttered, stopped. They were definitely *arms* around her; she hadn't hit the floor. Tension filled the air, made it thick and hard to breathe.

She peeked out into the darkness, daring to open her eyes.

The animal's face was inches from hers. He inhaled, deeply, blew the air back out, and inhaled again. Those teeth were curved and wicked, and the flat shine of the eyes reminded her of a cat's eyes at night.

It looked like it could eat her. But she'd still take this over Mark's plummy, contorted face any day.

This was one monster she didn't have to be afraid of.

"Zach," she whispered. He kept sniffing her. "Come back. Please."

He stopped sniffing. A shudder went through him. The strength in those arms could snap her in half, but she felt only a dozy faraway concern that she might pass out before he came back.

*That's funny, I can see him in there. Why can't they?*

There was a crackling, creaking sound like

boughs snapping under icy weight. Fur melted, and he shuddered. Bones restructured themselves as she watched, fascinated, the dimness down here suddenly kind.

He was shaking. So was she. The arms holding her thinned as his face rose from behind the animal's. He went heavily to his knees, the jolt going all through her, and Sophie raised her leaden arms.

"S-s-s-s—" He stuttered, his lips working over the word.

*He's still trying to say my name.* Her heart cracked again. She finally got her arms around him.

"That's nice," she murmured. "Do you do parties?"

And the darkness became complete, the heat of Cullen's drink deserting her at last. But this blackness was kind, and even as she drifted away she saw the *majir* smiling with approval, stroking Zach's trembling shoulders.

"Sophie—" He was hoarse, his voice scraped raw.

She was out.

# *Chapter 26*

Two days later Zach was still on the knife-edge between wanting to kiss her so hard she couldn't breathe—or shaking her so hard her head bobbled.

She'd been deep in shaman-sleep, that restorative, vulnerable unconsciousness that replenished more than just the body. She smelled like a shaman now, and a powerful one, too.

Zach held out his hand, watching it shake just a little. The rage wasn't completely gone, but breathing in her smell kept it leashed. It would probably take weeks for the adrenaline and violence to fade.

They were nervous around him. Not his

Family, but the sleuth who owned this house, and even the Tanuki healer-shamans who came to visit, smoothing their hands over Sophie and reassuring everyone that she would, indeed, be all right.

The sun had come out, and it filled the small room. Sophie's eyes were open, and she was looking at him.

He tried to figure out what her expression was, and failed. Down the hall Julia was humming in the bathroom, Eric was probably in the kitchen downing shots with a couple of the Felinii, and Brun was out looking for a new van. They all slept in this room, on the floor, Zach waking up every hour to make sure Sophie was still breathing.

Her lips were dry, and slightly parted. She looked at him for a long time, her gray gaze steady.

Zach stood, frozen in place. Was she disgusted? Still frightened of him? Angry? Had he tried to hurt her? Brun said he hadn't, but you never knew, with the Rage burning in your veins. She probably hadn't had any idea how to handle it—but she'd brought him out, hadn't she?

Silence stretched between them, the animal shifting restlessly inside his bones.

When she pushed the covers back he almost tripped over himself getting to the side of the bed. "Take it easy, Sophie. Just take it real—"

"To hell with taking it easy." She sounded hoarse but steady. "I want a shower and a toothbrush and some fresh clothes. I feel greasy."

*She sounds fine. Thank God.*

"Okay." He tried not to look at the tank top, all rucked up under her breasts and exposing a slice of perfect pale belly-curve. She looked so *soft*. And one of her hips hitched just a little, a lovely seashell. "I, um—"

She put her hands up, and he caught them reflexively. "Go easy on me, Zach. I feel like I've been pulled apart and put back together wrong."

"Sophie—" Where was he going to begin? With, *I'm sorry?* With, *Are you all right?* He braced her as she rose slowly, groaning, from the bed's embrace.

One little bare foot touched the floor, then the other. She spilled into his arms like grace itself, smelling of musk, the faint, fading trace of pain and exhaustion washed away by the cold moonlight of a shaman. She sighed and leaned into him, and the rage retreated.

He felt like himself again for the first time in days.

"Hello," she said to his chest. "It's good to see you."

Did she mean it? He only had the vaguest crimson-tinted memories of bursting into a dark confined space, the stink of murder all around him, clinging to his fur, and—

"Are you all right?" he managed. Everything else he wanted to say congealed in a lump right behind his Adam's apple.

"I need a shower. And a change of clothes. And breakfast. I'm *dying* for some coffee." She rubbed her chin against his T-shirt, and he had to swallow dryly.

"Sophie, I—" *I went right over the edge. What did you see me do?*

"They say you think I'm your mate." Her head tipped back, and without the glasses she looked even softer. He couldn't decide which way he liked her more. Curls fell in her face, and even unwashed and sleepy-eyed she was just about the most delicious thing he'd ever seen. "And that you killed a lot of vampires to get me out of there."

"Um." Words deserted him.

"That was my ex-husband." A shadow passed over her face, a devouring sadness. "He wanted to murder me. I guess he always wanted that."

*You never have to worry about that again. Anyone so much as breathes at you wrong, I'll hand them their spleen.* "Sophie—"

"You're no prize," she continued. "You kidnapped me, dragged me all over town, and your social skills are *so* totally nonexistent."

*Oh, Christ.* His entire body had turned to lead. "I—"

"Will you shut up? As I was saying…" She coughed a little, leaned farther into him. Her softness short-circuited his brain, but also soothed the animal. It curled up, satisfied, at the very bottom of his mind. "You're an arrogant werewolf and a kidnapper. But I've never had very good taste in men. I guess Mark was proof of that."

His arms were around her. She was leaning into him in a most definite way, and his stupid body was taking notice.

"Lucy told me it was time to get back into the dating pool, and I suppose I could do worse than a man who saved my life. But we're going to have to talk about your social skills. And

Julia, too. She's spoiled and neglected at the same time, and…" She coughed again. "But we'll take care of that in a little while. Right now I need a shower, and you can get me some coffee."

*What?*

She was still leaning on him. "I feel amazingly good, all things considered. A bit sore. How long was I out?"

"Um." *Two days.* "I, uh…" Where had all the wisecracking like a teenager gone?

She pushed at him, gently, and he let her go. His arms didn't want to relax. They fell at his sides like two pieces of wood.

Watching her take two steps back and gingerly turn away was like being fifteen and lonely again. Those curls were a messy glory, and she was wearing a pair of boxers. There was a fading bruise on her calf that begged to be kissed, just like the curve of her lower back peeping out from under the tank top.

That made the animal take notice, in a drowsy, sated way.

She paused at the door, her hand on the knob. Looked back over her shoulder. "How long? And *is* there any coffee?"

He was suddenly very sure he didn't want

her to step outside this room. *All the coffee you want. Just don't leave us. Don't leave me.* "Coffee. Yeah, there's some."

"And some clothes that don't smell like vampire?"

His hands curled into fists. The thought of *upir* threatened to bring the rage back. The animal in him perked its ears, bared its long muzzle.

"Hey." She came back, padding on those cute little bare feet, and the smell of her washed over him again. It wasn't familiar, and he had to concentrate for a long syrup-stretching moment before he realized why.

She didn't reek of fear. Not anymore.

"Zach?" Uncertain now. She stopped a few feet away. He had to look at the square of pale winter sunlight she was standing in, or he was going to do something unforgivable.

Like grab her and show her just how happy he was she was awake and alive. Like kiss her again. Like push her back down on the bed and get to know her in the best way.

"Don't leave us." The words were raw. "You're our shaman. Don't leave us. Don't leave *me.*"

"Zach—"

"You've seen what we are now. What I am. We were doing the best we could, Sophie. We *need* you. I—"

Her hand clapped over his mouth. Warm, soft skin. She was so close he could feel the heat of her, and *touching* him. "Shut up." She looked thin and tired, and absolutely beautiful. "I know you need me. The *majir* told me. They told me about your little brother playing with the matches, too, while your parents were sleeping. That was what started the fire. You never told anyone, and he always wondered if you knew. Both of you felt guilty. And now you wonder if you were too late and too slow because you loved him so much, but you hated having to keep the secret, too."

His shoulders slumped. He stared at her.

Her mouth drew against itself, the sadness and *listening* look almost too much to stand. "That was why you never took the alpha."

His eyes were hot, and incredibly full. Sunlight gilded her, turned her into a statue of living warmth.

"We both know about keeping secrets. I guess we're more alike than I thought. Now do me a favor and stop worrying. I'm going to learn how to be your shaman, and I'm going to do my best to keep you all together. You just keep your temper, and we'll get along just fine. All right?"

*Keep my temper? Yeah. That'll be the day.*

But he wanted to. If it would keep her around, he'd keep all the temper she wanted.

Her fingers loosened over his mouth. He reached up, caught her wrist, and pressed his lips against her palm. Stubble rasped—he hadn't had a chance to shave yet.

He hadn't wanted to leave her alone.

She swallowed, and the sudden wash of coppery heat through her scent told him she wasn't immune to him. It was a good sign.

"I would never…" He had to clear his throat. She was so goddamn *soft,* and he was all sharp edges and claws. "Never lay a hand on you, Sophie. Unless you wanted me to."

The smile that broke over her face was like Christmas and springtime and running under the full moon all at once. She actually *grinned* at him. "We'll get around to that."

She took her hand back, but not before he kissed her palm again, a slow lingering pressure of lips. And she actually *blushed,* a high flag of color rising in her cheeks.

"Sooner rather than later?" Thank God.

The wisecracks were back. It was a goddamn miracle.

"That depends on how soon you get me some coffee, Zach." She ran her other hand back through her hair and grimaced. "And some fresh clothes."

"No chance I could get you to walk around in just a towel?"

"In a house full of were-bears? Forget it." She retreated, step by step, still smiling.

*Hope springs eternal.* His heart did a triple backflip. "So, in a different house?"

"Coffee, Zach. And keep your temper." She swept the door open and was on her way down the hall, obviously knowing where the bathroom was.

He stood there, closed his eyes, and breathed in the smell of her filling the room, until the shower gurgled into life down the hall.

How had he gotten so lucky? It wasn't like things to work out.

But he was damned if he was going to complain.

## Chapter 27

It rained through the minister's graveside address, but stopped just in time for the casket to be lowered. The sun broke through, and golden light poured over the cemetery.

She sat in the passenger's seat, her fingers twisting together, and watched as the pearl-gray coffin descended. The window was down just a little, and she suspected Zach would have told her what was being said. If she asked.

The little jeweled purse lay in her lap. When her fingers weren't curling around one another, they were running over the absurd colored rhinestones, the big fake plastic jewels.

*Oh, Lucy.*

There were mourners—Battle-Ax Margo, her blue hair piled just as high and proud as ever, and everyone else from the office. Classmates. Quite a few of them, actually. Some of them were even crying. Margo dabbed at her eyes every so often.

And off to one side, in his grubby mackintosh, was Detective Andrews.

*I'm free.* It was a strange thought. Shadows moved like liquid through the van's interior; Zach had parked out of easy sight, in the shade of a huge cedar.

She watched intently, pushing her glasses up every now and again. When she looked over the top of the lenses, the world was a comforting blur of evergreen and gold, with the silver speckles of frozen rain dewing the blade-edged grass.

When she looked through them, everything was in clear sharp focus. Even the *majir,* swirling around the van, unhurried.

"You all right?" Zach asked again.

"Fine," she said, again. Quietly. "I'm watching my own funeral." *After all, I missed Lucy's.*

"Are you sure about this?"

She glanced at him. He held the steering

wheel, his hands steady, and was looking at the side mirror, checking around the van. It would be stupid to be seen here, but she'd wanted to come.

His hair fell over his eyes, that soft wave she could touch anytime she wanted—or the white streak sliding down the side of his head, a little coarser than the rest of his hair. Each time she did he would lean in, as if he liked it. As if he couldn't get enough. He would let out a little sigh, and sometimes close his eyes. Which meant she had to touch his cheek, too, trace his jawbone, and marvel at the complete and utter trust on his face, the vulnerable openness.

Which usually lead to him leaning in and kissing her. It was nice, and he was very slow. Very deliberate. Very patient.

She liked that about him. The more she was with them, the more she realized she *did* like all of them. She liked Julia's fierce loyalty and Eric's steadiness, and Brun's sweetness.

But most of all, she liked Zach.

"I'm sure. They've already reported me as dead. Why show up and have to answer questions?" *And I was so close to my degree, too.*

"You could go back to school. We'd tell whatever lies we had to, Sophie."

"Better just to start over with no lies." *Or, at least, very few.* She still wasn't used to the implicit assumption of "us against the world," but traveling werewolves probably had a lot of reasons to feel that way.

*Not werewolves,* she reminded herself. *Carcajou.*

And she was their shaman. She was beginning to learn what that meant. The next thing was singing Zach's brother into rest, a type of funeral they would perform privately. When she was ready to handle it.

"You might feel differently when we—"

"I started over once before, Zach. I can do it again." *There's a whole lot I didn't know I could do. But I can.*

Detective Andrews was staring at the grave. Some of the mourners were hugging one another. Margo blew her nose, and the sun slid behind a pall of heavy gray cloud, rain threatening. The golden flood of light faded as the coffin thumped home in its hole.

"That cop is going to be trouble." The words held a touch of a growl. It might have scared her, before.

"The Tribes will make sure he meets dead ends. Cullen told me so." *I'm not sure how I feel about that. That's someone else's body in there.*

"Damn bears." Zach sighed.

She watched as the mourners started moving away, the knot of people fraying, coming apart. Margo walked with her head down. Detective Andrews stood watching, even when the minister left. He was still there when the backhoe lumbered into place and started filling in the hole.

*That's Sophie Harris's grave.* She was cold for a moment, and the *majir* moved restlessly, their voices rising in a chorus of comfort. *Who am I now?*

Andrews turned and walked away, his shoulders hunched. Sophie crossed her arms over her chest, hugging herself. For a moment, the feeling of being invisible, inconsequential, nameless, or dead—she couldn't quite figure out which—was overwhelming.

*Who am I now?*

Zach's fingers met her shoulder. He didn't squeeze, just rested his hand there, warmth spreading from the touch down into Sophie's chest.

Andrews stopped. His head came up. The *majir* swirled, warning her.

*I know who I am.* "Time to go," Sophie whispered.

Zach's hand vanished and the van roused quietly. It crept forward, and Andrews turned. Fresh rain spotted the windshield.

The narrow, one-lane paved strip turned toward an exit onto Alderson Avenue. Sophie twisted in her seat, watching as Andrews looked—the other way. By the time he turned to his left, the van would already be gone behind a screen of junipers. Still, she held her breath until the wet greenery folded around the van. There were tinted windows and she wouldn't be visible at this distance, anyway, but…

"We'll pick up the others and head out of town." Zach turned the wipers on. "Do you know where you want to go?"

"Kidnapping me again." But she smiled, and when he glanced at her, he was smiling, too. It did wonders for his face. "I don't know, Zach. Anywhere's fine as long as it's not here. I don't think I ever want to come back here again."

It was funny. She should have felt like she was leaving home. She wouldn't even get to see Lucy's headstone.

But she felt light, and strangely happy

even though her heart ached. Was this what freedom was?

"You got it, shaman. South, then. It'll be nice and warm. I'll see you on the beach in a bikini."

Sophie settled herself in the seat, leaned her head back on the headrest. "I don't wear bikinis." *Or I never did before. I never even went swimming. Because of Mark. Because of the bruises.*

"Huh." He sounded more disappointed than she thought possible.

Sophie closed her eyes. The van's engine hummed, and its tires shushed on the wet road. The *majir* hummed and sang. And beside her, Zach tapped the wheel as he drove.

"But you never know," she said finally. "Anything can happen."

"Amen to that," he said, and Sophie laughed.

\* \* \* \* \*

## RENEGADE ANGEL
### BY KENDRA LEIGH CASTLE

Powerful Seth has a bitter need for vengeance. And he's determined to make mortal enemy Josslyn pay, despite the passion she arouses in him!

## GOLDEN VAMPIRE
### BY LINDA THOMAS-SUNDSTROM

Sophie never believed she was special, until sexy shape-shifter Zach kidnapped her—insisting she's a Shaman—someone with a rare gift for taming his savage side!

### ON SALE 15TH JULY 2011

## BLUE TWILIGHT
### BY MAGGIE SHAYNE

No other mortal knows as much about the undead as Maxie. But a dark force will use that knowledge to strengthen its hold on her. Can mysterious Lou break the spell?

### ON SALE 5TH AUGUST 2011

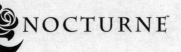

NOCTURNE

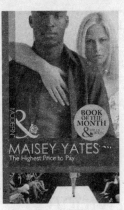

# Love and betrayal.
# A Faery world gone mad.

Deserted by the Winter prince she thought loved her, half-Summer faery princess, half-human Meghan is prisoner to the Winter faery queen. But the real danger comes from the Iron fey— ironbound faeries only she and her absent prince have seen.

With Meghan's fey powers cut off, she's stuck in Faery with only her wits for help. And trusting a seeming traitor could be deadly.

# Kaylee has one addiction: her boyfriend, Nash.

A banshee like Kaylee, Nash understands her like no one else. Nothing can come between them. Until something does.

*Demon breath*—a super-addictive paranormal drug that can kill. Kaylee and Nash need to cut off the source and protect their human friends—one of whom is already hooked.

But then Kaylee uncovers another demon breath addict. *Nash*.

*Book three in the unmissable* Soul Screamers *series.*

*They say that before you die your life flashes before your eyes*

You think it's going to be the good stuff.
Don't count on it.

I was Bridget Duke—the uncontested ruler of the school. And if that meant being a mean girl, then so be it! I never thought there'd be a price to pay.

Until the accident.

Now, trapped between life and death, I'm seeing my world in a new light. And I've got one chance to make things right. If I don't, I may never wake up again…

# FREE BOOK
## AND A SURPRISE GIFT

We would like to take this opportunity to thank you for reading th'
Mills & Boon® book by offering you the chance to take a special|
selected book from the Nocturne™ series absolutely FREE! We'r
also making this offer to introduce you to the benefits of the Mills &
Boon® Book Club™—

- **FREE home delivery**
- **FREE gifts and competitions**
- **FREE monthly Newsletter**
- **Exclusive Mills & Boon Book Club offers**
- **Books available before they're in the shops**

Accepting this FREE book and gift places you under no obligatio
to buy, you may cancel at any time, even after receiving your fre
book. Simply complete your details below and return the entire pag
to the address below. You don't even need a stamp!

**YES** Please send me a free Nocturne book and a surprise gift.
understand that unless you hear from me, I will receive 3 super
new stories every month, two priced at £4.99 and a third large
version priced at £6.99, postage and packing free. I am unde
no obligation to purchase any books and may cancel m
subscription at any time. The free book and gift will be mine to keej
in any case.

Ms/Mrs/Miss/Mr _____ Initials _____

Surname _____

Address _____

_____

Postcode _____

E-mail _____

Send this whole page to: Mills & Boon Book Club, Free Book Offer
FREEPOST NAT 10298, Richmond, TW9 1BR